MORE...

THE GIRL MOST LIKELY TO...

"An exceptional novel with humor and pathos and rich in detail, and the finely-put-together characters make this a story worthy of our Perfect 10 award and a must-read. You'll laugh, cry, and your heart will break over this brilliant story of a man and a woman—what most wondrous stories end up being about."

—*Romance Reviews Today*

"A wonderfully convoluted tale of love lost and found, secret pregnancies and spousal abuse, Donovan's latest shows us the healing power of forgiveness and the strength found in the love of family. It's peopled with complex characters who learn much about themselves and those they love through the course of this compelling story."

—*RT BOOKreviews*

THE KEPT WOMAN
A RITA Award finalist

"Sexy and funny. Donovan takes the marriage-of-convenience plot and gives it a fun update that will leave readers grinning...these characters are filled with genuine warmth and charm."

—*RT BOOKreviews*

HE LOVES LUCY

"A great book...terrific."

—*Fresh Fiction*

"A fun and sexy 'feel good' story and a 'must' title to add to your current romance reading list."

—*Bookloons*

"A story of rioting emotions, wacky weight challenges, and lots of love. This is one story you will be sad to see end. Kudos to Donovan for creating such a believable and realistic story." —*Fallen Angel Reviews*

"*He Loves Lucy* has everything: humor, sweetness, warmth, romance, passion, and sexual tension; an uplifting message; a heroine every woman...can empathize with; and a hero to die for."

—*Romance Reviews Today*

"An extraordinary read with intriguing characters and a wonderful plot...fantastic." —*Romance Junkies*

"Lucy is a humorous delight...fans will enjoy this fine look at one year of hard work to find love."

—*Midwest Book Review*

"A great romance...a top-rate novel...with its unforgettable characters, wonderful plot, and excellent message, *He Loves Lucy* will go on my keeper shelf to be read and re-read a thousand times...Donovan has proven that she will have serious star power in the years to come." —*Romance Reader at Heart*

TAKE A CHANCE ON ME

"Comic sharpness...the humorous interactions among Thomas, Emma, and Emma's quirky family give the book a golden warmth as earthy as its rural Maryland setting. But there are also enough explicit erotic interludes to please readers who like their romances spicy."
—*Publishers Weekly*

"Donovan blends humor and compassion in this opposites-attract story. Sexy and masculine, Thomas fills the bill for the man of your dreams. Emma and Thomas deserve a chance at true love. Delightfully entertaining, *Take a Chance on Me* is a guaranteed good time."
—*Old Book Barn Gazette*

"Full of humor, sensuality, and emotion with excellent protagonists and supporting characters...a wonderful tale. Don't be afraid to take a chance on this one. You'll love it."
—*Affaire de Coeur*

"Impossible to put down...Susan Donovan is an absolute riot. You're reading a paragraph that is so sexually charged you can literally feel the air snapping with electricity and the next second one of the characters has a thought that is so absurd...that you are laughing out loud. Susan Donovan has a very unique, off-the-wall style that should keep her around for many books to come. Do NOT pass this one up."
—*Romance Junkies Review*

"Susan Donovan has created a vastly entertaining romance in her latest book *Take a Chance on Me*. The book has an ideal cast of characters...a very amusing, pleasurable read...all the right ingredients are there, and Ms. Donovan has charmingly dished up an absolutely fast, fun, and sexy read!"   —*Road to Romance*

"Contemporary romances don't get much better than *Take a Chance on Me*...such wonderful characters! You want sexual tension? This book drips with it. How about a love scene that is everything that a love scene should be? There's humor, a touch of angst, and delightful dialogue...*Take a Chance on Me* is going to end up very, very high on my list of best romances."
                                                    —*All About Romance*

KNOCK ME OFF MY FEET

"Spicy debut...[A] surprise ending and lots of playfully erotic love scenes will keep readers entertained."
                                                    —*Publishers Weekly*

"*Knock Me Off My Feet* will knock you off your feet... Ms. Donovan crafts an excellent mixture to intrigue you and delight you. You'll sigh as you experience the growing love between Autumn and Quinn and giggle over their dialogue. And you'll be surprised as the story unfolds. I highly recommend this wonderfully entertaining story."   —*Old Book Barn Gazette*

St. Martin's Paperbacks Titles
by Susan Donovan

Cheri on Top

SUSAN DONOVAN

St. Martin's Paperbacks

This is a work of fiction. All of the characters, organizations, and events portrayed in this novel are either products of the author's imagination or are used fictitiously.

CHERI ON TOP

Copyright © 2011 by Susan Donovan.
Excerpt from *I Want Candy* copyright © 2011 by Susan Donovan.

For information address St. Martin's Press, 175 Fifth Avenue, New York, NY 10010.

ISBN: 978-0-312-53621-3

Printed in the United States of America

St. Martin's Paperbacks edition / September 2011

St. Martin's Paperbacks are published by St. Martin's Press, 175 Fifth Avenue, New York, NY 10010.

10 9 8 7 6 5 4 3 2 1

Dedicated with love to my friend Kris Larson Fagre.
I'm so glad you weathered your storm.

Acknowledgments

The author would like to thank Arleen Shuster for being my road-tripping BFF in North Carolina and in life; Becky and George Fain for graciously hosting us at the Inn at Iris Meadows in Waynesville, NC; Sean Lewis for tidbits from the world of small-town newspapering; Chad Smith, for helping me rediscover my "one percent"; and Celeste Bradley and Darby Gill for pulling my threads in the nick of time. Because of all of you, this book is a book and I'm still smiling.

"Storms make trees take deeper roots."
—Dolly Parton

Chapter 1

The phone rang out like an air-raid siren, causing Cherise to nearly dump her ramen noodles onto the dining nook floor.

"Woo-hoo!" her roommate shouted from the plastic lawn chair in the living room. "I hope it's Tampa Electric—I was starting to worry they just aren't into us anymore!"

Cherise set her bowl on the dinette table and blew on her burning fingers, chuckling at her friend's sarcasm. Everybody had their own way of dealing with stress, she supposed. Candy's was sarcasm. Cherise preferred cheap carbohydrates. Who could say which was better?

"I made a good-faith payment on the electric bill just last week," Cherise told her roomie as she headed toward the kitchen wall phone. "This is probably Bank of America."

"In that case, the suspense is killing me. Will this be in reference to *your* grossly overdue account, or *mine*?"

The ringing continued to ricochet off the studio apartment's bare walls.

"Don't answer it," Candy suggested.

"Ignoring them only makes matters worse."

"I'm not sure that's possible."

Cherise peered at the caller ID, and took a step back in astonishment. She'd expected to see the words "Incomplete Data," the euphemism for collection agencies and accounts receivable departments from Memphis to Mumbai. Instead, the caller ID display read "Newberry, Garland."

She snatched up the phone. "Granddaddy?"

"Hello, Cheri! How's my favorite redheaded Southern belle today?"

Cherise blinked. The sound of her childhood nickname spoken in her grandfather's North Cack-a-lacky twang left her breathless. She turned in time to see Candy run into the kitchen, looking as scared as Cherise felt.

How had everyone back home heard what happened? Their bankruptcy paperwork hadn't even been filed, and Cherise and Candy had sworn they'd never breathe a word to anyone back in Bigler.

Oh, God. This was bad.

"Did I lose you, darlin'?"

"Granddaddy Garland? Is that you?"

He laughed. "Of course it's me, silly."

"Did someone die?"

It wasn't that Cherise hoped anyone had passed, but she prayed there was a reason for her grandfather's call—other than the obvious.

He laughed. "No one I know of, but I'm hangin' on to life like a hair in a biscuit, myself."

"Don't say that!" Cherise tried to ignore Candy's interpretive dance of anxiety. Her friend was now waving her arms in circles over her blond head while twisting her face into a series of panicked expressions.

Cherise placed her hand over the receiver. "I don't know yet!" she whispered, gesturing for Candy to give her some space. "Just calm down and let me find out what's going on."

Candy retreated to one of the dinette chairs, where she propped her elbows on the table and let her head fall to her hands.

"Uh, hi again, Granddaddy," Cherise said. "So, Aunt Viv's okay? Tanyalee's okay? You're not ill or anything?"

"Everyone's fine. You've been on my mind lately, is all."

That was a fib, of course. The Newberrys didn't just think about each other out of the blue, and they sure as hell didn't call each other on a lark. Cherise's nuclear family had blown up a long time ago. Her extended family went for long periods without communicating. The Newberrys were estranged in addition to being just plain strange. So that meant only one thing: somehow, the family had found out what happened down here in Florida and Granddaddy was calling to get in his "I told you so"s.

He cleared his throat.

Here it comes.

"I suppose I should just fess up, Cheri. I'm calling you for a particular reason. You got to promise you'll hear me out."

They know.

Cherise sighed heavily and leaned her butt against the refrigerator. She knocked the back of her head repeatedly against the freezer door, dreading the lecture that was about to come, a lecture that was wholly unnecessary. Anything Granddaddy Garland could say to her she'd already told herself many times during the last nine months.

Fourteen million dollars' worth of real estate had slipped through her fingers, and she had no one to blame but herself. She'd been imprudent and selfish. She'd been materialistic and shallow. She'd allowed possessions to define who she was. She'd been drunk on greed and easy money and she hadn't exactly shared her bounty with the less fortunate. She deserved whatever misery had befallen her.

"Cheri, sugar, I want you to take over the *Bigler Bugle* for me. I want you to run the family business. I want you to come home."

Cherise straightened and pulled away from the fridge, not quite certain she'd heard correctly. "Excuse me?"

"Don't tell me to go suck eggs quite yet, darlin'. I know we haven't been close, but you're the logical choice. I'm near on eighty, and everything's changing far too fast for me to keep up."

She gulped.

"The paper's circulation is in the toilet and I've had to lay off nearly half the employees. Ad revenues are down. The technology is mystifying to me. I want the comfort of knowing the *Bugle* is in capable Newberry hands when I go to meet my maker. That means you, my darlin' girl."

Cherise slapped one of those capable hands to her forehead in disbelief. "But what about Tanyalee? She still lives in Bigler, doesn't she? She'd be interested, wouldn't she?"

It took a few seconds before her grandfather responded. "Your sister's talents lie elsewhere, bless her heart."

Cheri bit her lip, trying not to laugh at that classic example of Newberry-style diplomacy. Indeed, Tanyalee's talents were legion, and occasionally illegal.

"Besides, you're the only one in the family with a finance degree."

And without a criminal record.

"You would make an excellent publisher."

Cherise glanced at Candy, now staring with huge blue eyes, waiting for news. Cherise quickly gave her a thumbs-up to assure her friend that from what she could tell, no one back home had a clue that they'd lost everything.

Candy clasped her hands as if in prayer and raised her eyes toward the ceiling.

"Granddaddy?" Cherise asked. "Why me? Why didn't you just ask, well, you know—" It was embarrassing that she was incapable of saying her ex-brother-in-law's name aloud. Ridiculous. She was thirty years old. Yes, J.J. DeCourcy had been her first love, but it wasn't like she had any claim to him. Nor would she want any, she reminded herself. The sweet and funny kid she'd known had become a cruel man with a tendency to lie and cheat, a man who had treated Tanyalee like garbage. But all that pregnancy-wedding-divorce chaos had ended more than five years ago. J.J. DeCourcy meant nothing to her. So of course Cherise should be able to say his name.

"Why haven't you asked *him* to run the paper?"

"You're referring to J.J.?" her grandfather asked.

"He's a real journalist, right? And I thought he was the trustworthy type—you know, at least when it comes to his work."

She heard her granddaddy take a deep breath. "I love Jefferson Jackson DeCourcy like a grandson and I always will. He knows this newspaper inside and out. I've asked him to stay on as managing editor."

Cherise rubbed her eyes. This was getting worse by the second. Granddaddy was asking her to be J.J.'s *boss*?

"I need my own flesh and blood in the publisher's chair, Cheri. You know the *Bugle* is your birthright. The paper was started by our family right after the great unpleasantness."

"Yes, I know," she said, shaking her head. *Over a hundred and forty freakin' years have passed since the end of the Civil War! Say the words! Just say the freakin' words!*

But no, that wasn't the way things were done back home. Euphemisms were big in Bigler.

"It's the state's only surviving daily this side of Asheville," he added, as if she didn't know.

"I remember, Granddaddy."

"Your father had just taken his rightful place as publisher when—" Her grandfather's voice began to crack, which was something Cherise had never heard from him before. But he caught himself. "You're my only hope, Cheri girl. Please at least say you'll consider it."

Cherise looked around the depressing studio apartment she'd been sharing with Candy for the past six months, and had to ask herself, what, if anything, is left for me in Tampa?

Their on-paper residential and commercial real estate fortune had vaporized. She'd had to walk away from the mortgage on her own four-bedroom, three-bath home in Harbour Island. The Audi had been repossessed. The Miu Miu bags, Dolce & Gabbana sunglasses, and Stuart Weitzman peep-toe booties had found new owners via eBay. And Evan, the beautiful, go-all-night man-boy she'd shared two years of her life with, had turned out to be as shallow as piss on concrete and had hit the road at the first sign of insolvency.

This meant the only thing in Tampa that mattered to Cherise was Candace Carmichael, her lifelong best friend and business partner, who remained at the dinette set with her eyes heavenward, no doubt thanking the gods that no one back home had gotten wind of their spectacular fuckup.

"Maybe you could take a sabbatical of some sort from your business down there," Granddaddy said. "I know you have a successful life in Tampa. But would you at least consider my proposition? At least give it a try?"

Just then, the call waiting cut in. Cherise checked the display. "Incomplete Data" was on the line.

"The lake house is rightfully yours, so you could move right on in." Granddaddy paused. "After a good sweeping-up, anyhow. And I'll pay you fifteen hundred a week to start."

Her heart began to pound. Fifteen hundred a week? That was three times what she made at the temp agency!

"Oh, and of course Aunt Viv will set you up with

some home cookin' until you get settled. I know you were never a big cook."

Cherise took a sideways glance at her bowl of ramen noodles, a staple she bought in bulk for five cents a pack at the Dollar Store. True, cooking wasn't her thing, and that had never been a problem when she was dining out every night. But nowadays, she never "dined" at all, not out or in or anywhere in between. Her meals were consumed at the secondhand walnut veneer dinette set and consisted of freeze-dried noodles, canned goods, and off-brand frozen entrées.

Suddenly, visions of Aunt Viv's thick-sliced country ham began to dance in her brain. Her stomach clenched. She pictured a big slab of crumbly, hot, cast-iron-skillet cornbread slathered with sweet butter. Her head throbbed. She saw a helping of heirloom green beans cooked to desiccated perfection with onion and bacon. She began to get light-headed from hunger.

"I know how you've always loved Viv's sweet potato and pecan casserole."

Cherise gasped at her grandfather's cruelty! *That was so unfair . . .*

"And of course, there's her banana puddin'."

Cherise pursed her lips in anger as the breath sawed in and out of her nostrils. Clearly, her grandfather could be downright ruthless. Like all the Newberrys.

"Well, whad'ya say, darlin?"

"Uh . . ." Cherise glanced at Candy. Of course, the two of them would have to talk this over before Cherise made any decisions. They'd been a team since fourth grade. Maybe she could convince Candy to go back home to Bigler with her, just temporarily.

She put her hand over the phone again. "He wants me to run the *Bugle*!" she whispered to Candy excitedly. "Do you think you might ever consider—"

A look of horror spread over Candy's face.

"Never mind," Cherise said, returning her attention to the phone call. "I can't make you any promises, Granddaddy, but I'll think about it. I'll get back to you."

Crafty old coot, she thought, hanging up on her grandfather and the anonymous bill collector in one motion.

Why did he have to go and mention the banana pudding?

Chapter 2

"DeCourcy. Get your butt on over here."

J.J. dragged his attention from the drama unfolding in the drained lakebed and glanced at his grumpy friend, Cataloochee County Sheriff Turner Halliday. "Any sign of a body yet?" J.J. asked him.

Turner shook his head sharply. Then he gave a wide swipe in the air with his fingers, motioning for J.J. to walk with him. That kind of body language told J.J. all he needed to know. His best friend was not just irritable, he was downright pissed, which wasn't his style. J.J. and Turner had been buddies since kindergarten, and he could count on one hand the number of times he'd seen his laid-back friend in such a state.

"What's up?" He joined Turner near a grove of trees on the east bank of what was once Paw Paw Lake. Turner set a slow walking pace, and J.J. matched it. "Everything all right?"

Turner didn't look him in the eye. "Give me twenty-four hours before you go putting any details in the paper. That's all I'm asking."

"Say *what*?" J.J. gave a dismissive snort and stopped in his tracks. "You're joking, right?"

Turner ignored him. "We don't know what we're looking at yet. Since there's a remote chance were going to find a body, the FBI is on the way. This could turn into a huge fuckin' mess."

Well, that certainly explained the bad mood. Turner got testy when the Feds came to town and treated him like some backwoods bozo. Regardless, J.J. decided to point out the obvious. "It's already a huge fuckin' mess."

Turner kicked at the red dirt, saying nothing.

"And you and I both know what we're looking at here." J.J. crooked a thumb over his shoulder. "A big-assed hydraulic winch is about to rip a 1959 Chevy Impala from the bottom of Paw Paw Lake, and we're going to discover it's been the secret underwater tomb of one Barbara Jean Smoot for the last four decades. Remote chance? Come on, now. We've finally found our 'Lady of the Lake.'"

Turner looked up and narrowed an eye at him. "Sounds like you already wrote your damn story, DeCourcy—pretty words and all. I guess the facts don't even matter to you."

"Whoa!" J.J. held his palms out in surrender. "Hold up, Turner. This is the biggest mystery our town has ever laid claim to, and I'm watching it unravel with my own two eyes. It's my job to report what I see today for tomorrow morning's edition. Same as always, man."

Turner's laugh was tinged with sarcasm. "What you see is a vehicle of unknown age and make that's turned up in the mud at a construction site. Period." He scowled at him. "But go ahead. Write about Barbara Jean Smoot tomorrow if you want. I'll look forward to reading your front-page correction the day after that."

"Uh-huh." J.J. tipped his head and studied his friend. Turner was mean as a sack of rattlesnakes today. J.J. had seen him go through hell and back since June died, but that was a personal tragedy of the first order. His wife was only twenty-five when she was killed in a car crash four years ago, driving home to visit her folks in Chicago. But J.J. couldn't recall ever seeing Turner this jacked over *work*.

Unless . . .

"So this is personal," J.J. said. It wasn't a question. "Mind telling me how?"

Turner looked up at him, his hazel eyes smoldering. "Forget it."

"Tell me."

Turner sighed. "Barbara Jean was a pretty white girl who disappeared on a rainy night in June of 1964, right? The only person who ever claimed to know anything was a black man. And, as you might recall, Bigler wasn't exactly a hotbed of racial harmony in those days."

J.J. widened his eyes at the understatement.

"You know who that witness was, right?" Turner asked.

"Sure. A man named Carleton Johnston."

"Do you know what happened to that man?"

"As a matter of fact, I do," J.J. said. Just that morning, when police scanner chatter began buzzing about a possible vehicle found buried in the mud, J.J. asked a reporter to pull a slew of old news clips from the *Bugle* microfiche archives. Carleton Johnston was described as an out-of-town visitor who claimed he'd seen a white man jump from the passenger side of a car just before it drove off the pier into Paw Paw Lake—with someone slumped at the wheel—then watched the man scurry off into the woods. Johnston said he couldn't swim so he ran to get help. Less than a month later, it was reported that Mr. Johnston passed away of natural causes at his home in Charlotte, and no one was ever charged in connection with Barbara Jean's disappearance.

According to the clips, the Cataloochee County Sheriff's Department and North Carolina state troopers dragged the lake four times in the months after her disappearance, but came up with nothing. Johnston's story was never substantiated, and as the years went by, many people assumed he was responsible for her disappearance. In 1975, Barbara Jean's family had her legally declared dead.

"Did you know that Carleton Johnston was my mother's uncle, visiting from Charlotte? And did you know that the poor guy had some kind of learning disability? Back then, they just called him slow."

J.J. raised an eyebrow in surprise. "No. I did not."

"See—you don't know everything."

J.J. yanked a reporter's notebook from his back jeans pocket. "Why haven't you ever told me this?"

"Never came up." Turner scanned the scene, watching the progress of the dozens of recovery and emergency personnel working to extricate the car. "Now listen, Jay. I'm not saying shit on the record. But as your friend, I'm asking you to wait before you go blabbing some half-assed truth all over creation."

"But—"

Turner cut him off. "If we find human remains—and that's a big if—nobody's going to be able to positively ID anyone or anything for a very long time."

J.J. nodded.

"Whatever we find will only be one piece of a bigger puzzle. When this cold case thaws out, I'm afraid the whole thing is going to stink to high heaven."

J.J. let out a long and low whistle and began to write. "You're confirming that Carleton Johnston didn't die of natural causes. You're saying somebody killed him to keep him from talking."

"I'm not *sayin'* anything." Turner bit on the inside of his lip. "All I know are the ghost stories we heard when we were kids—that and the suspicions of my mother's family." Turner glanced over his shoulder at the crane. "But as of right now, for your news story, we don't even know whose car this is."

J.J. smiled. "Ah, well, I can help you with that. See that frail old lady over by the fire truck?"

Turner peered through the sun. "Yeah. Who's she?"

"That's Barbara Jean's sister, Carlotta Smoot Mc-Coy, from Maggie Valley. She stopped by to watch the recovery."

Turner's mouth fell open. "Did you call her, De-Courcy?"

He shrugged. "I had one of my reporters go over to her place for a quote, and she insisted on coming down."

"Shee-it," Turner said, wiping his mouth nervously. "I really don't want this turning into any more of a damn circus than it already is."

At that moment, real estate developer Wim Wimbley strolled past, coming within earshot. Turner stopped talking, and his back straightened noticeably. He tipped his hat. "Wim," he said.

"Sheriff." Wim acknowledged Turner coolly, giving just the barest nod of his head. Then he caught J.J.'s eyes. "DeCourcy."

Wimbley walked on by, nose high, hands in his chino pockets, a professionally made crease down the arm of his pale pink, button-down Ralph Lauren dress shirt.

"Little shit," J.J. mumbled.

"Yeah, well, he's the filthy rich little shit who owns the property we're standing on. And if this development takes off it will make him even richer."

J.J. took his gaze away from Wim and looked at Turner thoughtfully. "Haven't you ever found it ironic?" he asked his friend.

Turner shrugged. "You mean how Tanyalee's engaged to Wim?"

J.J. laughed. "Hell, no! That's not irony, man—that's a godsend! I'm talking about the fact that Wim comes in here and drains Paw Paw Lake to build a luxury waterfront retirement community. I know what he told the planning commission about his man-made jetties and maximizing lakefront homesites and all that crap, but I still don't get it. Is our society so removed from nature that we have to re-engineer a mountain lake to make it beautiful?"

Turner wasn't listening. His eyes had gone huge and now focused directly over J.J.'s right shoulder.

Though he wanted to turn around, something told J.J. to wait. A tingling began way down in his core. It warned him to stay sharp.

"Are the Feds here?" he whispered to Turner, not wanting to turn around and gawk.

Turner shook his head slowly. "It's worse than the FBI, man. It's CNN."

J.J. was about to spin around in disbelief when he realized what Turner was saying. For them, CNN wasn't just a moniker for a news network. It was their shorthand for Cherise Nancy Newberry, in all her glory.

She was two days late.

J.J. heard a car door slam behind him. He smiled, sliding his notebook into his rear pocket. "She coming this way?"

Turner nodded. "Ooh, yeah."

"How's she look?"

Turner shrugged. "Like she's been living off bib lettuce and Evian water, but other than that, everything seems to be in working order."

J.J. took a moment to center himself. He pasted a scowl on his face. Their first encounter had to be convincing if this was going to work. It was unfortunate Cheri had shown up in the middle of the biggest news story to hit Bigler in forty-seven years but there wasn't a damn thing he could do about that now.

"Stay cool, Halliday," J.J. said through gritted teeth.

"Scout's honor."

J.J. turned. It was all he could do not to fall to his knees at the impact. He hadn't laid eyes on her in over five years. He had to make sure she wouldn't see the relief in him, the hunger. He checked her out from tip to toe at lightning speed. Her dark, lustrous red hair was cut in some kind of trendy layered style and it skimmed above her shoulders. She wore a skirt that was real short, which was real thoughtful of her. Right then, J.J. decided that he may have been a lot of places and met a lot of women since he'd graduated from high school twelve years before, but it still held true: Cheri Newberry had the best set of female legs on the planet.

Unfortunately, her sexy four-inch heels were turning out to be a spectacularly bad choice for a visit to a drained lakebed, and J.J. watched her wobble and cuss under her breath as she stepped over deep ruts in the earth.

Except for the methodic *click-click* of the winch, everything had gone silent. The recovery crew had stopped talking and yelling. Every set of male eyes was on Cheri. And why not? Cheri Newberry stood out like a Thoroughbred in a field of pack mules.

Focus, he told himself. *Don't smile. Don't laugh. And for God's sake, don't stare at her legs.*

Cheri wobbled over to the two men. She used an index finger to nudge the big, dark sunglasses up the bridge of her nose. "Hello," she said, her hands nervously smoothing out the contours of her skirt. "I just drove into town. I decided to pull off the road when I saw all the commotion. What's going on?"

J.J. said nothing. He simply scowled at her. It struck him as amusing that she'd chosen that getup for her big entrance. It was still about image management for her, he supposed. His guess was that she'd driven most of the way in shorts and flip-flops, then hit the Tip-Top truck stop to change her outfit and freshen her lipstick before she rolled into town.

He had to give the girl an A for effort.

Turner took it upon himself to break the awkward

silence. "Sure is wonderful to see you, Cheri." He gave her a hearty, but quick, hug. "We're happy to have you back home."

"Oh." She laughed uncomfortably, as if she were surprised by the friendly greeting. "Well, thanks. That's nice of you to say, Turner."

J.J. was aware that the rules of social intercourse would require him to say something immediately. If he didn't speak now, the window for a polite welcome would slam shut. So he stayed silent. Cheri's eyes flashed from behind her dark glasses, aware of his rudeness.

Excellent.

Turner, however, was too much of a gentleman to let the uncomfortable moment continue.

"Did you have a nice drive up?"

"Oh! Sure . . ." She looked back at her car and laughed nervously. "I decided to leave my Audi down in Florida and drive my old car up here—you know, save on wear and tear and all that."

Turner nodded but kept a straight face.

J.J. did his best not to roll his eyes.

"So how's Candy Carmichael doing these days?"

"Uh, she's great," Cheri said, smiling stiffly at Turner. "You know, crazy busy, like always. The Florida real estate market is really starting to rev up again and we're juggling all kinds of deals, but she's fabulous. I'll tell her you asked about her."

Turner nodded. "Great. Well, if you'll excuse me, I need to get back to work. It's crazy busy around here, too. Let me know if there's anything I can do to help you get settled."

"Wait." Cheri reached out for Turner's arm. She

wrapped her fingers around his wrist, and that's when J.J. noticed she still had the same short, pink nails she'd had since high school. "Candy and I were so very sad to hear about June. You've been in our thoughts and prayers. I am so sorry."

"That's quite kind of you. Take care, now." Turner nodded quickly and turned away, not comfortable with talking about June, J.J. knew. But before he could take two steps, the ground shook and the air vibrated as the winch revved up for another tug at the car. As everyone watched, a loud squelching noise exploded from the muck and a pair of mud-covered chrome fins poked up from the goop like a perky set of boobs in an all-girl mud-wrestling match.

"I'll be damned," Turner said, just before he broke into a jog.

Cheri spun around and whipped off her sunglasses, staring at J.J., her mouth open in shock.

"Is that—" Cheri stopped herself. She gasped. She pointed behind her. Her voice went high and squeaky. "My God! What's the name of that missing woman from back in the fifties? The one we told all those ghost stories about—the 'Lady of the Lake,' right? Barbara Jean Something? Was it the fifties? The sixties, maybe? Is that her car? After all this time?"

J.J. didn't know how to answer her. All he could do was stare back at Cheri. She had the same soft, tawny brown eyes she'd always had, and they were wide with wonder at the moment. God, she was still so beautiful.

J.J. had made so many missteps in his effort to forget her. The biggest disaster had been Tanyalee, of course. But with Cheri now standing in front of him, just inches from his reach, he knew with certainty that it had all been in vain. He still wanted her. And he'd missed her lovely face, her sense of humor, her sweet mouth. He'd missed her something fierce.

"Oh, just go fuck yourself, DeCourcy," that sweet mouth said. Cheri laughed and tossed her hair. "You know, you could've at least *pretended* to be decent about this. It's not like I wanted to come here. Granddaddy begged me. I don't relish the idea of being your boss. I would have been fine with never seeing you again as long as I lived. Get the hell over yourself."

He had no time to react. Her hand was already on its way to making contact with his cheek. He couldn't blame her. In fact, she should have smacked him upside the head that awful day in Tampa more than five years ago. God, how it pained him to remember. He'd just finished confessing his love for Cheri when Tanyalee called with the joyful news—she was pregnant with his baby. Cheri had been too stunned to slap him. Too horrified to move. Too angry to cry. And the next time he saw her was at the wedding, where she wouldn't even look at him. It was as if he didn't exist, as if Tanyalee were walking down the aisle with an empty tuxedo.

There had been no such hesitation today, and as Cheri's hand sliced through the air and headed for his face, J.J. grabbed her wrist.

Their eyes locked. They both breathed hard. She yanked her arm and tried to spin away. He tugged back. She lost her balance and fell against him.

"Don't touch me," she hissed.

He stared at her open lips. Despite everything, he wanted her. Still. And now that she was here, warm and alive and in his grasp, he had no idea how to make it right. He didn't even know where to begin.

One thing was for sure—he was fixin' to kiss her.

Oh, *hell,* no.

Cherise felt herself frozen where she stood, her wrist imprisoned in J.J.'s grip, her knees starting to shake, her nose full of the crisp, clean scent of J.J. DeCourcy. She hadn't been this close to him since that fateful day in Tampa, when J.J. had gone from charmer to snake in a matter of seconds.

And after that, she'd sworn to herself that she'd never get this close to him again.

But here she was, her lips about to meet his, a full-scale war going on between her body and her brain. Cheri tried to pull away. He wouldn't let her go. Her skin was on fire beneath his fingers. Her mouth had gone dry. And Cheri's brain circled and whirled and twisted around one single thought. *You ripped my heart to pieces! You married my sister! You married Tanyalee when you were supposed to be mine!*

"My sister! Oh, dear God, my sister!"

Those words hadn't come from Cheri, yet she'd surely heard them. She gasped and spun around, pulling from J.J.'s grasp in time to watch a huge, muddy form begin to push up from the mud.

Chaos exploded all around them. Everyone began to shout and move into action. Cheri didn't know exactly what she was witnessing. Was that really the missing woman's car? Was the old lady her sister? What the hell was going on here?

Then, with a sudden, sucking whoosh of air and

mud, an entire car-shaped blob popped out of the ooze. Some of the recovery crew broke out in cheers.

J.J. moved close to her ear and whispered, "That right there, Cheri, is the sound of the past surrendering its secrets."

Out of the corner of her eye, Cherise saw him flip open his reporter's notebook and hastily scrawl some words down. She nearly laughed aloud. If anyone were already an expert on the subject of secrets, it would be J.J. DeCourcy.

"Has a kind of Edgar Allan Poe feel to it, don't you think?"

She ignored him, fascinated by the sight of the car, swinging from the end of a huge chain like a monster-sized mud dauber nest.

"Who's that tiny older lady?" she asked.

"Barbara Jean Smoot's sister, Carlotta Smoot McCoy."

That's when the woman began to sob, bending in half at the waist with agony. Cheri gasped in concern. "I'm going to go to her. She needs somebody to lean on."

J.J. responded but his words were overpowered by Carlotta's loudest scream yet. *"Barbara Jean! Oh, God, my sweet sister!"*

They watched as Carlotta ran under the police tape. She began clomping into the mud in a pair of worn house slippers. She didn't get far. Several deputies went in after her, dragging her out of the mire and carting her back to dry soil.

Carlotta's feet kicked in the air, flinging mud as she hollered, "HY-9871! Oh, it's Barbara Jean! I know it is! Just check!"

Cherise looked at J.J.

"Yep," he said. "That was the plate on Barbara Jean Smoot's missing Impala."

"Just check and see!" Carlotta screamed as she was restrained by deputies. "Oh, please, God! It's Barbara Jean! Just check the license plate!"

Cheri took a single step toward the lady when the car began to sway back and forth on the chain, moving through the air, destined for a tow truck backed up to the edge of the lakebed. Thick globs of muck rained down from the undercarriage and the chain groaned and creaked, its metal-on-metal screech painful to the ears.

"Stay back," J.J. said, placing his hand on her shoulder. "It's not safe."

"Good Lord!" Cherise shrugged away from J.J.'s touch. What a homecoming this was turning out to be! Cherise had no sooner crossed the Bigler city line than she nearly kissed a man she despised while a ghost got ripped from her grave! She hoped to God this wasn't some kind of omen.

As a kid, Cherise had loved sitting on her daddy's lap and listening to him and Granddaddy Garland talk about what might have happened to Barbara Jean. The newspapermen would stretch out in their rusted lawn chairs by the edge of Newberry Lake and rehash the story, the evidence, the possibilities, as Cherise cuddled into her daddy's chest. The story of Barbara Jean Smoot was Bigler's biggest news story ever, they'd say. It was the town's most enduring mystery. And as they talked, Cherise would let her imagination run free. Oh, how she'd thought the tale of Barbara Jean was the best scary story she'd ever heard.

When she'd gotten older, long after her parents were gone, she and Candy would retell the story for the thrill of its high drama—a girl, not much older than they were, too beautiful for their sleepy mountain town; a man seen running away from her car before it disappeared into the lake; and a handful of people who swore they could still see the figure of a woman in a dress and tight blond ponytail, pacing the dock at night, her head bent as if she were scanning the dark water for the clues to her own death.

In her secret heart, Cherise had always believed she had something in common with the Lady of the Lake. Cherise knew what it felt like to walk around with a heart and a spirit about to bust through the seams of this stupid little town. If Barbara Jean had done herself in—or run away without having the decency to say good-bye—Cherise wouldn't have blamed her one bit.

She sighed deeply. Yes, the dock and water had disappeared from Paw Paw Lake, but in her mind she could see the ghostly vision of a woman, searching in the dark for the pieces to her own puzzle. And the image was sharp enough to make her shudder.

J.J. studied Cheri as she stood with her arms clasped tight around her middle, shivering like she was cold. Turner had been right—she'd gotten a little too thin, though what remained looked damn fine packed into that short skirt.

She began to walk off.

"Cheri?"

She didn't answer. He watched her march back to

her decidedly low-end Toyota sedan, nearly taking a header into the dirt in her rush to get away from him and/or the drama of the crime scene.

J.J. wiped his hand roughly across his lips, his brain in flames, his head ready to explode. If he'd followed through with what he'd wanted—if he'd kissed her—it would have been the stupidest damn thing anyone had ever done in the course of human history. It would have ruined whatever remote chance he still might have to win her.

But.

Oh.

Her lips. How he wanted to taste them again.

"Back off!"

J.J. pulled his stare away from Cheri's behind. Turner had just shouted for everyone to move away from the Impala, now being secured to the tow truck. The sheriff stepped forward and hoisted himself up on the truck bed, and, using a latex-gloved hand, he began to shove away forty years' worth of mud from the car's plate.

Carlotta screamed again. J.J. made his way toward the woman, knowing Cheri had been right—little Carlotta Smoot McCoy needed somebody to stand next to her, somebody who wasn't wearing a uniform. And since J.J. was responsible for her being here, he knew it was the decent thing to do.

"Ms. McCoy. Is there anything—"

"I have nothing to say to you newspaper people!" She wagged a knobby finger in J.J.'s face and her eyes bugged out. "You did this to her! You left her to rot! *Murderers!*"

He took a step back, bewildered by her outburst, and

kept an eye on her as the deputies led her away to a squad car. J.J.'s gaze wandered to the banged-up Toyota. Cheri hadn't made much progress. She sat in her car, forehead against the steering wheel in defeat, trying to get the car to start. He listened to the engine grind away at itself, never even coming close to turning over, and called her a tow.

Chapter 3

It was a short drive from Paw Paw Lake into town, and Cherise spent it peering over the dirty passenger window of the tow truck, taking in the sights and sounds of the slice of Cataloochee County she knew best.

The sun was sparkling overhead and the late-spring trees were busting out into full leaf. As they rolled into town down the twisting state highway, Cherise noted the air smelled the same—clean and fragrant with an undertone of decaying forest and cold, clear creek water. They drove past the familiar concrete behemoth paper and fiber factory, out of commission since her childhood but still taking up space at the entrance to town. They drove up Main, past the liquor store, the hairdresser's, the post office, and a string of mountain crafts stores that catered to the tourists on their way to the nearby Smoky Mountains National Park. The old tannery down by the river was still up and running, and the Piggly Wiggly had undergone a no-frills renovation since her last visit, and Cherise had to admire the grocery's effort. Coming up on the right was the old three-story red brick

Bugle building, still dapper and slickly groomed despite its age. And of course, hovering over everything were the mountains—solid but always changing, never-ending, looming but friendly at the same time, immobile waves rolling through a color palette of greens, blues, purples and browns, as familiar to Cherise as the sound of her own name.

It took about two minutes to pass through four of the six traffic lights in downtown Bigler. They turned right at the corner of Main and Boscombe, then took a left onto Willamette.

Cherise grinned at the sight of her grandfather and great-aunt waiting on the front porch, waving and smiling as the tow truck pulled into the drive. Aside from the fact that they were both a little whiter and decidedly more stooped, the moment could have been right out of Cherise's high school days.

Little about the place had changed. Aunt Viv's clapboard two-story house was still painted the hideous mauve color Candy long ago dubbed funeral parlor pink. The edges of the tidy front lawn were still bordered by pink and white peonies crippled by the weight of their own gawdy blossoms, and the porch was trimmed in a wild explosion of white rhododendron flowers. The same giant poplar towered over the property, leaving most of the house in shade.

"Thank you," Cherise told the driver as she held out her last two twenties. "This is all I have . . . I mean, all the cash I have on me at the moment."

The previously silent driver shook his head. "Already paid for, miss," he said, jumping out of the truck.

Cherise exited the passenger side and headed toward

the house. She managed a few steps up the drive when she stopped cold. She didn't know whether to laugh or cry at what she saw. There he was—still at his politically incorrect post in front of the rhododendrons—Viv's concrete lawn jockey. He was outfitted in the same bright red topcoat and the same white gloves, but the jockey had received a Caucasian makeover at some point in the past. The mauve paint that graced the house now coated his once dark cheeks, forehead, chin, and lips.

Cherise had to press her eyes closed for a moment and tell herself that Viv must have meant well. Somebody probably told her that having Mr. Bojangles in the front yard wasn't exactly acceptable these days, and this was her way of evolving. Still . . . the expression "shoot me now" didn't even begin to cover it.

Cherise was back in Bigler.

"Oh, now just look at you!" Viv hollered, holding her arms out wide, her striped blouse bursting at the buttons. "Come on up here, Cheri! Hurry up, now! I've missed you something terrible!"

Granddaddy Garland held on to the railing and took a cautious step down. "Look who it is! The new publisher of the *Bugle*!" He held his arms out, too. "Get up here and give us a hug."

Cheri hurried toward them, and was immediately encased in kisses and squeezes. Aunt Viv smelled the same as she always had—a combination of Jean Naté, vodka, and sausage gravy with too much pepper. Granddaddy felt like a collection of bird bones under his short-sleeved dress shirt. Cherise was startled at how skinny he'd become—all the Newberry brawn was gone.

"Are you sure you're not sick or anything?" Cherise escaped the hugs so she could study Granddaddy. His eyes were watery. Skin hung in crinkled swags from his cheeks and jowls. "Are you okay?"

"Lord-a-mighty!" His laugh was the same, and it rang out through the tree branches. "Hell no, I'm not okay. I'm about to turn eighty stinkin' years old! I'm falling apart! And there's not a damn thing anyone can do about it!"

Viv grabbed Cherise by the elbow and pulled her toward the front door. "Garland, you're going to scare the girl before she even gets unpacked." Viv's arm went around her waist. "We're all getting old, sweetie, but we're healthy as can be expected. The Newberrys live long lives, you know. Always have, and always will."

Cherise had just barely stepped over the threshold when those words came out of Viv's mouth. She wouldn't correct her, of course. There was no need. Right there on the foyer wall hung Cherise's father's high school graduation portrait, and he was gazing down at them, a sardonic glint in his eye, gently reminding them that he'd bucked the family trend.

Loyal Newberry sported a buzz cut in the colorized photo, along with a bow tie and Buddy Holly glasses. He possessed a smile that could knock the wind out of a person.

By thirty-one, he was dead, along with Cherise's mother, Melanie, and the Newberry girls came to live with Aunt Vivienne in the pink house on Willamette. Cherise had been seven. Tanyalee, five.

The official story was that the couple just happened to be in the wrong place at the wrong time. Cherise knew better. It was her fault they were dead. She'd even heard Aunt Viv say as much. Cherise often wondered if her life would have been different if only she hadn't chosen that particular night to sneak downstairs and eavesdrop on the grown-ups. Would life have been easier if she'd never overheard that particular conversation, those particular words?

"Now you come on in here and relax yourself some," Viv said. "I'll get you a sweet tea and a slice of peach cobbler." Though Viv was only a few years younger than her brother, she was still a sturdy woman, and she shoved Cherise down into the armchair by the side window. This wasn't exactly unexpected. Viv had never gently "guided" anyone toward anything, whether it was a chair, a meal, a prom dress, or a man.

Cherise looked around the front parlor. She could have been inside a time capsule. The same white lace sheers hung at the bay windows. The same Hallmark Precious Moments knickknacks adorned the side tables. The same embroidered doilies were laid upon every upholstered head or armrest in the room.

Granddaddy situated himself on one end of the sofa and shook his head. "She'll never change," he said, wistfully. "Thinks she's in charge of the whole damn world."

Viv called out from the kitchen. "I'll holler down to Hazel and have her send up Tater Wayne! He'll unload your suitcases and take 'em up to the guest room! He's going to be so excited to see you after all this time!"

Cherise smiled bravely at her grandfather.

"Tater's been taking care of the place for Viv the last few years, mowing and weed-whacking and doing repairs she can't manage herself." He glanced over his shoulder and lowered his voice so his sister wouldn't hear. "She's slowing down some. I won't let her drive anymore. And since I had to let Tater go at the paper during the layoffs, it seemed like a perfect solution." Granddaddy lowered his voice another notch. "Tater didn't have much luck finding another job—what with his eyeball flopping around the way it does. It makes most folks a little uncomfortable."

Cherise nodded. "I remember." Of course she did. She'd known Tommy "Tater" Wayne and his wayward left eyeball since he moved to Bigler in the second grade.

"As a matter of fact, I've arranged for him to help you clear out the lake house." Granddaddy leaned forward and balanced his scrawny elbows on his knees. "It may take a few days to tidy things up over there."

She didn't like the sound of that. Granted, the last time Cherise had set foot in the lake house was a dozen years before, but she'd always cherished her memories of the old cottage and its rough-hewn beams, quaint but spotless kitchen, and shiny pine floors. It was a magical, light-filled place where the lake breezes blew the curtains, the screen door slammed all day, and the crickets and frogs ruled the nights. It was where she'd experienced moments of pure happiness and belonging before her parents died.

Maybe she'd been foolish to assume Granddaddy and Aunt Viv had managed to keep it up all these years. Maybe it was nothing like her memories.

"You said it just needed a good sweeping," Cherise pointed out. "I thought you meant how it is at the beginning of every summer season."

Granddaddy nodded soberly. "I did say that, yes I

did, but I might have misstated the situation a bit. See, we've not spent much time out there lately."

"Lately?"

"Well, let's see. Tanyalee and J.J. only lived there for six months, so that would make it 'round about five and a half years since anyone's been out there."

Cherise let the back of her head fall against the doily, a sense of dread settling over her. She'd been in town fifteen minutes and she'd seen a ghost pulled from a slime pit, discovered her grandfather was at death's door, and nearly locked lips with Satan himself.

And now Granddaddy admitted he'd lied to her, that the lake house—part of the package he'd used to lure her back to Bigler—had been abandoned for over five years and, worse still, had been the unholy love nest of her sister and J.J. prior to that. She wasn't aware the couple had set up housekeeping there, and never would have agreed to this if she had.

Oh, God—Candy had been right. She'd warned Cherise that the reality of her homecoming wouldn't be the pretty picture Garland had painted over the phone. And now Cherise began to wonder if she could count on anything he'd promised, including the paycheck.

What the hell was I thinking?

Her body began to tremble. She let out a small squeal of desperation.

"We're sure happy to have you back," Granddaddy said. Then he hollered over his shoulder. "I'll take some of that sweet tea!"

Viv scurried back to the living room with a tray, shaking her head. "He's a sly one," she said to Cherise. "He's waiting for the day I forget he's diabetic. Here you are, dear." She handed Cherise a glass decorated with yellow daylilies and green leaves, the same tumblers she'd had since Cherise was a kid. That was followed by a giant slice of warm peach cobbler, vanilla ice cream melting over its golden brown crust.

"Diabetic?" Cherise asked.

"And here's yours, Garland. Unsweetened as always." Viv handed him an identical glass followed by a microscopic piece of cobbler, then sat on the opposite end of the sofa.

"The doctor told me about three years ago, but I'm managing just fine," he told Cherise with a wink.

"Well." Aunt Viv clasped her hands on her lap and smiled. Now that her aunt had stopped moving, Cherise could get a good look at her outfit. Pink pedal pushers. A tucked-in pink-and-white-striped blouse. A pink sun visor. White tennies with pink laces. Pink lipstick.

One thing could be said for Viv—she was consistent.

"You look wonderful, Cheri," she pronounced. "So skinny you'd have to run around in the shower to get wet, but we'll fix that up in no time."

"I thought I'd take you down to the *Bugle* this afternoon, give you the grand tour," Granddaddy said.

"Uh . . . okay." A tour? Granddaddy knew she could find her way around the nineteenth-century office building blindfolded. From her toddler years on, Cherise, Tanyalee, and Candy had had the run of the place with his blessing. There wasn't a better hide-and-seek location in all of western North Carolina. But if he wanted to give her a tour, she'd go on a tour.

Cherise took a sip of tea, then buried her fork in the

cobbler. She brought it to her mouth, clasped her lips around the warm explosion of texture, and tasted the sweet, tart, rich perfection.

Oh, dear God. She had to close her eyes for a moment as the pleasure blasted through her taste buds, leaving her dizzy. She opened her eyes and dug in for another bite.

No wonder Garland had diabetes.

Eight bites later, Cherise placed the empty dessert plate on the side table. It was then that she noticed Granddaddy and Aunt Viv staring at her in silence, shamelessly scouring her from her heels to her hair, naked curiosity in their eyes.

"I ran into some commotion off Highway 25 on my way into town." Cherise offered that tidbit as she wiped her mouth with a napkin, hoping the conversation would end her elderly relatives' intense scrutiny of her appearance, not to mention her eating habits.

"You don't say?" Granddaddy asked. "Over at Wim's construction site, no doubt. There are always earth movers and trucks going in and out."

"No," Cherise said, noting that her grandfather must not have heard the news. Maybe he'd already vacated the publisher's chair in spirit if not in body. When she was a kid, nothing happened in Bigler without him knowing. "I think it's a crime scene. Turner's there with a bunch of his deputies. They're pulling an old car out of the muck, and I think it might be the car the police were looking for all those years ago, you know, Barbara Jean Smoot from the the 'Lady of the Lake' legend."

Every muscle clinging to Granddaddy's frail frame tensed. His eyes went wide beneath his bushy white brows. "I better call J.J."

"He's already there."

Cherise didn't miss the quick glance between her relatives.

"How nice he was there to welcome you to town, then," Viv said.

Cherise laughed, thinking that J.J. had been as welcoming as a sex-deprived pit bull. "A veritable one-man Welcome Wagon," she said.

"Breaking news, eh? All the more reason to head down to the paper." Granddaddy pushed himself up from the couch with some assistance from Viv, which he tried to shake off.

"I surely don't think Cheri wants to go to work right off the bat." Aunt Viv stood with him, steadying him at the elbow. "At least let the girl unpack and freshen up. And her car is out of commission. Do you think we should give her the Cadillac to drive while her little foreign car gets repaired?"

Granddaddy slapped at Viv's hand. "Stop fiddling with me, Vivienne. I'm perfectly fine. And a modern young woman isn't going to have the slightest desire to drive your pink houseboat around town."

Aunt Viv slapped the hand that had slapped hers. The slapping back and forth continued for several seconds while the brother and sister argued about the maintenance history of Viv's 1976 Coupe DeVille, a car that Candy had dubbed "the pimpmobile," a car that Cherise would never, *ever* be caught driving.

"Oh, for heaven's sake, Garland!" Viv said, smacking her brother on the shoulder.

Just then, there was a crisp little knock at the door. The hinges groaned as the door opened. "Anybody home?"

When Tater Wayne stuck his head around the living room archway, the senior citizen beat-down abruptly came to a halt.

"Cheri!" He smiled widely, even as his left eyeball began ricocheting around in his skull. He held out a bunch of familiar-looking pink and white peonies and moved toward her, smiling with the seven or eight teeth that remained in his mouth. "What in the world were you thinkin' stayin' away from Bigler this long?"

"I know, Tater!" Cherise pasted a smile on her face. "I was just asking myself the same darn thing!"

Chapter 4

The newsroom floors, walls, and ceiling were the same as they had always been. But nothing else about the place made any sense to Cherise.

She made a quick sweep of the long and open room and counted four bodies behind about a dozen desks. When she'd been a kid, the desks had been crammed in here back to back, people running through the narrow aisles with paper gripped in their hands, cigarettes dangling from their lips as they shouted at each other over the ringing phones and clacking and humming of electric typewriters.

Today's version of the *Bigler Bugle* newsroom was preternaturally sterile. Reporters spoke in hushed tones into earbuds, their fingers flying over laptop keys that barely generated noise. The air was smoke-free. Nobody's desk was piled high with papers. No one was running down the aisles to deliver news copy or photographs by hand to editors.

In fact, there were no aisles at all, just open space,

and Cherise saw only one editor and two people on the copy desk. The place had been decimated.

A wave of sadness rushed over her. The *Bugle* she knew was gone. The business had been gutted and drained of its lifeblood.

At that instant, J.J. came rounding the corner, his expression stern and his footsteps hurried. Cherise watched him point to a reporter who was wrapping up a phone conversation, then at the lone editor, motioning for them both to join him in the new glass-walled conference room.

Only then did J.J. notice Cherise standing at the far end of the newsroom with Granddaddy at her side. He stopped. Cherise watched something pass over his face—surprise and another emotion she couldn't immediately put her finger on. Probably shock. *She* was still shocked by that moment that they'd almost kissed, that was for sure. One thing she knew—that wasn't shame she'd just seen in his expression. J.J. didn't do shame, apparently.

"You, too," he said, pointing to Cherise. Then J.J. turned his back and headed for the conference room.

Her mouth fell open. *What an ass-hat.* She couldn't do this. She didn't need this. She couldn't stand to be in the same room with J.J., let alone masquerade as his boss. He'd been immeasurably cruel to her sister. What kind of person gets a woman pregnant, cashes out her inheritance, and kicks her to the curb when she miscarries, throwing her things into the rain?

Cherise could still hear Tanyalee's sobs over the phone. It would be a sound she'd carry with her for the rest of her life.

And she'd almost let that man *kiss* her?

She had to get out of there.

"Shall we?" Grandaddy asked.

No.

She would turn right around and drive back to Tampa. Or maybe it was time to start over somewhere like Raleigh or Atlanta or Charleston. She had a finance degree and years of experience—she would eventually find a job if she kept trying. And Candy could join her once she was settled.

That was that, then. There was no place for Cherise here. She felt no obligation to her crazy family, their obsolete business, or this ridiculous, has-been, hillbilly town that had nothing to offer but ghost stories and regrets.

"I'm really sorry, Granddaddy," Cherise said, turning to look up into his milky eyes. "I can't do this. I should never have agreed to come back here. I'm afraid this isn't going to work."

Her grandfather lifted his chin and laughed, all while guiding her toward the conference room with a hand against her back. "That's the thing about newspapering," he said, ignoring the fact that she was now digging her heels into the old wood floors in an effort to prevent any additional forward progress. "You just have to jump in, Cheri girl. It's what all the Newberrys before you have done. You're going to do great. It's in your blood."

"But . . ."

Granddaddy stopped pushing her and removed his hand. She nearly fell.

"You promised me you'd at least try," he said, his face pulled tight in seriousness.

"I—"

"Give it four weeks. That's all I ask. If you still feel this way in a month, I won't force it—you can go on back to your business in Tampa and forget this ever happened."

Cherise took a deep breath. "Will you shut down the *Bugle* if I don't stay?"

"More than likely."

Cherise blinked at Granddaddy. It was true—she'd given him her word. And she certainly needed the money. A few thousand dollars would be enough for a fresh start. Besides, she could survive anything for a month. Her foray into the world of temp work had taught her that, if nothing else.

"Is there a problem?" J.J. stood in the conference room door, his arms folded across his broad chest and his head cocked in annoyance at their slow progress.

What had happened to him? Cherise wondered. Sure, he was still insanely handsome with that thick, black hair and those intense, bottomless blue eyes. His body was ripped like it had always been, thanks to his fondness for hikes, mountain-biking, and rock climbing. But when had he become so serious? What had happened to the playful man she once knew? She couldn't remember the last time she'd seen a sincere smile on J.J. DeCourcy's face.

Cherise suddenly stiffened, a sharp awareness slicing through her. *Oh, yes she did. Of course she remembered.*

It was her last night in Bigler before she left for college. She and J.J. were sitting on the edge of the dock, their bare toes making circles in the warm lake water, their feet bumping against each other's, their bodies so close she was halfway on his lap.

He kissed her one last time. It was so sweet and hot and deep that her head reeled. She'd allowed herself to fall into it, melt away in the hot rush of that kiss. Just one last time. Then she'd pulled away.

That's when he'd smiled at her. He looked down into her face, the moonlight shimmering in his eyes, as his lips parted and his dimples deepened. It was one of those charming, lopsided, puppy-love smiles he'd been giving her since the middle school mixer, when he'd professed his eternal devotion and showed her the "CNN" he'd scrawled on his inner left forearm in permanent Magic Marker. "Permanent means it'll be there forever," he'd pointed out.

How many times had she explained it all to J.J.? What they'd shared had been fun and wonderful, but it wasn't meant to last. She had no intention of staying in some small town in the middle of nowhere. It wasn't the life she planned for herself. It might have been good enough for J.J., but not for her, and there was no way she was hitching her fortunes to a small-town boy with small-town dreams, a boy who couldn't even decide if he wanted to continue his education.

His smile had eventually faded.

Nearly seven years passed before she saw him again, bigger and harder and no longer a boy. He was standing on the doorstep of her first house in Tampa, a shy smile on his face and hope in his eyes.

The next time she saw him he was wearing a tuxedo with a white carnation pinned to his lapel and Tanyalee glued to his arm, and the smile plastered on his face looked more fearful than joyful. And all Cherise could think was, *Here comes the bride, and there goes J.J.*.

"There's no problem whatsoever," Cherise answered him. She smoothed out her shirt and raised her chin as she walked past J.J. and into the conference room, immediately introducing herself to the city editor and general assignment reporter waiting to meet their new publisher. Several other people began to file in, and Cherise took a moment to introduce herself to each—the sports editor, the business writer, the head of the graphics and photography department, and the schools and government reporter.

"Close the door, please," Cherise told J.J., taking the seat at the head of the conference table as everyone got settled. Granddaddy smiled proudly at her. She took that as her cue to get the meeting started. "Now, I'm assuming the most pressing concern today is the discovery of the old car? What's the latest? What do we know?"

Chapter 5

We?

J.J. widened his eyes in disbelief and looked sideways at Garland, the proud patriarch. It would take a superhuman amount of self-restraint to not bust out guffawing at this point.

We knew next to nothing. *We* might be a Newberry, but *we* had never worked a day at the *Bugle* and wouldn't know a news story if it bit a big hefty chunk out of our nicely shaped ass. *We* just rolled into town in a scrap heap of a car and ridiculously impractical shoes and plopped our tight skirt into the publisher's chair without so much as a howdy-do.

J.J. took a deep breath as he sat down, reminding himself that there was a reason she was here, and he now had a role to play. At least he hadn't blown everything by kissing her.

J.J. managed a patient smile. "First off, we know it's Barbara Jean Smoot's car. There's a match with the plates and the vehicle make and model. Turner said there are remains inside, but they are in such disintegrated condition that any forensic investigation will take longer than usual."

Cheri drummed her fingers on the tabletop, frowning. "That's just a technicality. Really, who else could it be?" She looked around the table. "Is anyone else missing in this town? Why can't we just put her picture on the front page and say the Lady of the Lake's car has been found and the body inside is hers and that she was obviously murdered?"

A sharp pain sliced into J.J.'s right temple. "Because that's not good journalism."

"Fine. I understand your point. I'm not an idiot," Cheri said. "What I'm suggesting is that we find a way to spice up the 'good journalism' so we can take advantage of this story and sell some papers."

Cheri waited for someone in the room to agree with her, but no one did. "Isn't that what we're trying to do here? Isn't it about time the *Bugle* got its sexy back?"

Mimi Grayson, J.J.'s only general assignment reporter, snorted in disbelief, then covered it up with a fake sneezing attack. Jim Taggert, the *Bugle*'s seasoned city editor, stared blankly ahead, the gray stubble on his upper lip glistening with sweat.

J.J. turned slowly to Garland for some guidance. The old man gave him a helpless shrug and a wink.

Oh, shit. What had they done?

"Madam publisher," J.J. began, wondering how the hell he could give Cheri a refresher course in journalism without making it sound belittling. "You are well aware, growing up as a Newberry and all, that the primary responsibility of a newspaper is to report the news as accurately and fairly as possible while making our home-delivery edition deadline, which is midnight, about eight hours from now."

"I know that."

"Then, of course, you know that the *Bugle* can't publish something without the facts to back it up."

I'm starting to sound like Turner, he realized with a shudder.

"I'm not asking you to," Cheri said, her voice growing snippy. "I'm asking you to make the most of the facts we do have."

"Uh-huh."

"It's Barbara Jean Smoot's car, right? So that's fact number one." Cheri said this with authority.

"Okay," J.J. allowed.

"Is Barbara Jean Smoot still officially missing?"

"Uh, yes."

"Is Barbara Jean Smoot the woman behind the 'Lady of the Lake' legend?

"Well, if you believe that stuff, yeah."

"Then that's fact number two," Cheri continued. "And from that flows some logical possibilities that we can use to attract readers. The body in Miss Smoot's car is probably Miss Smoot, so we'll just get the sheriff to say that. And she was probably the victim of foul play, because how else does a woman end up at the bottom of a lake, trapped in her car, forced to haunt the site of her hideous murder until justice is done?"

J.J. bit down on his bottom lip so it wouldn't land on the floor with a thud.

Taggert cleared his throat. "She coulda gotten lost and driven into the water."

"Maybe she was under the influence and thought the dock was a road," Mimi suggested.

Cheri frowned. "Who wants to read that? We need something juicier, something that will make people gasp and gossip to their neighbor and not be able to fall asleep at night!" She gestured toward her grandfather, her golden eyes shining with excitement. "Am I right, or what?"

J.J. squinted at Cheri, deciding that her enthusiasm greatly outweighed her grasp of reality. This imbalance might allow her to pass for the redheaded love child of Sarah Palin and Glenn Beck, but it had no place at a principled little Southern news outlet like the *Bugle*.

Someone knocked on the conference room door, putting an end to Cheri's fevered sales pitch. Whoever it was, J.J. wanted to hug and kiss them for their timing.

"Am I interrupting?" The perpetually pickled Purnell Lawson headed toward Cheri before anyone could answer, his arms outstretched and his smile wide. The finance and advertising director's belly pushed against his shirt buttons with such force that J.J. feared his red suspenders would snap off, poking somebody's eye out.

"The prodigal daughter has returned! Give ole Uncle Purnell a hug!"

J.J. watched Cheri stand politely and tap the old guy on the back as he embraced her.

"How are you, Purnell?" Cheri asked.

"Busier than a cat covering crap on a marble floor!" Purnell kissed her cheek. "How's my sweet Cheri?"

Garland looked embarrassed and cleared his throat. "There'll be plenty of time for a nice visit over at the house, Purnell," he said. "Right now we're in the middle of an editorial meeting."

"Getting her feet wet already?" Purnell laughed loudly, sending a breeze of Beefeater through the enclosed room. "Something big, I hope. We need a spike in street sales to stimulate advertising. What y'all got?" Purnell looked to Garland with his reddened eyes wide.

"Well, seems Barbara Jean Smoot's car was just pulled out from Paw Paw Lake."

Purnell sucked in air like he wanted his Beefeater fumes back. The old man's bloated face paled and his body stilled.

"You don't say?" Purnell asked, still smiling.

"Wim Wimbley drained the lake so he could start construction and they found the car this morning," Mimi said. "They got a winch and a crane out there right away."

Purnell nodded. "Well now, that *is* a good story." He chuckled. "I'll leave y'all to your business."

Suddenly, he was gone.

Chapter 6

Once Aunt Viv and Granddaddy were in their rooms for the night, Cherise pulled the short cord of the pink Princess phone from its hallway stand and into the bathroom. She shut and locked the bathroom door. She sat on the fluffy pink bath rug, pressed her back against the claw-foot tub and stretched her legs out under the pedestal sink.

Here she was, thirty years old and still hiding in the bathroom to make a phone call, just like in her high school years. She stared at the familiar pattern of pink and white ceramic tiles going halfway up the wall, inhaling the sharp mix of Jean Naté, Dial soap, and Pond's cold cream that had seeped into the grout over the decades.

Candy's voice sounded like the music of the angels. "I knew it," her friend said after Cherise had given her a detailed rundown of her first day home. "So when do you think you'll be back? It'll be great to have a car again. I hate the bus—it's full of pervs."

Cherise sighed, then whispered, "I got some bad

news about the car. It died. I have no idea what's wrong with it."

"Oh, well, you get what you pay for, I guess." Cherise heard her friend try to hide her disappointment. "How much did we pay for that car, again?"

"Five hundred."

Candy sighed. "So you'll be taking the bus home?"

"I'm not coming home. Not right away. I'm going to give it a month."

"You go, girl," Candy whispered. "That's a month longer than I figured you'd last. Have you talked to Tanyalee yet? I know you said J.J.'s still an ass, but is he still hot?"

Cherise frowned. "Yes," she whispered.

"I knew it," Candy whispered.

"Wait a minute. Why are *you* whispering?"

"Because you are."

"But I'm in Aunt Viv's bathroom. I have to whisper."

Candy burst out laughing. "My God! This is hilarious! I'm having déjà vu!"

Cherise hung her head and ran her free hand through her hair. "Good Lord, Candy. I swear I have no idea why I came back here, and now I've promised Granddaddy I'll stay for at least four weeks. I made a total fool of myself at that meeting today, pretending like I was Diane-Freakin'-Sawyer. And then Granddaddy took me to the publisher's office and asked me to pick out a paint color for the walls, and J.J. walked by several times just to sneer at me through the open door."

"Ugh."

"I'm not qualified for this."

"Just choose something in a neutral pastel."

"No! I mean the *job*! I don't know the first thing about what I'm supposed to do in this *job*!"

"I don't know about that," Cherise said. "You grew up around journalism and what you don't know now you can learn in a hurry. The important thing is that you demonstrated leadership today—charged right in there and took the bull by the horns. Besides, advance preparation has never been our strong point."

Cherise giggled. How very true. They'd launched— and lost—several businesses before they stumbled into real estate. Armed with only an online course and an abundance of enthusiasm, they'd managed to turn a three-thousand-dollar investment into a portfolio worth more than fourteen million.

The way up was nothing but one long, heady rush. The way down was all shock and pain.

"This is different," Cherise said with a sigh. "This is my family's heritage. What if I do nothing but hammer down the last nail in the coffin? They think I'm some sort of business genius. They think I can turn around decades of decay in a few weeks!"

"The important thing is you're going to try your best. You're keeping your promise to your granddaddy. That's all that matters." Candy paused. "Um, I just want to remind you that you can never tell anyone what happened down here. My mother can *never* find out I lost the money she gave me."

"I know."

"So what else?" Candy asked.

"What do you mean?"

"What aren't you telling me?"

"I'm not following."

"Come on now," Candy said. "The paper is on its last legs, Aunt Viv and Garland are as strange as ever, Tater Wayne's still hot for you, and the lake house has probably fallen to the ground. But what else aren't you telling me?"

Cherise rolled her eyes. "Isn't that enough?"

"Sure. But I know you. You're hiding something."

"God," Cherise groaned.

"Well? What is it?"

"He . . . he almost kissed me."

Candy was silent for a moment, then said, "Cherise, I've been telling you since second grade that it's nice you're always so sweet to Tater Wayne, but he misinterprets your good nature. He thinks you're hitting on him."

Cherise giggled. "I'm talking about J.J."

"Out at Paw Paw Lake? You mean, he almost gave you a 'hello' kiss on the cheek?"

"Uh, not exactly."

Candy whistled low and long. "Details, please."

"I was in the process of slapping him for being such a dickhead, you know, not saying a single freakin' word to me while Turner was nothing but a gentleman."

"How's Turner doing? He's always been a good guy."

"Actually, he seems very sad, even though it's been years since his wife died."

"I'm sorry to hear that."

"He asked about you."

"Really? That was nice of him. Tell him I say 'hey.' But we were talking about you—what did you mean by 'slap'? A real slap? You were trying to slap J.J.?"

"Yes, but he grabbed my wrist and yanked me up

against him and stared at me like some kind of sex-crazed, wild—"

"Cheri? Are you in there?"

The bathroom doorknob jiggled back and forth. This was followed by a series of quick little knocks on the door. *"Everything all right, sweetie? Can I get you anything? I bought you some sanitary pads. They're on the second shelf of the linen closet, behind the Dippity-Do."*

"I'll be out in a second, Aunt Viv."

Candy began laughing into the phone. "Better hang up before you get grounded! And save some of that Dippity-Do for me!"

"Oh, my God," Cherise whispered. "I don't care if I'm sleeping on a bed of leaves out at the lake. I gotta get out of here and get a cell phone."

"Maybe with your first check you can buy yourself one of those pay-as-you-go phones."

"I plan on it. I'll get you one, too."

"That'd be great! We haven't had cell phones since—"

"Cheri?"

"I better go."

"Hold up," Candy said. "J.J. was staring at you like he wanted to kiss you? Are you sure?"

Cherise laughed. "Of course I'm sure. He just grabbed me and—"

"Cheri? Did you find the pads?"

"I really gotta go. I miss you."

"Miss you more. Call me tomorrow. This shit is so good I don't even miss having cable."

* * *

Purnell pushed up from the rocking chair and stumbled through his living room to the front door, kicking over his bottle of gin in the process. He watched the remaining liquid soak into the carpet.

It didn't matter. Nothing mattered anymore.

The pounding on the door continued. He could pretend to be asleep, he supposed, but what was the point? The prick had a key. The prick was his landlord. The prick owned Purnell's home. The prick owned his soul.

Purnell yanked his suspenders onto his shoulders as he answered the door. "Fuck you," he said by way of greeting. Then he staggered back to the rocker and took a minute to catch his breath. When he looked up, the prick stood over him, disgust in his eyes and glee in his smirk.

Wim Wimbley had one hell of a smirk.

"Just love what you've done with the place, Lawson." Wim nudged the gin bottle with the toe of his polished loafer. "It's got a nice Late Stage Alcoholic vibe to it."

Purnell ignored him. He hooked his fingers into his suspender straps and rocked back and forth, the hate roiling in him. Sometimes he had to laugh at how he'd misjudged this young man. The senior Wimbley had been a soulless bastard his entire life—back in school, all the time he was Cataloochee County sheriff, and later when he started buying and selling every acre of land he could get his hands on this side of Tennessee. Even after Wimbley had gone and knocked up his third wife—becoming a daddy at fifty—Purnell used to tell himself that his nightmare would be over once the old bastard was dead. What a pitiful miscalculation that had been.

Wimbley's spawn was twice the prick his father ever was, and he'd inherited more than the land development company—he'd inherited the family's profitable little blackmail business as well.

The transition from father to son had been seamless. After Winston died, Wim continued with the collections. Six hundred dollars on the first day of every month, month after month, year after year, with a sixteen percent penalty for late payment. Thanks to the Wimbleys, the fear of being prosecuted for murder had turned Purnell into a thief and drained every bit of decency from his life.

"Of course, I'll have to charge you for damage to the carpet upon termination of the lease," Wim said.

Purnell howled with laughter. That statement was absurd and they both knew it. The lease would terminate when Purnell did. Besides, the carpet—like everything else in this little ranch house—had been purchased by Purnell a long, long time ago, when he still owned the place, back before Lizzie got sick, back when there was a reason to get up every morning.

"What do you want, Wimbley?"

He chuckled. "You could at least offer me a drink."

Purnell gestured to the gin-soaked carpet. "Help yourself. Straws are in the kitchen."

Wim laughed.

It never failed to disgust him how he'd gotten himself into this mess. After Lizzie got the cancer diagnosis, Purnell didn't have the time or energy to keep up with blackmail payments to Winston Wimbley. Out of the kindness of the bastard's blackened heart, the senior Wimbley offered to hold the house title in lieu of payments. Once Purnell was up to date again, he'd get the title back. Never happened, obviously. And now Purnell paid rent on his own home in addition to the blackmail payments. His wife was dead. His kids were grown and gone. The carpet—like the roof, the yard, the furnace, and Purnell's arteries—was beyond repair.

"I suppose you've heard the big news," Wim said.

Purnell looked away. "You came all the way over here to gloat? Is that it?"

"Not really."

Purnell produced a raspy chuckle and shook his head. "Don't be coy, son. No time to fritter away. My ticker could give out at any moment."

Wim looked around the room for somewhere to sit, then thought better of it. "I stopped by to tell you that you got a problem over at the *Bugle*."

Purnell nodded. "We got lots of problems over at the *Bugle*. Shitty advertising revenue. Shitty circulation. Garland installing his bimbo granddaughter in the publisher's chair."

"Hey, careful now," Wim said with a wry smile. "That bimbo is my fiancée's sister."

Purnell snapped his suspenders in surprise. "Well, now, that'll be as near perfect a marital union as this town's ever seen. Don't forget to purchase an engagement announcement in the *Bugle*. I can get you a discount."

"Of course you can." Wim smiled down at him. "The point is, you're going to need to keep J.J. from writing about that car. Nobody wants that."

One of Purnell's eyebrows shot high on his forehead. "Really now? What kind of sick game are you playing, Wim? You knew as well as I did what was on the bottom of Paw Paw Lake and you dug it up anyway—got all your permits in place and merrily sucked the lake dry. If you didn't want the truth to come out, why did you go and do that, boy? For sport? To see an old man squirm on the hook just one last time?"

"I didn't know she was down there," Wim said.

"That's horseshit."

"No. I'm telling you the truth." Wim suddenly looked nervous. He rubbed his smooth-shaven chin. Not for the first time, Purnell wondered how Wim was able to pull it off—he was just as handsome and golden as he'd always been. None of the rotten, stinking foul mess at his core had ever leached to the surface. It was another way in which the son surpassed the father.

At least with Winston, he'd been as ugly on the outside as the inside.

"Give me a fuckin' break, son," Purnell said. "Besides, J.J.'s not your problem. There are FBI agents in town. And I sure as hell can't do anything about the FBI."

"No. Listen to me." Wim began to pace back and forth. It occurred to Purnell that all he had to do was stretch out his foot and he could trip the little prick. Now wouldn't that be fun?

"I heard it's going to take a while for the police to get a positive ID on the body. I need you to keep J.J. from printing anything in the meantime. I gotta sell those lots."

Purnell laughed. "You're kidding me."

"Listen." Wim held his palms out. "Daddy always said there was nothing down there. Whenever I asked him about it, he'd laugh and say that you were too drunk to know what really happened that night, and there was no car in the lake. No ghost. No murder. Nothing. He said you blacked out. He told you that you killed the girl so he could use you."

Purnell didn't think he had it in him, but he shot out of the rocking chair, energized by a burst of clear, pure rage. He grabbed Wim by the collar of his preppy shirt. *"What?"*

Wim twisted himself free. "It's the truth! Daddy said you were so drunk you thought you killed her and he went along with your delusion because he could use you to get money to start buying land. Daddy said that he knew for a fact that Barbara Jean Smoot ran off and changed her name. He used to laugh at you all the time."

Purnell's chest tightened. He had trouble breathing. "Nonsense!" he whispered.

That was crazy talk. How many times had he relived that night in 1964? Barbara Jean had picked him up behind the newspaper offices and they did what they usually did—they got liquored up and went for a ride. Music blared from the dashboard radio, the wind whipped all that gorgeous blond hair of hers around her head, Purnell dragged his fingers across the bare flesh of her upper arm, tweaked a hard little nipple . . . that Barbara Jean had been something special, all wild and hell-bent on living life to the fullest. He was damn happy to help her.

Admittedly, the rest of the evening's events were fuzzy, but of course Purnell had been responsible for the girl's death! He woke up in the woods near Paw Paw Lake late that night, his fingers smelling like girl juice, dried blood under his eye, a little pair of white cotton panties shoved in his trouser pocket. What in the name of God had happened? Where did Barbara Jean get herself to? he wondered. It must have been one hell of a night!

Purnell had walked home in the dark. He snuck in his own front door without waking Lizzie. He showered and dressed for work, putting a dab of Mercurochrome on the cut and telling Lizzie he'd nicked himself shaving again. He staggered into the newsroom. It wasn't unusual for him to be a little rough around the edges first thing in the morning, so nobody seemed to notice.

But then again, no one was paying any mind to him that morning. The newsroom was buzzing—there'd been a possible murder! A witness told the sheriff he saw a car plunge into Paw Paw Lake with a woman behind the wheel! And a man was seen jumping out of the vehicle at the last instant. He ran into the woods. Police were looking for him.

Purnell thought he'd vomit. He escaped to his office and shut the door. He could barely catch his breath. What had he done? He and Lizzie had two kids at that point. He'd just been promoted to chief financial officer at the *Bugle*. He'd just become president-elect of the Bigler Chamber of Commerce. *This could not be happening!*

"You all right, old man?"

Purnell blinked. It took him a few moments to make sense of where he was, when it was, and why Winston Wimbley's son was standing in front of him. The pain in his chest helped Purnell regain his focus.

Of course he hadn't imagined anything. He'd killed that girl, no question. But it had obviously been an accident. And as Purnell had sat in his office at the *Bugle* that morning so long ago, he told himself he should confess. That was the only way out. He'd do it tomorrow. Or the day after that. But he'd do it.

Turned out, a confession wasn't necessary. Sheriff Winston Wimbley had figured it out by the afternoon. Of course he had—Wimbley knew all about Purnell's dalliances with the pretty and willing Barbara Jean Smoot, and might have had a few rolls in the grass with her himself. It was no secret she had a thing for older, successful men, after all.

And, oh! Purnell's body shook in terror as he watched that bastard stroll through the newsroom on his way to the business office, gun on his hip, badge on his chest, and a swagger in his step. Purnell was certain the first words out of his lifelong buddy's lips would be, "You're under arrest."

Instead, Wimbley shut Purnell's office door behind him and pulled its shade. "*Now* what have you gone and done, Purnell?" Sheriff Wimbley shook his head like he was straining to have patience. "Y'all probably don't even remember what happened last night."

Purnell started shaking. He fingered the cut under his eye. He was on the verge of crying. "I don't remember! Oh, God, what have I done?"

"Looks like she fought you pretty good, too." With a deep sigh, Wimbley settled into the chair across from Purnell's desk. "This is an unfortunate turn of events, no doubt, but it doesn't have to be the end of the world. I can get you out of this mess."

"What?" Purnell had looked at Wimbley in shock. "*How?*"

"I got a little proposition for you."

And that's when he got his marching orders. It remained unspoken, but Wimbley had to have been aware that Purnell didn't have the kind of money he was asking for. They both knew the only way he could comply with Wimbley's demands would be to steal from the *Bugle*. So that's what Purnell did.

For the first few years, he made a habit of skimming off revenues, hiding what he'd stolen by underreporting how much the paper was earning through retail advertising, classified liners and displays, and preprint inserts. But after Garland started asking questions, Purnell knew he had to find another way to pay Wimbley. That's when he got the idea to steal from the debit side of the ledger instead.

He began padding the costs of doing business wherever possible. This included payments for newsprint, ink, machinery, transportation costs, and especially the steady stream of technology upgrades needed from the eighties on. Perhaps Purnell's most ingenious move was inventing a series of shell "consulting" firms that were paid handsomely for services they never provided.

And that's how he'd managed it, month after month for more than forty years—a lifetime of stealing from Garland Newberry to pay Winston Wimbley. In exchange, Sheriff Wimbley made the witness go away. As he told Purnell that day in his office, "That Negro don't have the brains God gave a goose. Won't be much of a loss."

Oh, how Purnell had come to wish Winston had just gone ahead and handcuffed him that day, dragged him through the newsroom, and put his ass in jail. It would

have been the proper punishment for killing Barbara
Jean. It would have spared the life of that poor Johnston bastard, and many years later, Loyal Newberry
and his pretty young wife.

Why had Garland's son turned out to be such a goddamned do-gooder of a publisher? Why did he have to
go poking his nose into what was buried in the past?
*Ah, hell . . . Oh, Lord have mercy . . . of course I killed
Barbara Jean! Because if I didn't, it would mean Garland's son and daughter-in-law died for no damn reason at all!*

"You should probably sit down, you old fool," Wim
said. "You look kinda green all of a sudden."

Purnell fell back into the rocking chair, his throat
burning with bile. Then a sharp pain sliced through his
chest. He stared at the young Wimbley, suddenly unable
to get his breath. "You're a fuckin' liar," he wheezed.

Wim raised his hands over his head. "I'm not shit-
ting you! When I went to drag the lake, I had no idea
she was there! Now we've got a dead body and a big-
ass publicity problem. Who's gonna want to shell out a
third of a million for a retirement cottage at the scene
of a murder, haunted by an honest-to-God ghost? Fuck!
Do you have any idea how much fuckin' money I'm
about to lose on this?"

Purnell gasped. It was unthinkable. He couldn't grasp
it . . . his vision was going dark . . . "On the kitchen
counter . . . my pills . . . hurry."

Wim ran from the room. When he returned seconds
later, he shoved the bottle toward him. Purnell shook
out a single tablet and placed it under his tongue, waiting for the relief to come.

"Should I take you to the hospital?"

Purnell shook his head.

"Well. All right then, I guess." Wim cleared his throat and headed for the door. "Remember what I said about stopping J.J."

Relief washed through Purnell at the sound of the door shutting. He didn't want the little prick to see him cry.

The moon was off duty that night and the path was severely overgrown, but J.J. knew the way. He'd taken this walk hundreds of times in life, and again in his dreams.

When he reached the lake's edge, he saw that the water was as lifeless as black glass. No breeze rippled its surface. No stars peeked from the cloud cover to reflect in its mirror. And since it was still May, the nighttime symphony of amphibians, insects, and loons hadn't yet gotten their act together. It was all silence. Darkness. Memories.

J.J. held the flower arrangement against his leg and inhaled the cool night air. What everybody said about him was true—he belonged in hill country. He'd traveled the world, but these North Carolina mountains were in his blood and bone. Nowhere else rang true. This would always be home, and there wasn't a damn thing he could do about it.

He smiled and shook his head in the dark. He hoped Cheri would discover it was the same for her. In fact, he'd bet everything on it.

He remembered the day he and Garland discussed the possibility of Cheri coming to town. Yes, the publisher's job was supposed to be his, but he'd be all right if it went to Cheri. "She's a Newberry and I'm not," he'd told Garland.

"You sure, son?" Garland's white eyebrows twitched as he studied J.J. "It's not going to be an easy road, you know. Cheri has made a point of avoiding this family, and I can't say as I blame her. She's complicated, you know, always been a prickly girl. Still angry about losing her mama and daddy."

J.J. knew all that.

"As you know, this newspaper is at a crossroads, Jefferson, and it won't take much for us to go under for good. So if I bring her in as publisher, you'll still need to keep a hand on the wheel."

He'd nodded.

"Plus . . ." Garland cocked his head and peered at J.J. quizzically. "Shit, son—if Cheri comes home it'll open the whole Tanyalee can o' worms. You know those girls never sorted it out between them." Garland chuckled. "You'll be ripped apart like a sirloin at a dogfight."

J.J. knew all that, too, but he'd agreed with Garland—the two sisters couldn't go on forever without having it out, could they?

"It would all be worth it if Cheri came home and stayed, wouldn't it?" Garland smiled at him. "So you're up for this mess, son?"

"Of course," J.J. had answered. "I wouldn't miss it for the world."

By now, J.J.'s eyes had become accustomed to the dark, and he scanned the lake property, noting how the land gently leveled out at the water's edge. The Newberrys owned over twenty wooded acres on this side, with the summer house strategically placed for sunset views over the Smokies. The house was fairly isolated, though he could make out the lights over at the Mc-Caswells' around the bend, a trick that would soon be impossible when the trees reached their full abundance.

He'd always loved Newberry Lake. Looking back, he knew that living here for six months had been the only decent thing to come from his marriage to Tanyalee.

J.J. shook his head and headed to the front porch. He placed the flowers by the door so they'd be the first thing Cheri would see when she visited with Tater Wayne the next day.

And, unfortunately, that was all the seduction J.J. had time for that evening. He got in his truck and headed back to the newsroom, knowing it was going to be a long, long night.

Chapter 7

"Oh, for God's sake!"

Cherise picked up the shiny brass nameplate from the desktop and gawked.

CHERI NEWBERRY, PUBLISHER.

Why did these people insist on calling her *Cheri*? It wasn't what her parents named her. It wasn't even how she referred to herself. So why did they do it?

There was no excuse. So what if everyone in Bigler had called her Cheri from middle school on? If Candy had been able to make the transition, why couldn't everyone else?

Cherise opened the desk drawer, tossed the nameplate inside, and slammed it shut.

"Morning."

Cherise jumped at the sound of his voice. She managed a pleasant smile as she looked up to meet J.J.'s gaze.

Her heart thudded.

He stood slouched in the doorway, wearing yesterday's jeans and rumpled cotton dress shirt. He looked disheveled. Sleepy. He'd probably nodded off in his desk chair at some point during the night.

Though wrinkled and bleary-eyed, J.J. still looked unbearably, wildly *sexy*.

Cherise shook her head, startled by the thought. "Good morning." It embarrassed her that her voice sounded so unstable.

"Problem?" He looked at her askance.

"There's a spelling error on my nameplate. It's not . . . well, they spelled . . ." She lost her train of thought because, no, of course he wasn't sexy. At all. He wasn't even a decent guy. He was rude. Hostile. Cruel. A liar and a cheat. He was a bad man who happened to be good-looking. Period.

And he stood there staring at her, waiting for her to finish her sentence.

"Whom should I speak to about ordering a replacement?"

J.J. thought that was funny, apparently. He straightened from the door frame as he laughed. "A typo, eh? At the *Bigler Bugle*? Are you absolutely certain?"

"I know how to spell my name."

"See? That's why we hired you as publisher!"

Cherise crossed her arms over her chest, in no mood for J.J.'s caustic brand of conversation. "I don't go by Cheri anymore, as you are well aware. I've been known as Cherise Newberry since . . . well . . . for more than five years. I believe it sounds far more professional."

He produced a crooked smile. "It most certainly does."

"I have no interest in going through life as a Popsicle flavor."

J.J. nodded slowly. "Or lollipop."

Cheri narrowed one eye at him, regretting she'd even started this conversation.

"But I gotta tell you, there's nothing like a cherry Slurpee on a hot summer day." He winked at her.

"Are you done?"

"Actually, no." J.J. gave a thoughtful nod. "Did you know that 'cherry' is what gearheads call a perfectly restored old car? Or that virgins are sometimes—"

"Who's in charge of nameplates?" Cherise prayed her cheeks hadn't flared red. "Who's the point person for these things?"

"Ah, that would be Gladys." J.J. crooked a thumb over his left shoulder.

She frowned. That couldn't be right—Gladys Harbison was still at the *Bugle*? Cherise hadn't seen her yesterday and assumed she'd retired long ago—or gone to the great Frederick's of Hollywood in the Sky.

"Yup. Gladys still runs the joint."

When J.J. let go with a real smile, Cheri took a sharp breath in—now *that* was the smile she remembered. It engaged his entire face and pushed up at his sparkling, blue-black eyes. But it was Gladys that made him smile like that. Not her.

"She must be way past eighty," Cherise said, forcing herself to change the subject in her head. *He isn't handsome. He isn't sexy. He isn't good.*

"No one knows for sure."

"And she's here today?"

J.J. nodded, gesturing for Cherise to take a peek into the newsroom. She ventured to the office door and immediately snapped her head back. She retreated behind her desk, horrified, and began to shuffle papers on her desktop, thinking to herself that old ladies weren't supposed to wear that stuff! They were supposed to look like Aunt Viv, in pedal pushers and tennies!

J.J. laughed at her reaction.

"I . . ." Cherise looked up at him, at a loss for words. "I didn't think she'd still be dressing like a . . ."

"Ten-dollar hooker?"

She choked back a laugh. When Cherise was a kid, Gladys had preferred stretch miniskirts, dangly feather earrings, and bottle-black, spiked-up hair. Apparently, she still did.

"She's dabbling in Internet dating these days."

"Please—" Cherise held up her hand. "Can we talk about something else?"

J.J. laughed again. He was clearly enjoying this exchange. "Sure. I assume you've seen the front page of today's *Bugle*?"

Cherise didn't like the tone of his question. It sounded like he was testing her. She suddenly felt defensive. Was she supposed to read the paper before coming into the office? Is that what was expected of publishers? Especially if their managing editor had been working all night, like J.J. obviously had? "I planned to read it once I got here."

"Ah." He nodded, pulling a folded copy from behind his back and handing it to her. It felt warm in her palm, which meant he'd probably had it tucked into his belt, and the idea of that sent a shock wave through her. How much of his body had she touched? How well did her fingertips know him? Why couldn't she recall?

A memory flashed like fire through her muscle and

bone—the feel of his hard body on top of her, the old wooden deck pressed into her back, the shiver of pleasure as his hands covered her breasts, his lips claimed her mouth, and her thighs opened in need.

And just like that, Cherise felt on the edge of tears. What the hell was that all about? She hadn't cried in . . . forever.

"Read fast," J.J. said. "We have an editorial meeting in fifteen minutes. Would you like some coffee?"

She nodded quickly, trying to rattle some sense into herself. What was her problem? How had she let J.J. push and pull at her body and heart like this? It was ridiculous. She'd been on a carnival ride of sensation, emotion, and memory for the last two days, and it was looping and banking too fast for her to keep her grip. She felt intensely sad at times. Elated at others. Bewildered always.

J.J. smiled. "I'll take that as a yes."

It was true that Aunt Viv's too-cold cup of instant decaf had failed Cherise on all levels—no caffeine, no flavor, no creamy froth, no rush of soul-satisfying warmth. "That's a yes," she said, sighing. "So there's a good barista in town now?"

J.J. laughed yet again, taking a moment to boldly examine Cherise from head to toe, pausing for an inordinate amount of time on her spike-heeled black boots. This caused her to stand straighter, squeeze her arms tighter over her chest, and second-guess the outfit she'd chosen for her first day as publisher—a stretchy, short-sleeved black blouse and a taupe skirt with a black belt. And the boots, of course.

She'd wanted to look polished, but bring a little urban

juju into the small-town environment. God knew it needed it. Plus, it was one of the three decent outfits she still owned.

"Gladys can fix you up with a cup of coffee. She's also your go-to gal for expense forms, paper clips, USB cables, and whatever else you might need. Oh, and she'll get you your BlackBerry."

Cherise felt her eyes go wide. "A *BlackBerry*?"

Immediately, she regretted the outburst. She was supposed to be a finance whiz with a multimillion-dollar business back in Tampa. A person like that wouldn't become excited about getting a smartphone—she'd already have one, one with all the bells and whistles, too.

"Hey, don't take it out on me," J.J. said, misinterpreting her remark. "I know it's a pain to carry around multiple devices, but the publisher needs to be reachable at all times. Part of the job."

Cherise nodded, damn happy to have been misunderstood and thrilled with the idea of having a phone again. Then it occurred to her that J.J. was being kind. He was providing helpful information. He was smiling at her now, too, his face relaxed and friendly. She didn't understand it. She licked her lips in nervousness. His eyes darted to where her tongue had just been. Then he scowled at her.

Oh, this was just plain nuts! If Cherise and J.J. were going to work together, they needed to clear the air. She had to know how he could have been so awful to Tanyalee, and why he seemed to vacillate between sweet and satanic in every encounter she had with him.

And that moment at Paw Paw Lake, when they almost kissed? Somebody needed to say something about that completely bizarre incident. She took a breath. "Listen, J.J.—"

"Yeah. We almost kissed. I know—bizarre. Forget it. I already have. I was hepped up on the adrenaline of a great news story. It's not the first time that's happened. In fact, I think I kissed Gladys when we had the giant mudslide across I-40 last year. See you at the meeting."

He was gone.

After remaining frozen in bewilderment for a long moment, Cherise opened the newspaper she'd been holding. *Body Found at Construction Site,* the bold black headline said. Below was a color photograph of the mud-covered car swinging from a chain, a grieving old woman restrained by sheriff's deputies in the background.

Imbedded in the story was that iconic black-and-white school picture of Barbara Jean Smoot, the one Cherise remembered seeing as a kid, the girl's blond bangs cut straight and her ponytail visible as it cascaded from high on the back of her head. Barbara Jean had a smile more suited to Hollywood than hill country. She had an elegant neck. Delicate features. Bright, shining eyes. Under the photo was this question: "Have we finally found the 'Lady of the Lake'?"

Cherise looked up in time to see J.J. round the corner out of sight.

Chapter 8

"Oh, *hell* no."

Cherise stumbled out of the car and stood in the gravel lane, her whisper escaping just before her mouth unhinged in shock. She was supposed to *live* here? The place was a complete *catastrophe*! Thistles up to her ass. A thick carpet of decayed leaves squishing under her feet. Hanging gutters. Missing shingles. Cracked windows. Thick kudzu growing unchecked up the bungalow's stone walls. A crumbling porch. A dilapidated dock.

A squirrel on her foot.

Her shriek sent the birds scattering. The scream echoed across the lake, cut through the woods, and easily carried all the way over the Tennessee border.

She snatched her boot away from the filthy, destructive creature and jumped back, smacking up against the side of the DeVille. The nasty thing just sat there on its hind legs like a rat-sized circus poodle, its little jaw going a mile a minute.

Cherise stomped her boots in the gravel. The creature still didn't move. "No! Git! Go away!"

The rodent cocked its head and stared at her with curious little brown marble eyes before it finally swished its tail and scurried off.

"Ain't that bad." Tater Wayne stood in the front door of the lake house, yet another bouquet of flowers dangling from his grip, his limp blond hair falling into his eyes. "Looks worse than it is, Cheri. Ain't gonna fall on ya er nothin'."

She willed her pulse to return to normal.

"Now, the outside is the main problem, but I'd hire a cleaning crew for the inside if I were you. It's plenty bad, too."

Cherise shuddered, trying to shake off the image of how the vermin had actually touched her boot. She hated squirrels. She almost lost everything on her very first residential flip when squirrels chewed through brand-new electrical wiring and started an attic fire.

Besides, they carried rabies. Ticks. Fleas. And God knew what else.

Gathering her courage, she walked gingerly toward the rotting porch steps, keeping an eye on whatever else might be lurking in the overgrown mess.

"Don't be such a city girl," Tater Wayne said, chuckling. "There's always been critters and weeds and dirt out here. You just done forgot." He smiled broadly at her, which caused his eyeball to go off on its pinball journey.

Cherise carefully made her way up the stairs and onto the porch.

"Here," he said, shoving the flowers toward her.

She grabbed them and smacked them against the side of her thigh, not bothering to hide her annoyance. Candy had been right. She'd always had this problem with Tater Wayne—the nicer she was to him the more he misinterpreted her kindness. The time had come to make things clear.

"Please don't bring me any more flowers, Tater." At the risk of sounding snippy, Cherise decided honesty was the approach. "I like you as a friend, but I don't have any interest in you romantically."

Tater's eye began to ricochet at double speed. "Oh," he said, his work boots shuffling in the crunchy leaves. "Well now, I figured as much. Anyway, these ain't from me. They was here when I showed up to clean the gutters."

"What?" Cherise bent her elbow to examine the mixed bouquet and saw it was wrapped in florist paper, a dead giveaway that Tater hadn't raided someone's garden to win her affection. She put her nose down into the delicate pink roses, daisies, baby's breath, and ferns. Cherise frowned and looked up at Tater once more. "So who are they from, then?"

He shrugged. "Heckifiknow. I best be getting back to work 'cause Garland pays me by the job and I still gotta run some urns for Viv. You know, Spickler's Hardware and the post office."

Cherise smiled. "Ah. *Err-ands.*"

"That's what I said. *Urns.*" He looked at her suspiciously. "You don't even talk normal these days." With that, Tater Wayne jumped off the sagging porch and headed toward a tall aluminum ladder he'd propped against the far side of the house.

"Hey, thanks for all your hard work," she called after him.

He gave her a salute and a smile.

Cherise tucked the flowers under her arm and cautiously stepped over the threshold. Immediately, her nostrils were assaulted by the presence of mildew. One quick glance around the living room and Cherise was certain that everything made of fabric would have to go—the rugs, the couch, the curtains, the kitchen chair cushions.

She went through the room and opened every window that wasn't stuck, relieved that the fresh spring air helped her eyes to stop watering. *A good sweeping up, my ass,* she thought. Well, at least there was no wallpaper or wall-to-wall carpet to be dealt with, and the wood floors and trim could be scrubbed back to life with oil soap. Anything else would sparkle after some vinegar and elbow grease. A little fresh paint probably wouldn't hurt, either. Of course, paying for a cleaning service was out of the question, and how she'd accomplish all this scrubbing and sparkling while running a daily newspaper she had no idea.

Her mind snapped back to the editorial meeting that morning. Granddaddy hadn't even bothered to show up, leaving Cherise to sit at the head of the conference table pretending to follow along as Jim Taggert discussed the day's "news hole," and Mimi ranted about the FBI's tight-lipped media relations policy and how Carlotta Smoot McCoy refused to give an interview.

"The lady is crazier than a sprayed roach," Mimi had said. "She went off on me about how I'd never lost a sister and wouldn't understand her pain and that the newspaper had failed her family for over forty years and she wasn't about to do us any favors now."

"She's pretty traumatized by this," J.J. said. "Be kind to her, but keep trying."

That's when Cherise decided that, as publisher, she should contribute to the discussion. "If Ms. McCoy doesn't want to talk we can't force her," had been her brilliant appraisal.

J.J. lowered his chin and stared at her from under raised eyebrows. "Madam Publisher," he'd said, his voice dripping with sarcasm. "Just yesterday you wanted to bring the sexy back. Well, I hate to tell you, but a background piece on Barbara Jean's angry family is about as sexy as it's going to get at the moment."

Cherise hadn't known how to respond to that. Again, she was baffled by the way J.J. alternated between kindness and snarkiness with her. It was almost as if he were keeping her off balance on purpose. "Continue," she had said with a wave of her hand. Too late, she realized the queenly gesture had been laughable.

Cherise took a deep breath of mildewed air, reminding herself that she was doing the best she could. Once she'd reviewed the *Bugle*'s financials, she'd have a clearer picture of how she could help the paper get back on its feet. That was her area of expertise anyway, not news gathering. She decided that in the future, she'd resist the temptation to offer her opinion in editorial meetings.

She wandered past the living room and into the kitchen. It was dingy but intact, except for the battered old refrigerator, with its door hanging off its hinges. That was destined for the junk heap. Everything else seemed usable—the deep porcelain farm sink with a pump handle and wooden drainboard, a mammoth old stove that would probably survive the apocalypse, tall maple cupboards, bead-board wainscoting, and the same narrow-strip white pine floors that ran through the rest of the house. The utilitarian round oak table and four ladder-back chairs resided in the middle of the kitchen, as always, though the centerpiece was a recent addition. At some point in the past five and a half years, a big chunk of plaster had fallen from the kitchen ceiling to the tabletop, almost as if the house itself were daring someone to notice it was falling apart.

She laughed aloud at the irony. Not so long ago, she'd spent nearly sixty thousand to upgrade her Harbour Island kitchen, adding an environmentally controlled wine cooler, dual convection ovens, a separate beverage service island, and the finest black granite and brushed steel money could buy. Yet she never once cooked in that kitchen. In fact, she'd rarely even poured cereal into a bowl or prepared a cup of coffee in it. Catered dinner parties were the only times the kitchen was used for its intended purpose.

And here she was, two years later, her only asset a quarter tank of gas and, if she wanted any privacy, no choice but to cook for herself. Right here. In this Little House on the Freakin' Prairie kitchen.

Cherise shook her head as she opened one of the cupboards, taking down a dusty old Mason jar from the top shelf. Wincing, she turned it over to shake out the dead insects, then removed the florist paper and stuck the flowers in the glass jar. The bouquet was too big and the jar too small, but it would have to do for now.

She began to work the water pump, still laughing at herself. She'd graduated summa cum laude from the University of Florida, and landed a great job at one of the biggest accounting firms in Miami.

Pump. Pump. Pump.

She'd put in three years of accounting grunt work before she was moved to the auditing division of their Tampa office. She'd earned a reputation for sniffing out inconsistencics and rose quickly through the ranks. Two years later she was an account manager in their consulting division, specializing in forensic accounting.

Pump. Pump. Pump.

She started dabbling in real estate—it was a no-brainer in Florida at the time. She started with flipping a few single-family residential properties. Candy invested about ten thousand, and together they began flipping residential and commercial. At the three million mark, Candy sold her various businesses and came in full-time. The profits really started to flow. When they reached six million in assets, Cherise left the accounting firm and sank everything she had into the business.

Pump.

They more than doubled their net worth in a year.

Pump.

They bet it all on a single commercial deal.

Pump.

Fourteen million—gone. Her personal savings—gone. All the people she thought were her friends—gone. Her dream home—gone. Evan—gone. Everything—gone.

Gone. Gone. Gone.

Cherise suddenly stopped her futile effort to get water

out of the beat-up contraption. She was out of breath, she'd broken out in a sweat, and tears were forming in her eyes. She swiped them away. If she wanted water for her mystery flowers, she'd be getting it from the lake.

Then it dawned on her—of course water wasn't coming out of the stupid pump! It had to be primed first! How many times had she watched her father and grandfather pour buckets of water into the fill cap near the well?

Cherise leaned on the drainboard and laughed at her own ignorance. What other basic things had she forgotten how to do? Could she catch a trout out of Pigeon Creek if she absolutely had to? Could she operate Granddaddy's lawn tractor? The chainsaw? Could she patch up a hole in the rowboat?

Slowly, her gaze moved toward the window over the old sink. Tentatively, Cherise reached up to pull aside the blue-and-white checked curtains and smiled at the serene beauty of Newberry Lake, its deep mountain water edged with the lace of early summer. Though the view was lovely, her stomach clenched with a sharp sadness.

It had been a July night twenty-three years ago. Her mother smiled and sang to herself as she washed dishes by hand at this sink. A warm breeze ruffled the curtains and touched her mother's strawberry-blond hair.

As usual, Cherise and Tanyalee had been fighting like cats. Her parents had exchanged angry looks and deep sighs and separated their daughters. Cherise's mother took her into the kitchen and asked her to put away the leftovers, which made Cherise furious, because her father was out on the porch reading aloud to Tanyalee. Why had she gotten chores while Tanyalee got books with Daddy?

It's not fair!

That was the complaint Cherise was prepared to lodge with her mother when she slammed the refrigerator door and spun around.

But the words wouldn't come.

Cherise stood transfixed by the sudden transformation of her ordinary mother in the ordinary room. The sun had partially dipped behind the mountains and shot a beam of its richest light directly through that little kitchen window, gilding her mother's skin in gold. In that instant, her mother became magically beautiful, a singing angel framed by blue and white checks, with her eyes closed and her sweet, high voice causing a seven-year-old girl to forget what had been bothering her. In that moment, Cherise expected bluebirds to start twittering around her mother's head, like in the movie *Cinderella*.

"Do you still love Daddy?"

"What?" Her mother's yellow-red hair whipped around her shoulders when she turned her head, laughing. "Of course I do, sugar! I've loved Daddy since the first time I laid eyes on him! Now what in the world made you ask me something as silly as that?"

Embarrassed, Cherise shook her head and looked down at her feet. "You and Daddy seem angry sometimes, is all."

Her mother chuckled. "Sweetheart, it's a full-time job to keep you and your sister from clawing each other's eyes out. If your daddy and I seem angry it's

because we're exhausted from refereeing the two of
you all the time! I swear, you two need to learn to
share. It's just not right how you girls can't get along."

Her mother dried her hands on her apron and bent
down to hug her little girl. She smiled at Cherise.
"Sugar, you're the oldest, you know. It's your responsibility to set a good example for your little sister. You
need to show her how to be nice and how to take turns.
That's your job."

Cherise nodded. She'd heard this before, of course.
"I'll try, Mama."

And that's how it happened that a few weeks later
her mother and father were found dead in a little beach
rental in Nags Head, where'd they'd gone in search of
"a moment's peace" as Aunt Viv had described it.

After they died, Cherise wanted to be dead, too, but
she somehow kept breathing, sleepwalking through her
days and dreaming at night of that lost moment, when
her mother was golden and warm and alive, her hands
in the soapsuds and her face turned to the setting sun.

Why hadn't I been able to get along with Tanyalee?
Mama and Daddy would still be alive . . .

Cherise dropped her hand from the curtain, turned
away from the sink, and pushed the pain aside. She had
no time for this crap—she needed to wrap up her little
excursion down memory lane and get back to the newsroom, where fifteen year-end finance reports were waiting for her to wade through. She had a month to decide
if and how the paper could ever be profitable again.
Once she'd accomplished that, she'd take her earnings
and go.

Cherise walked quickly, making a cursory check on

the rest of the house. The two bedrooms needed painting. The old iron beds were fine but the mattresses and box springs would have to be pitched. The bathroom needed scrubbing from ceiling to floor and the whole thing needed regrouting.

Cherise stepped into the hallway and gasped at what awaited her. The squirrel!

"Ohmigod! Shoo! Get out! How did you get in here?"

The thing wouldn't move. Cherise stomped her boot and waved her hands. "Go! Git the hell out! I know how destructive you little shits can be."

"Is that how y'all greet each other down in Tampa?"

Tanyalee.

Cherise looked up. Her sister stood in the open front door. She wore a buttery linen suit and spike heels. A large metallic bag hung from her shoulder. Her reddish-blond hair was twisted back in a tidy chignon, held in place by beautiful mother-of-pearl hair combs that looked like expensive antiques. She had pearls at her ears, a smirk on her face, and hands curled into fists at her sides. She looked like she belonged at a Junior League meeting.

Cherise had never seen Tanyalee look so chic—or chilly. "Hi!" she blurted out. "What a nice surprise!"

"Aunt Viv told me I might find you here." Tanyalee let her eyes roam up and down Cherise while she produced a smile that did not spread to her eyes. "And, of course, Wim told me yesterday that you were back in town."

"Wim?" Cherise nearly stepped on the damn squirrel as she moved toward her sister. "Wim Wimbley?"

Tanyalee laughed. "Of course. How many men do

you know named Wim?" Just then, Tanyalee raised her
left hand to smooth an unseen stray hair, making certain the huge solitaire diamond caught the light to its
best advantage. "We're engaged. I manage his real estate office."

Cherise opened her lips to comment on her sister's
happy news, but her mouth simply hung open, lifeless
and silent. Her brain, however, shifted into overdrive.
*Wim Wimbley? Candy's one-time sleazeball boyfriend?
And Tanyalee? When the hell had this happened? I hope
Wimbley keeps the cash register padlocked.*

"You can't possibly be serious about living in this
dump," Tanyalee said. "Why don't you rent a loft downtown? Wim has some units more suited to your lifestyle.
Unless you have a newfound love for . . ."—Tanyalee
looked around again—"camping."

"Well, I—"

"No one said how long y'all plan on playing publisher, but I'm sure Wim would be willing to do a month
to month. As a favor to me, of course."

With that, Tanyalee reached in her metallic bag and
pulled out a brochure for Wimbley Real Estate. She
held it in front of her body with a straight arm, as if she
were offering a treat to a stray cat she couldn't trust.

Cherise blinked. She closed her mouth. She took the
five steps necessary to reach her sister, walked right
into the brochure, and extended her arms to hug her.

Tanyalee remained as stiff as a corpse. She patted
Cherise on the back awkwardly, then pushed her away.

"Here," she said, shoving the brochure in Cherise's
hand.

Cherise looked from the five-color glossy booklet to

Tanyalee and cocked her head, unsure how to handle her sister. "Are you free? Can we go for a cup of coffee and chat? Catch up? We haven't talked in years."

Tanyalee produced a quick little laugh. "Five years. And unfortunately, no. I'll have to take a rain check. I just wanted to stop by and welcome y'all back." Again, she examined Cherise from head to toe. "You look good. What are you, a size four? I bet you could almost fit into my clothes now."

Cherise smiled pleasantly, though her body hummed inside with a low-level warning. *What the hell is up with Tanyalee? No, we've never slobbered over each other with affection and there's still an undercurrent of jealousy here, but when did my baby sister turn into a freakin' ice queen?*

"I hear that J.J. has already moved in for the kill. That sure didn't take long."

Cherise shook her head, truly not understanding. "What are you talking about, Tanyalee?"

Her sister chuckled and raised an eyebrow. "Wim saw the whole thing. Told me you'd barely gotten out of your damn car before he started manhandling you in front of half the damn town—while a dead girl was being pulled from a lake, no less. Talk about *tacky.*"

Cherise froze. Had everyone seen that? But it was nothing! J.J. said so! And why was there such bitterness in Tanyalee's voice? "I don't under—"

"Water under the bridge, my dear sister," she said with a quick wave of her hand. "I forgave you a long, long time ago."

Cherise felt her belly tie itself into a sick knot. "Forgave me for *what*?"

Tanyalee let go with a full-bodied laugh before she patted her sister's shoulder. "You've always been so above it all, haven't you, Cheri? Always pretending you don't know what effect you had on him or how you managed to ruin my marriage from three states away."

Cherise stopped breathing. "What?"

"Come on now, big sis. I was praying you'd be more mature about all this by now, even though I waited and waited for you to come to me with the truth and you never did." Tanyalee withdrew her hand from Cherise and pulled her lips tight, then shrugged. "I know everything, Cheri. I know how J.J. never stopped loving you. I know how you were calling him from Florida and telling him to leave me. He confessed everything once the divorce was final. And the weird thing is that I think I knew all along—a wife's intuition and all that—and looking back, I'm pretty sure it was the stress of the betrayal that made me lose the baby in the first place."

Cherise's knees felt wobbly from shock. What Tanyalee was saying was so horrific that she could barely follow along. *I'm responsible for Tanyalee's miscarriage? I was calling J.J. from Florida? And J.J. had never stopped loving me?*

"I don't have any idea what you're talking about."

"Oh, Lord-ee." Tanyalee repositioned the bag on her shoulder and sighed, as if it took a great deal of patience to deal with her dim-witted sister. "Anyway, I'm sure we'll have time to revisit this before you leave town." Tanyalee frowned. "So how long are you here for, anyhow? A couple months? Three? And do you truly have any idea what a mess you've stepped in over at the

Bugle? Wim says there's no way it'll ever bounce back, that it's as good as dead."

Cherise closed her eyes and gave herself a moment to distance herself from the whacko world of Tanyalee Marie Newberry. How would she respond? Where to start? It was all a cesspool of twisted lies. She'd never spoken to J.J. on the phone—not once since she left Bigler! So why would he lie to Tanyalee about something like that? Or was it Tanyalee who was lying to her now?

When Cherise opened her eyes, Tater Wayne stood behind Tanyalee in the doorway. He held up a greenish, rotted piece of wood that might have once been a window sash. "The *sitch-ee-a-ashun*'s more fucked up than I thought," he said.

Cherise did her best to smile, noting that Tater Wayne was becoming downright prophetic.

Chapter 9

"More beans, Cheri?"

Cherise straightened her posture in the hope the adjustment would help her breathe. She'd already consumed one of Aunt Viv's breaded pork chops, two pieces of corn bread with butter, a baked apple, two helpings of green beans with bacon, and a glass of milk. She hadn't eaten with such abandon since high school. The waist of her skirt had cut into her flesh.

"No, thanks," she moaned, falling back against the dining room chair. "I'm about to pop as it is."

Granddaddy snickered. "Nonsense. We're having red velvet cake for dessert."

"I know how y'all love red velvet cake," Aunt Viv said, emptying the serving spoon of green beans onto Cherise's plate as if she'd requested them. "Remember how I made it for your graduation party, with a nice cream cheese frosting?"

Cherise nodded, placing her hands on her pooched-out stomach. "Of course I do. It was delicious."

"Now, I would have been happy to make a red velvet

wedding cake for Taffy and J.J., but she insisted on a
carrot cake. But who in their right mind wants carrot
cake for their wedding?" Aunt Viv cut another square
of corn bread and put it on Cherise's plate, then provided her with another pat of butter. "If you ask me,
any marriage that starts out with carrot cake is bound
to—"

Granddaddy's knife crashed down against the edge
of his supper plate, drowning out the end of Viv's sentence. "So, Cheri, did Purnell gather up all those reports you'd asked for? Do you have everything you
need?"

Aunt Viv sniffed and raised her chin at her brother's
interruption. She began gathering the dirty dishes with
passive-aggressive fervor.

"Let me clean up tonight," Cherise said, starting to
rise from her chair.

"I wouldn't even consider it," Aunt Viv said, her voice
overly chirpy. "Now you'uns just sit and discuss your
business while I go and get us some cake and coffee."

Granddaddy slowly raised his eyes toward Cherise
and shook his head.

"If it's all right with *you*, of course," Viv added, mim-
icking her brother with an eyebrow raise of her own.
Then she used one of her pink-laced tennis shoes to
kick open the swinging door to the kitchen.

Cherise stared at the clattering door until it fell silent, then she turned to Granddaddy. In her mind's eye
she pictured Lady Justice with her scales, one side holding a single pack of ramen noodles and a cutoff notice
from Tampa Electric, while the other was weighed down

with the newspaper business, her family of crazy people, J.J., the crumbling lake house, a rabid squirrel, and a huge red velvet cake.

She let out a weak squeal of alarm.

"Don't mind your aunt Viv. Her dark cloud will blow over as soon as she has a nip of her slush."

Cherise blinked a few times to regain her focus. "What were you saying?"

"The financials. Has Purnell given you everything you need?"

Cherise laughed uncomfortably, supposing there was no right time to ask the questions that had stacked up since that afternoon, when Gladys Harbison delivered some of the five years' worth of accounting and book-keeping reports to her office. A quick perusal was enough for Cherise to see that the *Bugle* hadn't just lost ad revenue and circulation over the years, it was a study in financial mismanagement. She'd tried to track down Purnell to talk with him, but he'd been out of the office the whole afternoon.

"The *Bugle* hasn't been audited in at least fifteen years, Granddaddy," she said matter-of-factly. "Were you aware of this?"

He brushed corn bread crumbs off the tablecloth. "Oh, it's been a lot longer than that, but there's no need for it, Cheri. We're a privately owned family business where every employee is part of the family. It's always been our way."

She fought not to roll her eyes. Her grandfather was clueless! "Even privately held corporations need au-diting, Granddaddy. Audits reveal how reliable your reporting methods are and identify the changing trends in your business. They help you manage risk, and keep you on track toward accomplishing your goals."

He said nothing, but avoided eye contact.

"Granddaddy, I can't even figure out where some of your numbers are coming from, and I used to make my living doing this!"

His lip twitched.

"How involved have you been with the business end of the paper?"

He shrugged. "Involved enough."

"It's pretty unusual to have just one person who operates as both head of sales and chief financial officer, isn't it?"

He shrugged again.

"In fact," she continued, "this arrangement is borderline illegal, Granddaddy. Separating revenue creation from accounting is standard operating procedure and important for fraud prevention."

He laughed. "Not if you're the *Bugle*, Cheri. We've always done it that way. There are three arms of the company—finance, circulation, and editorial. The finance arm includes all our ad sales and it's all under Purnell. Editorial was mine. Since Chester Wollard passed, I've been handling circulation, too. It's always worked well for us."

Cherise shook her head. "I have to disagree."

"What are you saying?" His watery eyes blinked several times.

"I mean I've never seen such sloppy accounting in my life! The paper is hemorrhaging money, and I haven't yet been able to figure where all the bleeding is coming from. You've got serious problems."

He frowned, and when he shook his head, his jowls jiggled. "I'm sure if you just sat down with Purnell, he'd clear everything up."

"Granddaddy, that's what I'm trying to tell you— Purnell is a big part of the problem."

He laughed. "Sugar, I've known Purnell Lawson my entire life. He's a good man and the only remaining friend-of-my-heart from my childhood. Now, I will admit that he's had some health issues recently, and his drinking sure doesn't help the situation, but—"

"At best, he's incompetent. At worst—"

The swinging door burst open, and Aunt Viv swept in with a coffee tray and two dessert plates. She served Granddaddy first. His slice of cake was so thin it couldn't support its own weight and had fallen into a tiny mound of red velvet dust. Cherise received a piece as big as her head.

"Cheri, dear, would you like sugar and cream?" Viv asked this as she began adding both to the coffee cup.

Granddaddy rolled his eyes.

Aunt Viv plopped down into her chair and sighed, her work done. She reached for her tumbler.

"No cake?" Cherise asked, knowing full well what her aunt's response would be.

"All I need is my risky slush," she said with a wink. The smell of vodka and strawberry daiquiri mix was strong enough to bring tears to Cherise's eyes. She sighed.

"Did Taffy come by to see you today?" Viv savored

a long swig of her alcoholic confection. "Did you two have a nice, long talk? I sure hope you took some time to get reacquainted."

Cherise's attention wandered to the cake. As if on autopilot, she stuck her fork in the spongy perfection and brought it to her mouth, reeling from the sweet shock. She opened her eyes with a start, put down her fork, and pushed her plate away. If she didn't get out of this house soon, she'd end up bat-shit crazy. Three hundred pounds worth of bat-shit crazy.

Granddaddy reached across the table to pat the top of her hand. "I'll have a chat with Purnell. Don't worry about any of that mess. Now, I understand from Tater Wayne that the lake house needs some fixin' up. Don't you mind any of that, either. I've already called a few boys and they'll start work tomorrow."

"Good," Cherise heard herself say. "Because I want to move in right away."

"What?" Viv's eyes went wide.

Cherise was just as surprised by her decision as Aunt Viv. But what alternative did she have?

"I'll have to borrow some cookware and dishes and stuff—and I'll need to round up a decent box spring and mattress, linens, curtains, maybe a secondhand couch." Cherise saw her aunt frown. "Everything in there is covered in mold and mildew, Aunt Viv. It has to be pitched."

Viv sighed deeply. "Some of those things are family heirlooms, Cheri. You can't just roll into town and start throwing things out willy-nilly, though I know you never were the sentimental type. Not like Taffy, God bless her heart."

"Vivienne." Granddaddy smacked his hand on the table.

"Well, I have a right to know why Cheri doesn't want to stay here! Is there something wrong with this house? She only picked at her cake! Is there something wrong with the cake, too? And why is it so hard for Cheri to give her own flesh-and-blood sister the time of day?" Aunt Viv turned her pursed lips in Cherise's direction. "Well?"

Cherise felt her face go hot. She counted to five as she placed her napkin on the table and gathered her untouched coffee and barely disturbed dessert plate. "I'm used to being on my own, Aunt Viv. I would feel more comfortable having my own place." She stood, took a step toward the swinging door, then turned around. "And yes, Tanyalee did stop by today. We spoke for about three minutes, which was more than enough time for us to get reacquainted. There was even time for her to try to rent me one of Wim's condos and then blame me for her divorce *and* her miscarriage. So yeah—it was a really *nice talk.*"

"Now, Cheri—"

She didn't wait to hear what Granddaddy had to say. She kicked the swinging door with her high-heeled boot, dumped her dishes in the sink, and ran up the back staircase to her old room.

I must have been insane to come back here.

She slammed the door behind her and threw herself on the bed.

Was there any conceivable reason for J.J. to lie to Tanyalee about those phone calls? Was he trying to cover for his own bad behavior in some way? And why would Tanyalee believe him—a man she said treated her so badly—without even checking with her own sister?

Or was this all about Tanyalee and her ability to twist and turn at a lie until it had a whiff of truth to it?

This is why Cherise had left Bigler and never wanted to return. Shit! She'd almost wolfed down that big-ass piece of red velvet cake when she was already too stuffed to breathe! And why? Because this town made her second-guess herself. Suddenly, she didn't trust her own eyes, her own ears, or her finely tuned gut instinct. And she wasn't going to allow it. She wasn't going to let herself get sucked in that way.

Cherise was on the verge of screaming. She wanted to beat her fists into the bed and howl.

But she didn't. Cherise raised her head from the coverlet. She patted the bed, suddenly aware that she hadn't bounced all over creation on contact with the mattress. This was not the mattress and box spring she'd had in high school. This bed was new. Firm. Plush.

Tomorrow, she'd be strapping this sucker to the roof of the pimpmobile and moving out.

Chapter 10

The tap on the door made Cherise raise her head from the computer screen. When she saw it was Gladys Harbison, a little hum of disappointment traveled through her.

As hard as it was to admit, she'd hoped it might be J.J. She couldn't go much longer without talking to him about what the hell had really happened with Tanyalee and why—God, *why*—he had blamed Cherise for their divorce. It was driving her crazy. But J.J. had managed to avoid her all morning, almost as if he knew Cherise was on to him.

It made perfect sense, of course. Jackasses rarely enjoyed being called on their jackassish-ness.

"Where do you want me to put these?" Gladys asked, bent over by the weight of the documents, which did wonders for the view of crinkly flesh down the front of her peasant blouse. Cherise averted her eyes. She jumped from her desk chair, relieved Gladys of the stack, and placed it in the far corner of the room. With all the accumulating paperwork, the office was already in a state of disorganization, but with the addition of the painting supplies, ladders, and drop cloths, it had advanced to chaos.

"You sure you want this room painted gray?" Gladys asked, looking around. "Won't it be depressing?"

Cherise chuckled softly, knowing the wall color was the least of her depression-causing concerns. She gestured to the paint can. "The color's called Tradewind Azure."

"Funny name for gray. Here." Gladys held out the nameplate Cherise had given her the day before. "You left this on my desk by accident."

Cherise raised her hand, palm out. "Actually, I left it for you along with a note asking that you correct the spelling error."

She frowned. "I thought you meant there was an error on the ad sales summary. I've been looking for a misspelling all morning!" Gladys adjusted her bifocals and held the shiny brass up to the light. "I don't see anything wrong with this."

"It's just that I prefer Cherise. C-h-e-r-i-s-e. Would you mind arranging for a reorder?"

Gladys shrugged. "You're the boss. But it's gonna take a couple weeks. I'll have to redo all the business cards, too, I suppose." She put a fist on her hip. "That's why I did all this in advance, you know, so you'd feel welcome, so you'd walk in and know where it was you were supposed to sit and all."

Cherise smiled again. "That was very kind of you."

"Just doing my job."

"Gladys, could you stay for a minute? There's something I want to discuss with you."

The secretary nodded, moved aside a large canvas drop cloth, and sat in a chair across from Cherise's desk. Her skirt rode up, displaying a complex web of varicose veins and a pair of platform ankle-strap heels more often seen on women one fourth her age. Gladys crossed her arms over her low-cut peasant blouse.

"You probably want to talk to me about the Barbara Jean Smoot case, right? Because I was working here in 1964 and I remember that day—complete pandemonium."

Cherise hadn't expected that offer. "Uh, no. I mean, not really. I'm not a reporter. But you could tell J.J. what you remember from that day. I'm sure he'd appreciate it."

"Already did."

"All right."

"So this is about my outfits, then?"

Cheri pulled her head back in surprise. "Excuse me?"

"I told Garland I was fine with you steppin' in as publisher and all, but that I wasn't about to stop dressin' the way I like to dress, the way that makes me feel beautiful, so don't even start with me about that." She raised her heavily penciled brows, waiting for a challenge.

"Uh." Cherise paused, trying to collect herself. "I just wanted to ask you about the way the financial records are kept here at the *Bugle*."

"Oh." Gladys waved her hand through the air. "Ask away, then."

Cherise had to stop herself from laughing out loud. For six months now, she'd really believed that she'd been in the thick of doing her penance. All this time, she thought the bill collectors, the empty studio apartment, the crappy car, the sparse wardrobe, the temp bookkeeping jobs, the worry, the embarrassment, the regret—she'd thought *that* was the price she would be paying for an ego run wild. Not so, apparently. All that had only been a warm-up for the purgatory that was Bigler, North Carolina.

"Purnell should really be the one to answer your questions. I just do what he tells me."

"I understand," Cherise said, nodding politely. "But Purnell doesn't seem to spend much time in the building. He hasn't returned any of my calls."

"Oh, since the cutbacks he's always off visiting with clients personally and selling ad space. He's a real people person."

He's sure as hell not a numbers person, Cherise thought, folding her hands on the desktop. "So tell me about the bookkeeping routine, Gladys."

Gladys was a terrible driver, which wouldn't have been any of Cherise's business if she weren't riding shotgun in the DeVille, hanging halfway out the window to steady the poorly tied-down set of bedding.

"Holy hell, Gladys! Slow down! I'm losing the pillow top!"

"Sorry," she said with a shrug, taking another curve of Randall Road fast enough to cause her dangling feather earrings to smack against her cheeks. "When you're my age, there's no time to waste."

"Well, I'm not ready to die, so slow down."

"You're the boss."

Cherise shook her head and laughed. That seemed to be Gladys's response to most every comment she'd made today.

Could you get me an extra charger for the Black-Berry?

You're the boss.

Would you please tell J.J. that I'll be out for the rest of the day?

You're the boss.

Would you mind driving over to Newberry Lake with me this afternoon?

You're the boss.

Gladys lifted her platform shoe from the gas pedal and Cherise sighed with relief. "It's up here at the top of the hill on the left."

"Oh, I know where it is, Miss Cheri," Gladys said, her coral-pink lips curving into a smile. "There was a time I came up here nearly every weekend. Your grand-father wasn't always an old fart, you know. We used to have some big parties at that little house."

Cherise cocked her head. "Seriously?"

Gladys took the turn onto Newberry Lane and howled with laughter. "Sweetie, I doubt you've ever been to a party better than the ones your granddaddy used to throw back in the day."

She smiled to herself, thinking of all the parties she'd gone to in Tampa, Naples, Ocala, and South Beach—the most beautiful of beautiful people, the most private VIP rooms in the most exclusive clubs, and the most opulent private estates. Gladys's idea of a good time was not quite the same as hers, obviously.

"Everybody'd show up with nothing but their swim-suits and a towel and spend the weekend." Gladys wagged her eyebrows at Cherise.

"Say what?"

"Oh, yes. And there was plenty of booze. We'd put us some Elvis and Ray Charles and James Brown on the record player. There'd be dancing till the sweat poured and you had to go jump in the lake to cool off. Barbecue so tender it fell apart in your hands and the juices dripped off your elbow. Lots of sleeping under the stars. And sometimes there'd be marijuana. Person-ally, I never liked the way it made me feel—all out of control and silly like."

Cherise swallowed hard. "Granddaddy Garland threw pot parties?"

"Oh, we never called 'em that. We just called them shindigs."

Cherise pointed ahead. "The turnoff is on the left."

"Like I said, I could find this place blindfolded."

"So when was all this partying going on?"

"Back in the mid-fifties, before Garland married your grandmother—that put an end to all the fun, I'm afraid."

Cherise was having trouble wrapping her brain around the house's wild past. "What about Aunt Viv? Did she approve of these parties?"

Gladys roared. "What? She *was* the party! In fact, it was one of her boyfriends, a trumpet player from Char-lotte, who brought along the wacky to-backy. Viv was real popular with the boys, if you know what I'm sayin'."

Cherise frowned. No, she *didn't* know what Gladys

was saying. She refused to know what she was saying. "But Aunt Viv never married," Cherise said.

"Ha! That wasn't from lack of offers, let me tell you! She liked to play the field, is all."

Cherise turned her face into the wind and used her free hand to rub her brow. What to do with this new information? Her grandfather hosted weekend bacchanals. And her great-aunt was the teenie-weenic-bikini-wearing town slut, dirty dancing to raunchy James Brown tunes with a pot-smoking, beatnik trumpet player. Cherise felt a sick headache coming on.

The BlackBerry rang.

She fumbled for the smartphone and saw it was J.J. Her heart began pounding. "Hello?"

"Where are you?"

Cherise sniffed. "Hello, J.J. I'm just fine. Thanks so much for asking."

He chuckled. "And I'm fine, too, thanks. Now, where exactly are you?"

"Out of the office. I have some personal things to take care of. I borrowed Gladys for the day. We're headed to . . . Asheville . . . to do some shopping."

Cherise ignored Gladys's clucking sounds.

"You have a paper to run, Miss Newberry."

"Is there something I can do for you?"

"Nope—just wondering when you'll be back in the newsroom."

"Not till evening."

"Have fun in Asheville." *Click.*

Cherise took the phone from her ear and tossed it in her purse.

"My, my, my," Gladys said. "Three days home and you're already torturing that boy?"

Cherise fiddled with her hair. "My home is in Tampa, and I have no idea what you mean by 'torturing.'"

"Uh-huh. Now, I don't blame you. If I were only fifty years younger, or even forty years younger, oh, what the hell, even *thirty* years younger, I'd be all over—"

"Stop! Turn here!"

Gladys huffed. "Well, I never . . ." She shook her head at Cherise the whole way up the gravel lane. She stopped the car and turned off the engine, and the two women sat in silence for a moment.

"Sorry for cutting you off like that," Cherise said.

Gladys shrugged. "You need to relax, Cheri. You've got nothing to worry about. He's never wanted anyone but you, anyhow."

In slow motion, Cherise cocked her head, not sure she'd heard right. "Excuse me?"

Then Gladys slapped Cherise on the shoulder playfully. "Now, just looky at what we got here!" Both women stared out the windshield at the army of workers swarming the cottage. There were at least a dozen men of various physical types, hues, and ages climbing on and milling around the house. Men pounded on the roof and the porch. They wiggled under crawl spaces. They perched on ladders. They shored up cracked stone. There were even men hacking away at the overgrowth and putting down mulch. Cherise counted six pickups, an electrician's van, and a plumber's truck.

"Granddaddy told me he'd hired some workers," she whispered. "Boy, he wasn't kidding!"

"He wants you to be happy here, I guess." Gladys

craned her neck to follow three shirtless men as they hauled a wooden beam down to the water's edge. "I know *I'm* happy here."

"Let's just get this over with and get back to town." Cherise managed to keep hold of the tie-downs while exiting the passenger side of the car. "Could you give me a hand with the—"

She froze. Her jaw fell open. She pressed the front of her thighs against the car for support, so she wouldn't fall off the earth's crust. Oh, god-*damn*, she couldn't help it. What was *he* doing here? She would recognize him anywhere, in any context.

She watched him hand off his end of the wooden beam to another man. Then with one motion, he ripped off his T-shirt and tossed it to the grass, the muscles in his back rolling and twisting as he moved. It was a dance. It was a dance of male power and sexuality, and it made Cherise's mouth go painfully dry.

She swallowed hard as she watched him stroll to the water's edge, still in his work boots and a threadbare pair of jeans that showed off his ass to perfection. He jumped into the water. A second later he emerged with a big splash, twisting in midair, shaking his dark hair wildly and sweeping his hands over his face to shove the water from his eyes.

Cherise's boot heel slipped in the gravel. She felt the blood rush, hot and violent, to that sweet spot between her legs.

This was so wrong. She shouldn't be staring at J.J. like this. But how could she not? He was all wet and half naked, his muscular arms rising above his head to catch a piling being lowered into the water. The wooden beam must have weighed a ton because his biceps and triceps strained and bulged. His neck corded with effort and his chest—his bare, dripping-wet chest—rippled with the exertion.

Cherise let go of the rope she'd been clutching. She barely noticed the slow-motion slide of the box spring and mattress along the trunk and into the gravel.

Wrong. Wrong. Wrong.

Her knees shouldn't be shaking. Her panties shouldn't be wet. J.J. was a liar. He was cruel and rude and surly and . . .

Gorgeous.

Damn. J.J. was *gorgeous*.

And at just that instant, his lake-blue eyes flashed Cherise's way. An instant of surprise showed on his face, just as the beam's full weight settled in his hands. He looked away and frowned, concentrating as he lowered the wood into the water, his muscles undulating with the effort.

Gladys whistled low and soft. "Asheville, my wrinkly old ass," she muttered.

Chapter 11

"Thank you for everything, Tater Wayne." Cherise stepped away with satisfaction, relieved to see that the mattress and box spring fit perfectly inside the old iron frame in the front bedroom. It was the room her parents once shared, the one with an unobstructed view of the lake.

"Happy to help, but I really think it's a bad idea to stay out here tonight. The house ain't ready. Viv said—"

"*I'm* ready. I have everything I need." She gestured to the boxes, suitcases, and plastic trash bags on the bedroom floor, stuffed with her clothes, linens, and kitchen things. Cherise patted him on the shoulder. "I'll be fine, Tater."

He scowled, which sent his left eyeball into a spasm. "There ain't even any lights in here, except over the kitchen sink!" Tater threw his hands up in exasperation. "You know you can't use the tub until the grout sets. There's hardly a stick of furniture in this place, and I barely brought over enough firewood for one night!"

"It'll be fine, Tater."

"But Viv told me to make sure y'all went back to her place tonight. She said—"

"Doesn't matter what she said." Cherise motioned for Tater to exit the bedroom ahead of her, then shut the door behind them. It gave her great comfort to know there was one room, one little corner in Bigler, that was all hers.

"She's gonna tan my hide."

Cherise chuckled, walking behind Tater down the hallway. "You're a grown man. Just tell her to fuck off."

Tater spun around, his dirty blond hair whipping across his forehead, his eyebrows raised in shock. "You ever tell Vivienne Newberry to fuck off?"

Cherise had to acknowledge that she had not. "But I'm this close," she said, holding up her thumb and index finger. That made him laugh.

The two of them strolled into the living room, still laughing, when Cherise caught sight of J.J. out in the front yard, close to the water's edge. He had his back to her and he was still half naked. His jeans were soaked through, clinging to his lower half like a wet suit. Had his ass always been this tight? Had his thighs always been this cut? As she pondered these important questions, the sexual need sliced through her once more, hot and sharp. She gasped.

"Y'all all right?"

She whipped her head around to Tater. "Fine."

He offered her a tentative smile. "It's nice that J.J. pitched in. I didn't ask him. Viv and Garland said they didn't ask him, either—said it must have been his idea."

She crossed her arms over her chest and tried her hardest to appear disinterested. "It's a free country."

Tater shook his head. He ran the toe of his work boot through a patch of sawdust that had drifted in from the new porch. "J.J.'s a good man, Cheri," he said, looking up. "Seems not many people know how to be decent anymore, but he does. Y'all ought to try to be nice to each other again."

Cherise's mouth fell open in surprise. *Decent? J.J. DeCourcy?* Cherise decided to change the subject. "So how late y'all staying today, Tater?"

He sighed. "Not much longer. The sun's getting ready to set. Most of us will be back tomorrow and we should finish up before supper, but we ain't gonna get to cleaning the inside."

She patted Tater on the shoulder. "I'll take care of that."

He frowned. "You sure?"

"Yeah," she said, guiding him out onto the porch. "At least you got all the old moldy stuff out. In a way, I look forward to cleaning the place."

"Don't that beat all," he said. "I figured you for the type that has a maid."

Cherise laughed. "Oh, I used to, let me tell you. Those were the days." When she glanced up at Tater's confused expression, she was horrified by her own carelessness. She kept forgetting to remember that she was wealthy! "What I mean is I miss the housekeeping service I retain back in Tampa."

"We got 'em here, too, you know. I'll just make a phone call—"

"That's okay. Anyway . . ." Cherise scanned the front yard for something else to talk about—anything else to talk about. She found it immediately. Gladys was making a beeline toward the slicked-down J.J., a hungry look in her heavily made-up eyes.

"I better get Gladys back to town before she makes a spectacle of herself," she said, heading down the steps. "See you tomorrow, Tater."

"That you will."

Cherise made it as far as the gravel driveway that curved around the house when she stopped. J.J. had just lifted Gladys playfully off the grass. Gladys squealed and beat on his shoulders like she couldn't stand the idea of being tossed around by a half-dressed man less than half her age. J.J. eventually put her down, laughing.

Cherise froze. Her face went hot. Her knees shook. Her chest felt like it was weighted down with a huge boulder of sadness. And just like that, she was on the edge of tears. Something about the sight of J.J. dripping wet and laughing, standing in the grass by the lake, the sun setting behind him . . . and her heart had begun to split open. Memories began to pour out.

The days she'd spent with J.J. before college were happy ones. She had no way of knowing it at the time, but she'd never experience happiness like that again. Not in a way that was so simple. Real. With so much laughter. Gentleness. Patience. Water, sunshine, kisses . . .

Her heart nearly exploded with joy that day he showed up on her doorstep in Tampa, the same old J.J., smiling, handsome, making her laugh, telling her he'd missed her like hell and refused to go another day without seeing her.

Maybe it had been so good with J.J. because she'd been loved and had loved in return—effortlessly.

Cherise heard herself gasp. She prayed no one else

did. She turned on her heel and jogged to the DeVille, climbing behind the wheel. She started the engine, moved the car so it faced the main road, and waited for Gladys to get the hint that it was time to go.

With an eye on the rearview mirror, Cherise told herself she was crazy. She had to be PMS-ing. There was no other explanation.

Tears? Seriously? Tears for *what*? For *whom*?

Tears for a fantasy, that's what. The J.J. she'd held in her most private heart for all those years wasn't real. The real J.J. was the man who'd impregnated and then abandoned Tanyalee. The real J.J. couldn't decide whether to kiss Cherise or slice her to ribbons with his sharp words.

She needed to remember that.

Gladys threw open the passenger side door and slid onto the white leather bucket seat, giggling like a middle schooler. Cherise drove back to town so fast that Gladys's earrings swung against her cheeks and she clung to the overhead strap with a white-knuckled desperation.

"You're a terrible driver, Cheri," she said.

Chapter 12

Turner whipped his department-issued SUV into his designated parking space, and immediately began shaking his head and grinning at J.J.

"What's so funny?" J.J. asked, uncrossing his legs and pushing himself off the exterior brick wall of the Bigler Municipal Complex. "I wouldn't have to stalk you if you'd just answer my damn phone calls."

Turner didn't even bother to hide the glee that showed in his eyes as he stepped down from his vehicle. "How's the evil plot progressing, Jay? Has she succumbed to your charms yet?"

J.J. shook his head as he opened the glass entrance door and gestured for Turner to go ahead of him. "I'm here on official business."

"Uh-huh." Turner yanked off his ball cap and rubbed his close-cropped hair. J.J. followed him as he wound his way past the one-man 911 call center, the empty animal control office, and his secretary's desk. Like most people with normal jobs, she'd gone home hours ago. "Have a seat," Turner said. He shut his office door behind them. "Coffee?"

"Nah, thanks."

"Good, 'cause I don't think there's any made around here." Turner gave him a lopsided grin, but despite the cheerful demeanor, J.J. could tell his friend was bordering on exhaustion.

"The FBI still staying at the Tip-Top Motel?"

"Yeah, and bitching and moaning about it every minute of the day." Turner leaned back in his chair and cupped his hands behind his head. J.J. could see dark circles under his eyes. "I told 'em if they wanted five-star accommodations they shoulda stayed in Raleigh-Durham."

"What's the latest?"

Turner shrugged. "This ain't like the TV shows, Jay. You don't just drop off a slice of forty-year-old water-logged flesh and get all the answers before the commercial break. The FBI crime lab has its priorities, and this ice-cold case ain't one of them, sad to say."

J.J. nodded. "So nothing new?"

Turner smiled. "Not since the last time you asked, which was three hours ago."

J.J. let out a groan of frustration. Even to his own ears it sounded overly dramatic.

Turner raised an eyebrow. "Problem?"

"Carlotta Smoot McCoy won't talk to us. She's thrown Mimi off her property twice and told me to go to hell today for about the tenth time. She says the newspaper abandoned her family a few days after her sister went missing, when it stopped putting Barbara Jean's disappearance on the front page. She claims it's the *Bugle*'s fault that justice was never done."

Turner nodded. "Carlotta's not much interested in talking to us, either. She blames the sheriff's department as much as the *Bugle,* ranting about how old Sheriff Wimbley had Barbara Jean's blood on his hands."

"Jesus," J.J. said.

"Outside my mama's family, she's the only person I've run across who doesn't suspect poor Carleton. She told me, 'That poor man went to heaven with a pure heart.' "

"What kind of learning disability did you say he had?" J.J. asked.

"I didn't say." Turner straightened in his chair and ran his hands quickly over his face, trying to keep himself awake, no doubt. "Mama thinks it was some kind of attention deficit problem with some dyslexia thrown in—shit they didn't know about back then. He only made it to the eighth grade. She said he was a sweet man, and a hard worker."

"Now that's an odd thing," J.J. said, leaning an elbow on Turner's desk. "I noticed there isn't a single article where anyone comes right out and names Carleton as a suspect, although Sheriff Wimbley gets pretty close. He's always referred to as a 'witness.' And I haven't been able to find any record of a charging document being filed against him, unless you know something I don't."

"Nope."

"So there's nothing in the department archives you're not sharing with me?"

"Not a damn thing."

"So Carleton was a witness, nothing more. So why do you keep saying that everyone in town just assumed he was the murderer?"

Turner chuckled. "In North Carolina in 1964, the word 'witness'—when applied to someone of the slow-witted, black, and male persuasion—was spelled s-u-s-p-e-c-t."

J.J. frowned.

"Besides," Turner continued. "People want closure. It's just human nature. It was easier to blame it on a feebleminded black man from out of town than worry that the killer could be one of your nice, white, next-door neighbors."

There was an edge to Turner's words tonight. "I see," J.J. said. "So the FBI doesn't want you saying anything, is that it?"

Turner made a face, but stayed silent.

"So was there?"

"Was there what?"

"A nice, white, next-door neighbor killer on the loose?"

Turner shrugged. "I got nothing for you, Jay. Sorry."

"All right." *Figured as much.* "I finally got a copy of Carleton Johnston's autopsy report today. The Mecklenberg County coroner said he died of some kind of seizure that caused him to fall and crack his skull."

"Yep. That's what the report says."

"But?"

Turner shrugged. "Mama insists that Carleton didn't have seizures. Her family's always maintained someone whacked him over the head to keep him quiet, plain and simple."

"Then why in God's name hasn't your family had his body exhumed to get some answers?

Turner shook his head. "Jay, what do you think I've been trying to tell them for the last fifteen years? But Mama and her sister are the only family left who remember Carleton, and they've flat-out refused. They think it would be dishonoring the dead. They don't see things the way we do."

"So Carleton's killer gets away with murder? And Barbara Jean's, too?"

Turner averted his eyes and began shuffling some papers. "Not if I can help it."

"Tell me," J.J. said. "Maybe I can help put the pieces together."

Turner stood abruptly and put his ball cap back on.

"I've got to get home and get some rest. But I'll have something for you next week. Something worth waiting for. I promise."

"You mean *news*?" J.J. laughed. "An actual piece of *news* I can attribute to Cataloochee County Sheriff Turner Halliday and publish in the *news*paper?"

"Yeah."

"Shee-it!" J.J. hopped up from his chair. "I hope I remember what to do with it!"

Turner grinned at him. "You talking about a piece of news or a piece of CNN?"

Since J.J. had just transferred his weight to his feet, he froze with his knees bent and his back stooped. He stayed locked in that awkward position for a few seconds.

"You're right," J.J. said eventually, standing upright. "You need some sleep."

Turner put his hand on J.J.'s shoulder as they walked down the hallway and out the back door of the sheriff's station, chuckling the whole way. "Just go talk to the woman, Jay. Tell her what really happened with Tanyalee. God only knows the kind of poison that viper has been spitting out to Cheri over the years. It's probably even worse than the shit she's told Viv and Garland."

"Garland doesn't believe a word of it."

"Well, that's because he was one of Tanyalee's victims. Plus, he's worked with you every day for the last six years and knows the kind of man you are. Cheri, however, doesn't have the benefit of that. She hasn't said a peep to you since your wedding day."

J.J. shivered at the sound of those two words. *Wedding day.* D-day was more like it.

"Seriously." Turner grabbed J.J. by the shoulders and turned him so they stood eye to eye. His friend had a no-nonsense look on his face. "Cheri's in Bigler, man. It's real. She's back home. But that's only half the battle—she needs to know what really went on with you and Tanyalee."

J.J. closed his eyes a moment. "You know I don't believe it's my story to tell." He looked at his friend again, aware that he was scowling at Turner. "Cheri's got to find out the truth on her own, by confronting her sister. She wouldn't believe me if I told her, anyway. She'd just think I was doing whatever I had to do to get in her pants."

Turner's eyes sparkled under his ball cap. "She'd be right. That's *exactly* what you're doing, man. You're busting your ass so she feels needed at the paper and gets settled out at the lake house. And why are you doing all this shit?"

J.J. considered his point. "To get in her pants."

"No wonder I make the big money around here."

Turner slapped him on the shoulder before he headed to his car. J.J. left soon after, with every intention of heading back to the newsroom. But he drove right on through the old downtown, past the Ace Hardware and the diner and the library and the courthouse, until the red brick *Bugle* building receded in his rearview mirror. And soon he found himself driving up the twists and turns of Randall Road, heading into the night woods.

She finished her nightly phone call to Candy a little after ten, thrilled that the lake house and the BlackBerry gave her the privacy to laugh and dish all she wanted, at normal decibel levels, *and* without having to hide in the bathroom! It was comforting to hear Candy's voice, and laughing together about the events of the day had been just what she needed to unwind.

Cherise changed into a pair of thick socks, her favorite drawstring pajama pants, and a camisole tank top that was past its prime. She added a cardigan sweater and headed out to the kitchen. After she'd boiled some water and thrown a tea bag in a cup, she took her hot drink out to the top step of the new porch and plopped down. She breathed deeply, getting a nose full of rich lake air and fresh sawdust. She pulled her sweater tight and let the night settle around her.

Truth be told, Candy was the only thing Cherise missed about Tampa. Well, Candy and a decent cup of coffee. Everything else about the place seemed part of some faraway dream—the malls and boutiques, the sweltering heat, the gated neighborhoods she could no longer afford. It was fascinating how the memory of Tampa had already receded to a faraway place in her brain, reduced to a sun-bleached, flat blur, a barren strip of nothing special. Cherise took a cautious sip of her scalding hot tea and smiled to herself in the dark.

Florida was about as different from Bigler as you could get—which was probably why she moved there in the first place. And with each year she had stayed away, her life here in western North Carolina seemed less and less real. Less and less a part of who she really was. When acquaintances would ask her where she was from, she'd answer, "Tampa." If they persisted, noting her accent, Cherise would answer again, "Tampa," and work even harder at ditching her Cack-a-lacky curse.

But a thick black line had been drawn on that day J.J. showed up on her doorstep more than five years ago, all sweet and shy and sexy and telling her he wanted another chance with her, that he'd never forgotten her. Looking back, she felt sick to her stomach to think how close she'd come to falling for it, how she had started to believe him. Thank God Tanyalee called when she did.

From that day forward, she'd referred to herself as Cherise. She no longer wanted one foot in her present and one in her past. She no longer wanted any ties to Bigler or J.J. or Tanyalee or that stupid, naïve girl who had been Cheri Newberry.

So when she returned to Bigler for Tanyalee's wedding, she returned as Cherise. And Cherise and Candy made a point of staying overnight at a B and B in Waynesville. Anywhere but Bigler. They'd promised each other they'd never again spend a night in this town. It all sounded ridiculously pretentious to Cherise now, but she had money in those days, with more money on the horizon, and it would have seemed preposterous then that she'd ever find herself in a position where she'd have to come home to Bigler for a paycheck, a hot meal, and a place of her own.

After the wedding, the disconnect to her past was complete. She put most everything about her hometown out of her mind, the lake house in particular. That's why she'd been surprised to see how solid its walls were. How the years of heat and sun and mountain air permeated the floors. How quiet it was here. Peaceful. Real. And as strange as it was to admit, Cherise found herself enjoying the beauty of the rolling green-blue mountain vistas and the lakes and the forests of Cataloochee County, its familiar roads, the particular quality of light in its sunrises and sunsets. It was almost as if she were seeing things for the first time, like how there was a moist and teeming world under all the stillness that she'd never noticed before. Insects. Birds. Wildflowers. Streams.

This part of the South was intoxicating. It was a raw and boundless place, a magnet for songwriters, painters, and poets determined to capture the essence of its wild beauty. And try as she might to deny it, the story of this place was her family's story, and, in turn, her own. She might not be proud of that fact, but it didn't change it. So she supposed there was no shame in her taking advantage of her enforced stay here to take stock, make some changes, think things through, all while enjoying the view.

But she knew she couldn't hide here forever.

Cherise sighed deeply, the familiar money worries pushing into her brain. She'd get her first paycheck in another couple of days, and it was already spent. She planned to send more than half of her after-tax earnings to Candy to pay her portion of their bills, even though her friend had expressed her desire to ditch the studio apartment and stay with an old boyfriend to save money.

"Don't panic—I'll be sleeping on his futon," Candy reassured her. "And when you get home, we'll get a nicer place."

Cherise didn't have the heart to tell her she'd imagined starting over somewhere new, somewhere that wasn't Tampa. When Cherise had something specific to tell Candy, she would. Right now, that's all it was— her imagination.

Whatever was left of that first paycheck would go to groceries and savings, not to mention gas for the pimp-mobile, an expense she hadn't planned for. The gang down at the garage had dropped the bomb on Cherise that afternoon—the gas-friendly Corolla needed eight hundred dollars' worth of work. They said something about a fried cylinder head and a complete valve job— conditions that Candy thought sounded vaguely porno-graphic. Porno or no, the two of them had opted not to fix the Corolla for the time being, and Cherise had it towed to Viv's for storage.

Cherise set her cup down and wrapped her arms around her knees, hugging herself tight. It was getting chilly, just as Tater predicted. She sure hoped she'd carted off enough of Viv's blankets. She could always grab an extra armful tomorrow, she supposed, though she'd have to survive another of her aunt's displays of raised eyebrows and pursed lips.

Cherise closed her eyes, feeling it in her bones as the cold rose from the lake and the soil and slipped from the silent woods all around her.

Food. Gas. Bills—the ones she could pay and the ones she couldn't. And there was still the bankruptcy decision to make. All it would take was a phone call.

She sighed. Sometimes she couldn't even remember what it felt like back then, when she could drop a few hundred on a pair of shoes without thinking twice, or spend a fortune on restaurants and clubs. How many hours had she spent shopping, all in the pursuit of adorning herself and her house with baubles? To what end? What in God's name had she been doing? Who had she been trying to impress? Her business associates? Loan officers? Herself?

Was it possible she'd tried to use the money and stuff to build a wall between herself and Bigler?

Her motivation aside, the lifestyle was addictive. There were plenty of times when she felt the need to spend just to spend, as if the act itself were the reward, the best thing about being alive. Looking back, Cherise knew that she believed nothing was more satisfying than getting exactly what she wanted whenever she wanted it.

The ultimate high had been the day she and Candy closed on their sweet little sixteen-storefront strip mall in a rebounding neighborhood. Sure, they may have paid a little too much for it, and yes, they leveraged everything they had to qualify for financing, but by that time, she and Candy could do that kind of deal in their sleep.

They made it happen on a Tuesday afternoon, and

she and Candy went out for mojitos to celebrate. Laughing, they'd clinked their glasses together and toasted to "a whole 'nother level" of success.

By Thursday, a bit of startling news came out—median property values nationwide had suddenly dropped. Some even predicted the end of the housing bubble due to lenient mortgage lending practices. She and Candy decided to keep an eye on things, but refused to believe the naysayers. Real estate was the safest investment there was, and always would be.

It wasn't long before they'd hit a "whole 'nother level" all right—of disaster. The signs were confusing at first. Subprime lenders were folding while the Dow soared over 14,000 for the first time in history. Things couldn't be that bad, right? But then the big boys started going under—Merrill Lynch and Lehman Brothers and Washington Mutual—and it was like a landslide. Tampa's real estate prices imploded. Cherise and Candy suddenly owned property worth a fraction of what they'd paid for it. They started to go under—personally as well as in their business balance sheet—and they weren't alone.

They had held on longer than some of their social circle, but when the dust had settled, they were millions in debt. Desperate. Jobless. Stunned.

Cherise took another breath of sawdust and let her forehead drop. In her heart she knew she'd fought off the inevitable as long as she could. Tomorrow she'd call her attorney and give the go-ahead for her Chapter 7 personal bankruptcy filing. With that, the party really, truly would be over.

"Chit, chit, chit."

Cherise nearly fell off the steps as she scrambled to a stand, her heart racing under her sweater. "Oh, shit. Oh, God." She clutched her chest as her eyes adjusted enough to get a good look at the source of the eerie sound. "No! Not you again! Shoo! Git!"

The squirrel stared at her, his funny little face looking almost quizzical. His black marble eyes reflected what little light managed to spill from the kitchen. His whiskers twitched. He looked possessed, she thought. And most definitely rabid. Rabid, possessed, and probably looking to chew through some wiring.

Slowly, Cherise backed toward the door, her hand reaching behind her for the latch.

"I said go away!"

With disbelief she watched the rodent scurry up the steps, pausing at the teacup. He touched his little squirrel lips to the edge of mug and recoiled.

Great. That was one of only two cups she'd managed to lift from Viv's kitchen, and now she'd have to throw it in the trash.

"Chit, chit, chit." The squirrel's tail spun around over its back as it glared at Cherise, as if to complain about the evening's beverage selection.

"Scat!"

It didn't.

"Git!"

It didn't.

Cherise was about to slip inside and bolt the door when she heard the unmistakable crunch of car tires on the gravel lane. Who the hell would be coming out here at this hour?

As the car's high beams lit up the front yard and

bounced off the water, a strange thought occurred to Cherise—she was alone out here in the middle of nowhere. It never even dawned on her to be concerned about her personal safety, squirrels notwithstanding. And now, it was too late for caution. Whoever was hellbent on disturbing her privacy was about to pull up in front of the house.

A midsized pickup slid to an abrupt stop. It was a truck she'd seen out here earlier in the day. Maybe one of the workers had come back for something he'd left behind.

She nearly choked when she saw J.J. round the back of the truck, tuck his head down, and break into a jog up the porch steps.

Chapter 13

Cherise pressed her back against the door, flattened her palms to the wood, and braced herself.

His boots made a lot of noise as they crashed against the floorboards, but he froze the instant he saw her plastered against the door.

J.J. said nothing. Cherise watched his chest rise and fall like he'd just sprinted halfway across town. Suddenly, she realized she was breathing just as desperately. They stared at each other in the dim light. J.J.'s eyes looked hard. His face looked almost angry. For an instant, fear spiked through Cherise.

What did this man want from her?

"Chit, chit, chit."

J.J. paid no attention to the squirrel's protests.

"Chit! Chit! Keet-keet-keet-keet!"

Slowly, he turned his head toward the noise, then looked back at Cherise. His smile was faint, but it was there. Then he let his eyes trail down the front of her body and back up again, from her socks to the exposed expanse of skin above her cardigan. She wondered if he could see her heart pounding just below the surface.

"Why are you out here in your jammies? In the cold?"

Cherise raised her chin. "Because it's my house. I can sit out here in the cold, in my jammies, if I want."

J.J. nodded soberly, as if they were having a deeply philosophical exchange. "So," he said, jerking a thumb toward the little noisemaker. "Do all Florida business-women get themselves a personal security squirrel these days?"

"Of course not," she said, slowly ungluing herself from the door and unclenching her spine a bit. "The stupid thing is stalking me. I hate it. I think it has rabies."

J.J. shoved his hands in his jeans pockets. "I think she sounds mad at you. What'd you do to the poor thing?"

"I haven't done anything to it!"

J.J. shook his head in surrender. "You used to have a sense of humor, Cheri."

"You used to be a decent human being."

"Lord-a-mighty, Cheri!"

"*Cherise.* My damn name is *Cherise.* What's y'all's mental block with that? And why'd y'all come out here? You weren't invited. Nobody was invited! And I am so sorry to inform you that I'm not about to start hosting wild bikini pot parties out here, if that's what you were expecting!"

He raised an eyebrow. "Not as sorry as I am," he said, dryly.

"Just leave me alone."

J.J. opened his mouth to speak, then stopped himself. He winced. Obviously, it caused the man actual pain to be nice to her. God only knew what snarky comment was fixin' to fly off his tongue.

"All right. No wild parties—I can live with that. Your name's not Cheri—I'm all over it. Now that we got all that out of the way, do you think you could take off the boxing gloves for once? Just temporarily?"

J.J.'s voice had become softer and scratchier than usual, and his dark hair slipped down over his forehead, reminding Cherise of the seventeen-year-old he'd once been. "I came out here to talk to you. Do you think we could do that? Just talk? Like two grown-ups?"

Cherise laughed. She hadn't meant for the laugh to sound cold, but seriously—what a ridiculous question! There was only one immature jerk on this porch, and it sure as hell wasn't her. "That's up to you, J.J."

He shut his eyes and shook his head. "Nope. It's up to both of us." When his gaze connected with hers again, Cherise felt her cheeks flush. For just an instant, he looked almost innocent. Almost like he did back in middle school, when he'd pledged his undying love to her via permanent marker.

"We've got to work together, Cherise. We need to reach an understanding. What we've been doing the last few days is just pure crazy. I'll most certainly claim my part of it, but we can do better."

She held her breath, the tightness in her belly coiling tighter as she stepped away from the safety of the door. Of course they had to have this conversation. She'd even tried to start it before. But now that J.J. was here, standing in front of her, in the dark, taking the initiative and acting halfway decent, she felt scared to death.

Then . . . she exhaled and smiled. It occurred to her that her fear was ridiculous. How many iffy business situations had she breezed through in her life? How many deals had she made on a wing and a prayer, and how many times had she stared down her own coward-ice? "You're absolutely right," Cherise said, summoning the savvy professional she'd been before she'd come back to Bigler. "Come on in, J.J. Would you like a cup of tea or something?"

"Sure," he said, holding the door for her and smiling down like an actual gentleman. "Mighty kind of you to ask."

Don't look at her ass. Don't look at her ass.

"I'm sorry I don't have a couch or chairs—had to throw them all out because of the mildew."

J.J. ran a hand through his hair and tried to avert his eyes as Cheri walked ahead. Those drawstring pants were as thin as tissue paper. As she moved, he could see the slight jiggle of her flesh, the loose way her body swayed unobstructed, and, with the kind assistance of the harsh kitchen lightbulb, he could actually see the blush of her bare skin beneath. Bare thighs. Bare calves disappearing into thick socks. The bare, round, luscious globes of her ass.

She wasn't wearing any fuckin' panties.

Shee-it.

"No problem," he croaked out, looking around the room for something else—anything else—to focus on. He noticed a stack of wood next to the huge creek stone fireplace. "How about I make a fire? Hate for you to be chilly."

Seeing that you're not wearing any fuckin' under-wear.

"That would be great," Cheri said.

As he set about arranging the newspaper, kindling, and logs, J.J. had to admit to himself that he was glad most of the furniture was gone and the house seemed hollowed out. He'd spent the six longest months of his life living in this place with Tanyalee, and anything that didn't summon those memories was thoroughly welcome.

J.J. found a box of matches on the mantel and lit the paper, standing to watch last Wednesday's *Bugle* go up in flames. "So, you getting settled in?" he hollered to her. "Has Gladys got you everything you need?" J.J. kept himself busy by fetching two kitchen chairs and pulling them up to the fire. He refused to gawk at the lower half of her body like some kind of lecher.

"Pretty much."

"She tells me you're sorting through years of accounting reports. Finding anything interesting?"

Cheri walked back into the room with one of Viv's distinctive coffee mugs in her hand. She handed it to him and sat in the chair opposite.

"It's a mess, J.J. I told Granddaddy that Purnell doesn't have a clue what he's doing, but he wouldn't even listen to me. In fact . . ." She pulled the bulky sweater tight around her midsection and crossed her legs. "I think the guy might even be criminally negligent." Cheri turned away from the fire and made eye contact with J.J. She looked almost apologetic. "I used to do some forensic accounting down in Florida. I've seen this before."

J.J. nodded politely and bit his tongue. He knew that about her, of course. He'd kept track of most everything related to Cheri over the years. He knew she'd worked her ass off at that big, fancy corporation, and got herself promoted several times. He knew that she walked away from a vice president offer to go into real estate. He also knew that she had a habit of hooking up with dudes who looked like models and acted like morons. Maybe someday, when everything was sorted out between the two of them, she'd open up about all those years they'd been apart. J.J. had often wondered what she regretted, what she would have done differently, if given the chance.

Cheri frowned at him. "What?"

He must have been staring too intently. He needed to chill out. "Just thinking about Purnell, is all. I've been on Garland for years about him, but he always says he can't force him out because the guy's got nothing else. He says losing his job would kill the old codger."

Cheri shrugged. "If the gin doesn't do it first."

J.J. smiled sadly. "So are you going to fire him?"

"No. She shook her head. "I have no interest in firing people before my office is even painted."

He laughed.

"Besides," she said, "the records are such a disaster that I can't even get a clear picture of what's going on. I think I need to keep digging. When I do know, I plan to put together a report for Granddaddy. I'll give you a copy, too."

"I'd be much obliged."

They sat quietly for a moment, the wood popping and crackling as it began releasing heat. Since the exchange was going so smoothly—the kind of talk any two professional associates might have—J.J. tried his best not to sneak a prurient peek at Cheri. But it was impossible. He watched her tug her sweater tighter. He saw how her brow furrowed and her mouth was pulled tight in seriousness. None of that could hide the fact that Cheri was so beautiful she seemed lit up from the inside. Her warm skin and rich auburn hair burned brighter and hotter than anything J.J. had ever laid eyes on. He'd always seen her that way.

Cheri's gaze shot his way and she narrowed an eye in suspicion.

J.J. smiled at her. "Do you remember that day we all scared the livin' shit out of Viv, hanging around on her front porch after doing belly flops all day in the mud pit over behind Cee-Dee Creswell's smokehouse?"

Cheri's eyes opened as wide as her smile. "Oh, God, yes. Viv scrubbed me to within an inch of my life that night. Candy got her butt whopped."

"Turner did, too."

"But it was so worth it," Cheri said, giggling. "The look on Viv's face when she opened the door and saw us all on the porch swing, hair all stiff—"

"Nothing but the whites of our eyeballs showing."

Cheri shook her head and chuckled. "How old were we? About ten or so? Remember how she made us hose down her porch and sidewalk?"

J.J. nodded. "I'm still scarred by it."

Cheri turned her body to face J.J., tipping her head and grinning even bigger. "You remember our armpit serenade cruises?"

J.J. laughed. "Hell, yes. It was as close to culture as

Bigler ever got." He looked at Cheri's happy face, and the memory flooded through him like it was yesterday. They were sixteen that summer, and Turner would pick him up and they'd drive out here in the middle of the night, and Cheri and Candy would already have the rowboat ready. The four of them would pile in and head out to the middle of the lake, where he and Turner would take off their shirts, stick their hands under their armpits, and begin their duet. The racket carried across the lake. Some people's porch lights would go on.

"My favorite was always 'Islands in the Stream,'" Cheri said.

"Yep, that got the loons worked up somethin' awful."

"I laughed so hard once, I fell out of the boat."

"I think the twelve-pack of Bud Light probably had something to do with that, Cheri."

She looked at him sideways. "We had a lot of fun."

"That we did."

Their eyes locked for just an instant, and J.J. felt a knot form in his throat. He wanted to tell her everything, just like Turner recommended. But he couldn't. It was not his place to destroy the sisters' relationship. But he couldn't remain silent, either. Turner had been dead-on right about that.

"I owe you an apology," J.J. said, his voice nearly a whisper.

Cheri pulled away and blinked at him.

"Don't look so shocked," he said, chuckling. "I was an ass when you first got here, and I'm sorry."

Her lips parted. She cocked her head. She couldn't manage to say anything.

"It's a long story."

She nodded. "I just bet."

"Look, Cheri—"

"*Cherise*. And if you can't manage that small request, then I'm going to go around calling you Jefferson Jackson on a daily basis, like I did from seventh to ninth grades. How would you like that?"

He nodded, remembering that he'd liked it just fine back then and wouldn't mind it now, either. "You could come up with something a lot worse these days, I suppose."

"No shit."

They laughed together, but after a raucous few seconds, the sound died away, leaving the nearly empty cottage ringing with silence. J.J. felt an awkwardness creeping between them, which was the last thing he wanted. He couldn't let this moment pass.

"Listen, Cherise—"

She held up her palm. "I know you expected to be publisher, J.J. I know that Granddaddy goin' off and deciding to bring me up here must have surprised the hell out of you and really pissed you off. It was *your* job, and rightly so. I get it. But relax—I don't plan to stay more than a month, just enough to sort out the financial picture for Granddaddy, and then you can have your job back."

J.J. took a sip of his tea so he could carefully plan his response. Garland had told him about their little negotiation, of course, but he'd seemed confident that Cheri would decide to stay on after the one-month mark. J.J. knew it was up to him to set the stage for that. It was now or never.

"You didn't think I'd amount to much," he said softly.

"That night before you left town for college, you told me that I was a small-town boy with small plans." He looked up at her and grinned. "So I set out to prove you wrong."

"Seriously?" Cheri leaned her elbows on her knees and grinned.

"At first, oh, yeah. Then in my second year at Chapel Hill, it was like my brain caught fire, and I discovered I was into ideas for their own sake. Did you know I spent my junior year in Italy on a history fellowship?"

Cheri's lips parted. "No. I didn't."

J.J. figured as much—Tanyalee would conveniently forget to share any of the good stuff about him. "After I graduated, I backpacked for a year all over Central and South America, then went to work for a news service in New York."

"*City?*" Cheri's eyes were huge now. She propped her jaw in her palm.

"Yeah. But after a year or so of the subway and the noise and the rotten air and living in an apartment the size of an outhouse, I came on home and started working for Garland. I've been here ever since."

Cheri nodded thoughtfully and let her gaze wander toward the fire. "J.J.?"

"Yeah?"

"What the hell happened with Tanyalee?"

J.J. couldn't help it. The bluntness of the question—and the sheer enormity of it—made him laugh.

"I don't think it's all that funny," Cheri snapped, sitting up straight and tugging on her sweater again.

"Neither do I, let me assure you."

Cheri crossed her arms tight under her chest, then recrossed her legs. J.J. heard loud and clear what the body language was telling him. *Keep your distance. Watch what you say. Don't you dare lie to me.*

"Let me start with what I will not share with you," J.J. said.

Cheri rolled her eyes like she was expecting a load of horseshit.

He paid her no mind. "I will not tell you the details of what went on between Tanyalee and me in the privacy of our marriage. I don't believe that's right."

Cheri shifted around on the old kitchen chair. "That's very noble of you. Go on," she said.

"What I *will* tell you is this: I did not cheat on her. I did not steal a dime from her. I did not leave because she had a miscarriage. And I never should have married her in the first place."

Cheri blew air from between her lips. "Should have thought of that before you slept with her."

J.J. steeled himself. It was bad enough to know the truth in his own heart, but to say it out loud—to Cheri, no less—was going to take some balls.

"As soon as I settled in and started working for Garland, Tanyalee was all over me. She hit on me nonstop for a couple years, and one night I caved. A couple months later . . ."

Cheri's eyes flashed at him. She was fighting back tears. He didn't need to finish that sentence, obviously. Cheri knew exactly what happened a couple months later, because she was part of it. J.J. was in her house and in her bed and Cheri had just started undoing his belt when his cell phone rang.

God, how it sickened him to remember what happened next. Cheri had slipped her slim fingers into his pocket and removed the phone. It was Tanyalee calling. J.J. would never forget the shock and confusion he saw on Cheri's face as she hit the speaker button and placed the phone on J.J.'s stomach.

He looked at her now, took a deep breath, and decided to continue. "The first thing I did when I got back to Bigler was demand an in vitro paternity test. The baby was mine. And, as you recall, there was a wedding."

Cheri rocketed up from the chair and ran out to the kitchen. Clearly, she wanted to get as far away from him as possible. J.J. watched her lean on the rounded edge of the old farm sink and drop her head. He stayed quiet, figuring she'd come back when, and if, she was ready. It took a full minute for her to turn around, and when she did, J.J. instinctively jumped to his feet—Cheri was as sad and lonely as he'd ever seen a person.

"Stay there." She straight-armed her palm toward him. He could see her arm shake. "I gotta say some things."

J.J. nodded, his hands hanging uselessly at his sides, his heart aching for her.

"You got my sister pregnant," she said, giggling nervously. "You know, it may sound crazy but I might have been able to get over that . . . with time . . . a lot of time." She stopped and shook her head.

"Cheri—"

"I only spoke to Tanyalee occasionally, you know. She called when you two got engaged, of course, all happy and sparkly and clueless that you'd been with me when she called about the baby."

I wouldn't be so sure about that, sweetheart.

"Then later she called to give me the details on the wedding. She also called me to tell me about the miscarriage, and soon after, that you'd filed for divorce."

J.J. said nothing.

"Tanyalee made you sound like an absolute monster. You can't *imagine* how hysterical she was, telling me all the horrible things you'd done to her."

J.J. laughed bitterly. "Oh, I can imagine it just fine."

Cheri took a deep breath. "Tanyalee said you were bonking several of the Biltmore tour guides the whole time you were together."

"I was faithful to her."

"She told me you emptied her trust fund."

"If her money got itself gone, it sure as hell wasn't my doing."

"She said you threw her shit out into the rain! Now I realize she meant *here*! On this property! Which doesn't even belong to you!"

"Okay, now *that* I did do. So shoot me."

Cheri rubbed her face with both hands, like she was clearing something away from her eyes. Then she sighed like she was pushing out every last molecule of air in her body. "Tanyalee came to see me the other day. She told me that after the divorce, you told her I'd been calling while y'all were married, trying to get you to leave her."

The roaring in J.J.'s ears felt like it would shatter his skull. *What the fuck was Tanyalee up to? Was she that insanely jealous of Cheri?*

"I did not say that, of course."

"And she said she lost the baby because she . . . the

stress of—" Cheri choked back a sob. "She said she always suspected we were plotting against her, and the stress made her lose the—"

"Hell no, Cheri! *Fuck,* no!"

Cheri stood stone-still, her breath going too fast. The sweater had fallen away and J.J. could see her tummy quiver under the thin little tank top she wore. She was fighting to keep calm, and doing a far better job than he was, apparently.

J.J. took a step toward her. "No, Cheri. Listen to me, please. She did not lose the baby because of you, or me, or anyone else, or anything that anyone else did or said. That's a low-down, nasty lie with only one purpose—to hurt you, to hurt you *bad.* I am so sorry she did that. You didn't deserve it."

Cheri's brows knitted together and her mouth tightened. He watched her ball her fists at her sides. "What exactly are you saying, J.J.?"

He took another step closer. "You'll have to ask Tanyalee what happened. You just need to know with absolute certainty that you aren't to blame for anything."

Cheri's nostrils flared. Her knees shook under the thin pajama pants. "She told me something else." Cheri stopped, and her rich amber eyes began searching J.J.'s face. "Tanyalee said that you'd never stopped loving me, that you'd always been hung up on me and still are. Was that another lie?"

Her question landed with a thud in the empty room, and J.J.'s mind went blank. Nada. Zilch. Zero. He could think of no way to answer her without all hell breaking loose in his heart and his world. But if he lied, he'd be no better than the likes of Tanyalee.

"Oh, just forget it, J.J."

"Wait."

"You should probably go." Cheri headed toward the front door and reached for the handle.

It was exactly like a few days ago out at Paw Paw Lake. The instant J.J. grabbed her wrist, a wild heat ripped through his brain and body, blinding him to all else but Cheri and what he wanted—needed—now that she'd come back to him.

"Damn, Cheri."

He pulled her hand from the door and gently turned her arm so that it pressed against the small of her back. J.J stepped into her, molding his body against hers. He held her like that for a moment, fully in his grasp, her eyes locked on his, her lips open as if to dare him to do it, to make it happen, to make it become the only choice either of them had—the only choice they'd *ever* had.

He must not have moved fast enough for Cheri, because she reached up with her free hand and grabbed a hunk of hair at the back of his head, then yanked him down.

Wet, hot, slick, full of lightning and yearning, the kiss was the one thing, the only thing, that kept them tethered to the earth. As his lips danced with hers, J.J. dropped hold of her wrist and slid his arms up and around her body, lifting and pulling her into him so hard that he worried he might hurt her. That thought evaporated as Cheri's hands gripped the sides of his face, then raced down his throat, then kneaded his chest, all while her mouth moved on his with a ferocious hunger.

They moaned in unison and grabbed at each other

like they had to convince themselves the moment was real.

"Cheri, baby."

Suddenly, her legs were around his waist and her thighs gripped him tighter than a tick on a hound. He slapped his hands on her ass and squeezed, all while managing to turn them both and take a few steps toward the hallway, and the bedroom that lay beyond, just inside the gates of what he knew would be heaven.

Chapter 14

Wim pounded on the door long and loud enough that even a deaf old fart should be able to hear the racket. As he slipped the key in the lock, he hoped to God the drunken bastard hadn't kicked the bucket. Losing the blackmail payments—even as sporadic as they'd been of late—would put a dent in his cash flow, just when he was in danger of losing his shirt with the lake project.

"Lawson?" Wim shoved at the door only to have it catch on some kind of chain. "What the fuck? Purnell! Open the goddamned door!"

Nothing. As much as Wim hated to scuff his new Gucci tassel loafers, he wasn't left with much of a choice. He drew back his right foot and kicked the center bottom of the door.

It hurt like shit, but the chain broke away from the wood frame. He hobbled into the small foyer, shut the door behind him, and wandered into the barely lit living room. He gasped at what greeted him.

Dammit to hell! Purnell Lawson was dead, sprawled out on the chair with one arm flung out to the side and booze soaking into the carpet again. Wim figured he couldn't have been gone long since his skin still had a pinkish cast to it. As much as it pained him to have to deal with hip-hop Halliday, he pulled out his cell phone and began to dial the sheriff's office.

"Schnorrf!"

Wim nearly pissed himself. The sound Lawson just made must have been some kind of snort in his sleep. With a sigh, Wim slipped his phone back into his pants pocket and tapped his loafer against Lawon's pants leg. "Git up! I thought you were dead!"

Purnell smacked his lips and waved his hand around like he was chasing off a fly.

"Wake up!"

The old man's eyes flew open and he tried to right himself in the chair, an ordeal that was painful for Wim to watch. Lawson looked like an old walrus flailing on dry land.

"What the hell do you want? How did you get in here?"

Wim shrugged. "Kicked your door in, you old fucker. Now wake up. We need to talk."

Lawson groaned loudly and held his face in his hands. "Leave me alone," he mumbled.

"Not an option." Wim kicked the old guy in the shin.

"I should just blow your head off," he slurred.

"Here's the situation," Wim said, deciding to cut to it. He didn't want to stay in this rotten-smelling hole any longer than he absolutely had to. "Four preconstruction contracts fell through today. All after the *Bigler Bungle* started running pictures and sob stories about that little dead slut."

Purnell make a pathetic croaking sound, face still buried in his hands.

"And at nearly three hundred grand per, we're looking at a lot of fucking money! *My* money, Lawson! You're responsible! You got to do something!"

The old pecker shook his head but didn't raise his eyes. Wim had reached the end of his patience. "Fine," he said, pulling out his cell phone again. "Who gives a shit, right? I'll just call Sheriff Snoop Dogg and have him come pick up your sorry ass for murder. It's long past time somebody went to jail for killing her, right? Hey, maybe I'll get a reward."

That got his attention. But instead of looking fearful when he glanced up, Lawson seemed amused. "Even *you* wouldn't do something that stupid," he mumbled, shaking his head. "You're just as guilty as I am, son. If you turn me in, you expose your daddy for the devious, lying blob of spit he was—and yourself for being his idiot accomplice. Then guess what happens?"

Wim began trembling with anger. "What the fuck do you know about anything?"

Lawson laughed hard, his laughter changing to a hacking cough within seconds. "I know you ain't got the sense God gave a goat, boy, because as soon as you turn me in, your blackmail scheme gets exposed, and every piece of property and every building and every parking lot that dirty money has paid for over the last forty-odd years gets *taken away*. Is that simple enough for you? Now get your ass out of here or I'll shoot you where you stand."

Wim's eyes flew wide as Lawson reached down into the chair cushion and pulled out a handgun.

"Git," the old man said. "I'm just starting to understand how your daddy stole my life from me—it would only be fair if I took yours."

"Right," Wim said, managing a smile while checking that the gun's safety was still engaged. "Shoot me, you old motherfucker."

Lawson's hand shook violently. At this rate, Wim figured he'd be dropping the gun in about three seconds.

"The worst is your kids and grandkids, isn't it?" Wim continued. "Just imagine how they'll react to the news that sweet ole Pappy murdered an innocent girl. And what about Garland? Don't you think when this whole mess unravels it's gonna kill your best buddy to know how you've used him all this time? That you've lied and stolen from him half your lives?"

Click.

"Forget it," Wim said. "You're useless to me. To everyone." He turned around and headed for the door, fairly confident Lawson wouldn't pull the trigger. And even if he did, he'd be shaking too much to hit his mark.

Chapter 15

Cheri's whole being flooded with raw sexual sensation, painful need, crazy jumbled feelings of love and desire and regret and hope, all while she felt J.J.'s hands tighten their grip on her ass.

His lips were hot, slippery, first rough then achingly tender, then back again. His lips were everything. The feel of his rock-solid waist clasped between her thighs was heaven. The taste of him. The smell of him—it was all just right. And the heat shooting from his body—it had burned through the layers of caution, questions, and common sense. Somewhere in the back of her mind, Cheri told herself she wasn't being smart, that things weren't unfolding the way she'd planned—not with J.J., or Tanyalee, or Viv and Granddaddy. Not with the paper. Not with the lake house. Not with the way her heart was cracking open with the force of this place, this little town in the mountains, its memories and ghosts.

By the time Cheri felt her body being laid upon the bed, she told herself she was no victim. This wasn't all

J.J.'s doing. This was something she'd agreed to—no, *demanded*—the second she'd grabbed the man's hair and pulled his mouth down on hers.

She wouldn't lie—she wanted this. She'd always wanted this. She'd always wanted J.J.

She'd always belonged to him.

"Cheri," he mumbled as he dragged his lips up her cheek and over her ear, down her throat, and down into the valley between her breasts.

"Cheri," he said again, just before he clamped his teeth on the nipple threatening to poke through the worn fabric of her camisole.

"Cheri," he groaned, as his hands ran the length of her sides and over her hips and across her belly.

"Yes," she hissed. "Oh, God, *yesss*. Please!"

"You like that, don't you?" J.J. asked.

"Yes," she groaned. "I like everything."

She heard and felt J.J. chuckle. Soon he'd pulled himself up so that his face hovered over hers in the palest light. His fingertips pushed away a sliver of hair that had stuck to her damp cheek.

"You like it when I call you Cheri." J.J.'s lips curled up when he made that statement—it sure wasn't a question. "You like it because it reminds you of who you once were and who you are still—a sweet, fun, smart, beautiful, real young woman with a whole lifetime ahead of her."

Cheri took a gasp of air. She blinked. She stared at J.J.'s face. There was no teasing there, no snarkiness. It was not the face of a man who was toying with her.

It was the face of a man who wanted her to know she

was safe, that she could be herself in his company. That she was loved.

"You never answered my question, Jefferson Jackson," she whispered, feeling her chest and belly tremble with the significance of what she was about to ask. She could hardly believe she had the guts to utter the words— not once, but twice in one night. "So . . . is it true?" Cheri waited, the breath she needed to ask the full question suddenly not available to her. "Did you—"

"No," he said.

"No?"

"Absolutely not—I never stopped loving you. Ever." J.J. ran his fingertips over her bottom lip, then leaned in and nipped that puffy lip with his teeth. "And I never will. You can count on it."

It wasn't what she wanted—in fact, she'd fought all night to stop it from happening—but Cheri felt a tear run sideways down her face.

"Ah, baby. You're crying."

"What? I am not! I don't cry."

J.J. chuckled, leaving a sweet kiss on her lips, then several more along the path taken by her stray tear, from the corner of her eye to her hairline.

"Nothing wrong with a good cry now and again. Cleans away the cobwebs in the heart."

Cheri felt herself frowning. "You tellin' me I got cobwebs in my heart?"

J.J. offered her a crooked smile. "Hell, yeah, you do. We all do sometimes."

"And you're gonna help me do some spring cleaning?"

J.J. leaned his head back and laughed. "Absolutely. And when we're done with your heart we'll get to this place—we'll paint the walls and find you something to sit on and put your clothes in. It's not too late to plant some annuals if you want. And you've already got a whole mess of irises coming up in the back. Did you see them?"

That's when she just plain gave up. Cheri let the tears flow until she felt her back spasm and heard her own sobs. It was too much—that J.J. loved her was mind-blowing enough, but that he'd want her to be happy and help her paint and even noticed there were irises in the back? It was all too much.

His arms went around her and slipped under her back. She felt him roll so that she lay on top of him. Cheri buried her face in the crook of J.J.'s neck as he squeezed her tight.

He held her as she cried. Then cried some more.

"I said I'm not in the mood, babe."

Tanyalee chuckled, nibbling his neck again. "But I know how to get you there real quick-like."

Wim spun around in his home office chair. "Are you deaf? I said *not tonight.*"

"Well." Tanyalee straightened and put her hands on her hips. Truly, she could not remember the last time Wim had said no to sex, and she didn't much like it. Besides, saying no was *her* trump card. "Bad day at the office, honey?"

Wim released a half sigh, half laugh and shook his head. "Are you trying to be funny? Because I assure you, losing four contracts in one day is nothing to laugh at."

She threw up her hands, disgusted that she'd showered, shaved, and reapplied her eyeliner for *this* crap. "Excuse me for bothering you." She turned to go.

"Ah, shit, Tanyalee. Come back here."

"No, that's all right, honey," she said, producing a sad little pout, which she accented with a sexy arch of her back nicely framed by the doorway. "I know how important business is to you, Wim."

"Come back here."

She shook her head sadly. "Really, I understand. I'll just head on to bed."

"*Goddammit*, Tanyalee."

"Good night then, honey."

He was on her in a flash, pressing her against the doorjamb and nuzzling her neck like a piglet looking for a teat. Sometimes, she just had to laugh at the man. It had been disgustingly easy to train Wim Wimbley. He was as complex as a road sign. As unpredictable as sunrise. Once she finally agreed to go out with him—after damn near a decade of his begging and pleading—it required about two minutes of effort on her part to figure him out. It took two days for him to offer her a job, two weeks to pledge his unwavering devotion, and two months to propose with a two-carat marquise-cut diamond. Obviously, a man like that wouldn't be much of a challenge for a woman with her skills, but real property, interest-bearing investments, and cash on hand made up for a multitude of inadequacies.

"Oh, Wim," she breathed, rubbing her left thigh against his chief inadequacy.

"Don't be mad at me, baby," he said, sticking his tongue in her ear.

Oh, she fuckin' *hated* when he did that, but she was stuck with it now, because on their second date he'd stuck his tongue in her ear and got so excited he nearly unloaded his ammo right then and there. *"Do you like that, baby?"* he'd cooed. *"Oh, yes, Wim! Do it again!"* she'd cried. And so here she was, four months down the road, his tongue still wiggling in her ear like a slug on the sidewalk.

"Are you mad, baby?"

"Of course not, Wim."

"Good, because I have to get back to work."

"What?"

"Sorry." He kissed her cheek and patted her bottom before he headed back to his desk chair.

I can't believe it.

"I'm so pissed at that fuckin' DeCourcy that I wouldn't be any good for you tonight, anyway."

Don't laugh, don't laugh. Tanyalee bit down on her tongue in an attempt to prevent the slightest escape of sound. Had that fool just admitted he wouldn't be good in bed? And had he just mentioned himself, sex, and J.J. DeCourcy in the same sentence? God, but that was screamingly funny.

By the time Wim glanced over his shoulder to check her reaction, Tanyalee had assumed a position of sympathy—head tilted to the side, brow wrinkled, hands clasped demurely at her front. "What did J.J. do now, honey?"

"The same ole shit. The stories he's running on that dead bitch are getting picked up by big-city newspapers and TV stations. Right in my target markets! Atlanta! Raleigh-Durham! Charleston! Charlotte!"

"That jerk."

"I know! I'm spending a fortune marketing the fantasy of unspoiled Smoky Mountain retirement living to people sick of crime and rap music and urban decay and he's blabbering to the world about our dead bodies and ghosts and murder mysteries! He's hell-bent on ruining me!"

"He's a lying, cheating loser, honey. Just ignore him."

Wim swiveled around in his chair to face her again. "I damn sure wish you hadn't fucked it up with Garland the way you did. Maybe you'd be able to convince him to drop the subject, just stop covering the story altogether."

Tanyalee had never been so close to whopping Weenie Wimbley upside his hair-sprayed head. "Really?" she said, folding her arms over her chest. "So it's my fault that J.J. turned my own granddaddy against me? It's my fault Granddaddy won't listen to anything I tell him about J.J., and never will? It's my fault that J.J. has convinced Granddaddy that he's the Jesus of Journalism and not the cold-blooded bastard who ruined his favorite granddaughter's life?"

Wim blinked in surprise, then chuckled. "Tanyalee, darlin', you alienated your granddaddy all by yourself. He doesn't trust you because of the shoplifting, the check kiting, the computer hacking, and how you forged his signature on that credit application. He pressed charges against you for that, remember?"

Tanyalee felt the heat flare up from her chest and spread over her neck and face. *Oh, no, he did not just go there.*

"Besides," Wim said, letting his gaze roam up and

down her body, stopping momentarily on the sparkler that adorned her left hand. "You look pretty well-heeled for a 'ruined' girl."

Tanyalee's mouth fell open in shock. Wim had never spoken to her in this manner. In the past, he'd always taken her side when it came to the Newberrys. Or J.J. Or the incompetent Sheriff Halliday. And the fucked-up court system. And her idiot probation officer. And the whole Bigler rumor mill that had besmudged her good name. And now he was turning on her? Like everyone else?

"Oh." She made her voice as small and vulnerable as possible. "I see how it is. Good night, Wim."

By the time Tanyalee made it halfway down the hall, she realized Wim wasn't going to call after her or beg for the chance to smooth things over. As she proceeded down the central staircase, her eyes began to sting, probably from the blinding light splashing off the Swarovski crystal chandelier. Sometimes this new house seemed too bright, too clean, too perfect, too big. Sometimes she hated it. Like she hated Wim. And every fucking thing in her life.

Tanyalee grabbed her keys and purse from the foyer table. She got into her Mercedes coupe and started the engine.

Sometimes, the disgust and the rage got so hot inside her head that she felt like killing someone with her fists. Or running over somebody in the road. Or beating somebody's face against a big ole tree trunk.

Her head began to throb. Her eyeballs felt like hard rocks. She wondered if this is what it felt like to have a

stroke. Then about a mile down the road, it hit her—
and she began to laugh uncontrollably.

Everything had been going just dandy last week!
She was planning her wedding and honeymoon. She'd
convinced Wim that a prenup wasn't necessary. She'd
smoothed over the prickly spots with Viv and Garland
as best as she could. J.J. DeCourcy was nothing but a
distant—albeit hot—memory. But most importantly, last
week her damn sister was five hundred miles *g-o-n-e*.

Tanyalee took a right at Randall Road and headed
up the hill. She wasn't sure what she'd say to Cheri
when she got there. There were so many options, of
course. Tanyalee could remind Cheri that it was her
fault their parents died. She could mention that Viv always loved her more. She could point out that Cheri's
money didn't make her better than her sister, who, after
all, would soon be rich herself. And she could remind
Cheri which Newberry sister J.J. DeCourcy had married, and which sister had carried his child—if even
temporarily.

Tanyalee Marie Newberry, that's who.

Chapter 16

By the time Cheri finished crying, J.J.'s shirt was a wet mess stuck to his skin. This embarrassed her, apparently, and she started undoing the buttons and peeling the shirt from his body.

"Might want to get the jeans while you're at it."

Cheri giggled. "Nice try, but only your shirt's wet. Let me get you something dry to wear home."

"You kicking me out?"

Cheri sighed, pushing herself up and out of J.J.'s embrace. "Yeah. I guess. For tonight. I've got a lot to figure out, J.J. It's late and I'm whupped." He watched her bend down and begin rummaging through her suitcase. "Here you go."

J.J. caught the shirt in midair as he sat up on the bed. The instant he turned the shirt around he began laughing. "Seriously? You still have this?"

Cheri laughed. "Of course I do. A girl never forgets her first Dave Matthews concert."

"A night of many firsts, as I recall." *The first time*

she let me get my lips and tongue on her sweet pussy.
The first time she put her mouth on me.

J.J. removed his damp button-down shirt and pulled
the concert T-shirt over his head. He caught her gawking
while he did this and it made him smile. "You know, I
saw you checking me out today when I was working on
the dock."

She turned away, busying herself by shoving clothes
back into the suitcase and pretending she hadn't heard
him. She was probably blushing, too.

"You're not even going to bother denying it?"

Cheri shrugged. "No point. I was gawking. You caught
me. I want you. But let's continue this conversation tomorrow."

"Shee-it, you really are kicking me to the curb." J.J.
jumped from the bed and walked over to Cheri. When
he bumped up against her bent-over body, he heard her
moan.

He couldn't help himself. His arms went around her
waist and he pulled her upright, bringing her back
against his belly. J.J. lowered his lips to the side of her
cheek and squeezed her tight. He heard her breath
quicken.

"Just promise you won't wake up tomorrow with
amnesia and go back to hating the sight of me."

Cheri laughed. "Only if you promise not to follow me
around the newsroom tomorrow with 'CNN' scrawled
on your forearm. It wouldn't be professional."

"So you remember?" He *loved* that she did.

"Of course."

His hands began to slide up inside her sweater, around
her ribs, and up and over her breasts, each a perfect

handful. Immediately, her small nipples tightened and poked against his palms.

"J.J.—"

"Don't make me go, Cheri. Don't make me go another second without you."

She began to wiggle under his touch, and he couldn't tell what she was trying to do with the movement—get closer or get free—but he gave her the room to make her choice. It wasn't long before her head fell against his chest in surrender. That was his go-ahead, and he immediately tipped her face enough to latch his mouth over hers, her kiss desperate and hot, his hands moving rougher all over her body, feeling every contour and swell of her flesh.

That's when Cheri began pressing her ass against the front of his jeans. He released a moan of relief. To have her want him felt like a homecoming, a reward for all the years, all the loneliness. He turned her around the rest of the way, cradling her face in his hands and sealing her mouth with his once more. Cheri's lips were hot and damp and trembling and before he knew it, J.J. tasted her sweet, small tongue as it slid into his mouth.

His hands flew from her face to her sides, hips, ass, going from tender to demanding in mere seconds. He gripped the swells of her bottom and she lifted one leg around his hips so she could grind against him. That's when she lost her balance.

They crumpled back to the floor, J.J. hitting the hardwood first so he could cushion her collapse. She fell against him and it felt like her body shaped itself to fit his perfectly. Her legs parted and her breasts heaved against him and he had to get the clothes off her. He didn't want the layers. He was sick of the layers between them—of time, of distance, of twisted lies. He wanted to feel her naked and real and sliding all over his flesh. He wanted the feel of his Cheri on top of him once more.

He got his hands under her little shirt. Her skin was on fire. Cheri's fingers began to fumble with his belt buckle. They both panted.

That's when they heard it.

"Chit, chit, keek-keek-keek!"

"Oh, shit!" Cherise jumped up to a stand above him, her sweater half off and midriff exposed and her hair all messed up. God, she was gorgeous, even as she pointed at the squirrel in the doorway and screeched.

"Git! Git! Oh, you destructive little shit!"

J.J. propped himself on an elbow. "You talkin' to me or the squirrel?"

"The squirrel!" Cheri suddenly turned her head to look down on him. "You, too. I can't do this tonight, J.J. It's too soon. I can't sleep with my sister's ex-husband until I talk to her about it. Oh, God . . . what am I doing? I must be crazy. But yes, please go and take the squirrel with you, if you don't mind."

With a loud sigh, J.J. jumped to his feet and fastened his belt, all while trying to hide his laughter. He didn't succeed.

"What the hell y'all laughing at?" Cheri demanded, balling her fists on her hips. "Why is this damn squirrel after me? That's what I want to know. What did I ever do to him?"

J.J. peered at her through his messed-up hair. He

shook his head. "As I said before, I believe *she's* mad at you, and I mean really pissed."

"She?" Cheri's head swung wildly as she stared at the small rodent in the doorway. "How do you know it's a she?"

"I'm no wildlife expert, but I think this one is about to have babies."

"What?"

"See her belly all puffed out? My guess is she'd already picked the lake house as her nest when you showed up and ruined her plans."

"Seriously?"

J.J. watched Cheri crouch down very slowly for a close look at the critter. Her fingertips touched the floor for balance, and J.J. noticed how she was coiled to make a quick getaway, should the hideous beast decide to attack. But the squirrel looked just as fascinated with the woman, its whiskers twitching and its dark eyes focused like lasers.

"I see what you mean," Cheri whispered. "She looks like she's ready to pop."

Suddenly, the squirrel freaked out, skittered away, and let loose with a high-pitched screech. Cheri screamed in surprise and ran to J.J. for protection. They both watched in amazement as the squirrel shot through the living room and began barking like some kind of crazed little dog.

J.J. burst out laughing, but his amusement didn't last more than a moment, because a pair of headlights had just flashed in the front windows.

"Who the hell could *that* be?" Cheri asked, breaking away from J.J.'s embrace. He followed her down the hall. "I swear I get more unannounced visitors in the wilderness than I ever did in the city."

No, the bright red paint job wasn't visible in the dark, but J.J. could make out the sleek lines of the Mercedes coupe, and a heavy lump of dread fell to his gut. "Cheri, I hate to tell you this—"

"Oh, damn," she said.

Standing in the empty living room before the bare picture windows, J.J. figured the two of them were on display for Tanyalee's viewing pleasure. Thank God they were fully dressed.

He took a deep breath, steeling himself for what promised to be the nightmare of all nightmares, when suddenly, the car turned around and drove off.

Chapter 17

J.J. entered the editorial meeting with some kind of plastic zip bag in his hand and a scowl on his face. Cheri sat up straighter. Was that scowl for her? How did they get back to *that*? What happened to all the good stuff they'd shared the night before?

As she recalled, once Tanyalee finished her little drive-by, J.J. had agreed it wouldn't be wise for him to stay. So had he suddenly changed his mind? Why would he do that? Maybe she shouldn't trust him yet. Maybe she should keep her distance from J.J. a little longer, make him win her trust slowly. Something like that could take a while, of course. Days. Weeks. Months, even . . .

As J.J. plopped into a conference room chair, he gave her a quick wink and a sly, sexy smile.

Cheri had to look down at her legal pad to keep from blushing.

"Check this out, everybody," he said, throwing the plastic baggy to the center of the table. Everyone leaned in to get a look at the object of interest. Mimi Grayson snatched it, then held it up to the light.

She laughed. "Is this a joke?" She lowered the bag and peered over it at J.J. "We're being threatened? Why would anyone threaten the *Bugle*?"

"It's pretty self-explanatory," J.J. said.

"Maybe we got ourselves our very own Unabomber," the photo editor said.

Mimi read aloud. " 'Leave the past in the past, or some of you won't have a future. This is the only warning you will get.' " She tossed the plastic bag back to the table. "Sounds like something written by a fifth-grader—probably some kind of prank."

Jim Taggert pulled the plastic-covered sheet of notebook paper his way, shaking his head. "The handwriting's legible. Everything's spelled correctly, too, and that right there puts this little missive head and shoulders above our usual letters to the editor. I say we slap it on the front page."

"Gladys has already scanned it to graphics," J.J. said.

"How'd y'all find it?" the government reporter asked.

J.J. leaned back in his chair. "It was shoved under the Main Street entrance this morning. Turner's gonna swing by soon and collect it for evidence."

"Evidence of what?" Mimi asked with a dismissive snort. "You're really taking this seriously? You think this is connected to the Barbara Jean story?"

"Sure I do," J.J. said. "What else have we been covering that would prompt a threat like this? The spate of flattened tires at the Piggly Wiggly? The new metal detectors at the county courthouse?"

Cheri reached out for the baggy, then snapped her hand back, second-guessing herself. She'd sworn not to intrude on editorial decisions, hadn't she? She glanced J.J.'s way. "Do you mind if I take a look?" she asked.

"Of course not, Cheri," he said, grinning warmly. "Just don't take it out of the plastic, okay?"

She smiled back at him. "Of course not."

Cheri took a moment to read over the two sentences, and she knew immediately that it was no child's prank. The words felt menacing. The handwriting was strong. And angry. A shudder moved through her.

Cheri returned the bag to the tabletop and looked up—only to find Jim and Mimi and the rest of the assembled editorial staff staring at her in shock, eyes big and mouths open. Had she said something rude? Stupid? Ridiculous?

Had she said much of *anything*?

Uh-oh. They were probably shocked by her politeness and the downright gentlemanly way J.J. had spoken to her. Or maybe it was worse. Maybe they'd seen more than civility in their exchange.

J.J. cleared his throat, and everyone snapped to attention. "Jim, we've got room to run that playground feature Sunday. We can even make it a double-truck if you've got enough content."

"I thought you wanted to hold it another week," Taggert said, frowning.

J.J. shook his head. "Unfortunately, Gladys just gave me the ad count, and we've got plenty of room this week. In fact, we'll be going to press four pages lighter than last Sunday, even with the feature."

The room stayed silent. Everyone kept their eyes cast down. Even Cheri could translate that bit of newspaperese, and she knew J.J. had just informed them that the paper lost advertising during the last week, even when the Barbara Jean story had brought a significant spike to street sales.

No one said a word. She watched J.J.'s large hands grip the armrests of his chair so hard that the veins and tendons stood out on his wrists.

"J.J.?" Cheri heard herself ask. "Did the *Bugle* lose any active accounts last week, or was it an expected seasonal downturn, part of a cycle we've seen before?"

J.J. shook his head. "To the contrary—we normally get a big boost from lawn and garden retailers and landscapers around this time, but it didn't happen this year. It's been a growing problem during the recession— automotive, real estate, Christmas, want ads, back-to-school—the cyclical ad revenue we used to take for granted isn't there for us anymore."

Cheri looked around the conference table, knowing J.J.'s words weren't a revelation to these employees. They'd seen dozens of friends and colleagues lose their jobs while the size and scope of the newspaper delivered to people's doorsteps continued to shrink. J.J.'s comments just meant they were one step closer to being unemployed.

She hadn't planned to do it, but she felt herself stand. All eyes followed. She saw a variety of expressions on the faces—curiosity, surprise, and even contempt. She didn't blame them. After all, it wasn't even a week ago that these people showed up at work to see their publisher gone and taking his place was some chick from Tampa, a woman who didn't talk like them or dress like them, a woman who'd spent her time thus far debating paint colors, complaining about the design of her nameplate, and suggesting the newspaper get its sexy back.

"This is my issue to worry about, not yours," she said. "Your job is to put out the best daily newspaper possible for the citizens of Cataloochee County. The fact that we've done exactly that every damn day for nearly one hundred and fifty years should make you proud."

Mimi Grayson sat up straighter.

"The *Bugle* has survived world wars and the Great Depression and the digital revolution and it's going to survive this. Now, here's what I want us to do——" She looked at J.J. "How much has our single-copy sales gone up since the Barbara Jean Smoot story broke?"

J.J. thought for a moment. "A lot. We're up twenty-five percent in nonsubscription sales."

"Okay, then," Cheri said, looking around the room. "Then this is the time we need to beef up the page count of the *Bugle*, not gut it. We need to grab these new readers and give them a reason to subscribe. Show them what they've been missing."

"Uh . . ." Jim Taggert's eyes swiveled from face to face at the table. "What if all we end up doing is losing more money? The price of newsprint alone will make that a losing proposition."

Out of the corner of her eye, Cheri saw J.J. shove his chair away from the table. She wouldn't look at him. If he was scowling at her, she didn't want to know. In fact, it didn't matter if he was displeased. This was her job.

This paper was her family's legacy and it was now her responsibility. She had a right to say whatever needed to be said. In fact, she had a duty to say it.

"Look, I know y'all don't know me from Adam's off ox, but Grandaddy hiring me wasn't some kind of joke or act of desperation. I agreed to take on this job and I mean to do my best by every one of y'all. I'm not giving up on this paper and I don't want you to, either. And Jim . . ." She looked at the city editor and smiled. "We're already losing money. And we are guaranteed to keep doing so unless we take a different approach."

Glances were exchanged. Mimi chuckled. Jim Taggert looked uncomfortable.

"As publisher, I'll take any heat that's due me," she continued. "But if you want me onboard when the plane crashes, I damn well better be on it when it takes off."

J.J. rose from his chair and Cheri was sure he was about to tell her to shut the hell up—but she refused to look at him. She kept talking.

"Now, my top priority is untangling the financial mess we're in. However, I want y'all to know that my door is open. If you have any concerns, any questions, any suggestions you think I should hear—about any aspect of the newspaper—I will listen. And . . ." Cheri felt J.J. arrive at her side. He didn't touch her, but she felt the heat of his body, the solid presence of him. Suddenly, it dawned on her that he wasn't trying to shut her up. He was offering his support. She risked a quick glance at him and saw the warm smile in his eyes. Cheri took a deep breath.

"I give you my word—no one will lose their job in

the next month. I don't care how bad things get. Nobody currently employed at the *Bugle*—in delivery and circulation, or the pressroom, or the newsroom—not one person will lose their job this month. That is my promise."

The room was silent. Cheri gathered up her legal pad and pen and thanked everyone for their time. She felt their eyes burning a hole in her back as she exited the conference room.

She found Gladys at her desk. This morning's wardrobe selection consisted of a red nylon-spandex wrap dress, red espadrilles, and red and black earrings in a skull-and-crossbones motif.

"Morning, Gladys."

"Morning yourself," she said with a wide, smeared-lipstick smile. "Getting settled in?"

"Slowly," Cheri said.

"Hmph! I hear you've got round-the-clock help out there at the lake house, if you know what I mean!"

Cheri didn't have the time to deal with the comment. "Gladys," she said evenly, "I want you to e-mail me with the contact information for all the lawn and garden and landscaping advertising accounts we've had in the last ten years. Where is Purnell this morning?"

Gladys narrowed her eyes at Cheri. "He called in sick."

"What's wrong with him?"

Gladys shrugged. "His heart condition, most likely, though he didn't rightly say."

Cheri nodded. "Does he still live on Warmsprings Road?"

Gladys tipped her head. "Yes, but . . ."

"Thanks," Cheri said with a polite smile. "Ten minutes, please."

Cheri was mad as hell by the time she arrived at Purnell Lawson's shabby single-story ranch house. She regretted that she hadn't eaten anything since lunch the day before, because she couldn't tell whether her current light-headedness was from going twenty-four hours without food or from being as hacked off as she'd ever been in her fucking *life*!

She'd visited every one of those lawn and garden and landscaping accounts. Half the landscaping services were no longer in business, but the others bought ads on the spot. "Where you been?" one landscaper asked. "I expected you around here a month ago!"

Of the fourteen brick-and-mortar retail establishments that had done business with the *Bugle,* five had gone out of business. Three said they'd agreed to advertise and never received contracts or a follow-up call. Two others said they'd been hounding Purnell to run their ads, to no avail. The remaining four said they'd simply given up on the *Bugle* because of a combination of declining circulation, high rates, unimaginative ad design, and piss-poor customer service.

And every business lost to the newspaper had moved their advertising dollars to the Internet, the Yellow Pages, radio, and the Waynesville and Ashville papers.

When she found Purnell, Cheri swore she might strangle the old fool with her bare hands.

She pounded on the door. Nothing. She pounded some more.

"Purnell!" Cheri shouted against the door. No answer. Sighing in frustration, she hopped down into the tangle of weeds below the front windows and stood on her tiptoes to peek inside. There he was, slumped down in a rocking chair.

"Purnell! Are you okay?" she called out, banging on the window. He didn't respond.

Cheri raced back to the door and tried the knob. The door flew open, and it was then that she noticed a chain had been torn from the frame. Had someone broken in to his house and attacked him? As she ran toward Purnell's limp form, she pulled her BlackBerry from her bag and dialed 911.

"Cheri."

She jumped in surprise, then stared blankly, as if she couldn't make sense of the sight of J.J. standing in the doorway.

"Didn't mean to startle you," he said.

"You didn't. I just . . . I was lost in thought. How's Purnell?"

J.J. entered the publisher's office and took a seat across from Cheri's desk. The painters had finished, and he had to admit the pale gray-blue color looked nice against the sturdy white of the woodwork, though the space now looked devoid of personality. Garland had labored in this room amid an avalanche of photos, personal mementos, and just plain junk from his half-century tenure. Now, with Cheri, the slate had been wiped clean. He wondered what she'd do with it.

Which reminded him . . .

"That was a great speech this morning, Madam

Publisher," he said.

She shot him a scowl. Did she suspect he was messin' with her? *Still?* It wasn't so far-fetched a worry—she'd only been in Bigler a week. It was going to take some time, he knew.

"I only speak the truth, Cheri," he said. "You inspired the troops, and then you went right out and pounded the pavement for ads—you walked the walk. It's all anyone's been talking about around here today."

In addition to the scowl, she now lowered her chin and drummed her fingers on the desk. It was all J.J. could do not to laugh.

"What are you implying?" she asked.

"I'm not *implying* a damn thing. I'm telling you—you're gonna make one hell of a publisher. It's in your genes."

Cheri's eyes briefly flashed toward her computer screen.

"Is this a bad time?"

She sighed, a few shiny, dark red strands of hair clinging to her cheek when she shook her head. "Just tired." She gave him a brave smile. "So, what about Purnell? What do the doctors say?"

"He's stable, but still refusing any kind of treatment other than medicine for the pain. The doctors say it's a combination of liver disease and congestive heart failure. Garland's sitting with him, but it looks like the guy has just given up—he made the doctors draw up a do-not-resuscitate order."

Cheri rubbed her forehead and sighed. "What about his family? Doesn't he have some kids and grandkids living close by?"

J.J. raised an eyebrow and shrugged. "All of them live around here, but nobody seems to be in a hurry to get to his bedside."

"How sad," Cheri said, stretching her arms over her head. This gave J.J. a nice view of her breasts moving beneath an otherwise perfectly businesslike blouse. Then again, the girl could make a burlap sack sexy—always could. "It's a shame how families can fall apart like that," she said with a yawn.

He opened his mouth to reply, but thought better of it. The hesitation wasn't lost on Cheri.

She smiled at him. "Go ahead, Jefferson Jackson. Make your pithy observation."

"About what?"

Cheri laughed, then groaned in frustration. "I'm a big ole hypocrite—that's what you were going to tell me, right? That I got a lot of nerve commenting on other people's screwed-up families when mine should have its own exhibit in the Dysfunctional Family Museum?"

"Not my place," J.J. said, smiling, tapping his fingers on the armrest.

"Ha," she said. "And no, I haven't talked to Tanyalee yet and I haven't spoken to Aunt Viv since I ran from her house and now I've got a headache bigger than all hell."

"You eat yet?"

"Just a handful of nuts and a carrot stick I stole from Gladys." J.J. watched Cheri close her eyes tight for an instant, then glance at the computer screen again. With a definitive smack of her fingers on the keyboard, she closed the spreadsheet she'd been viewing. "I'm about ready to keel over from hunger, actually."

"Can't have that." J.J. stood up and offered his hand to her. "How does Lenny's sound?"

Cheri grabbed her bag off the back of her chair, laughing. "My God! That place hasn't been closed down by the health department? Do they still make those grilled pimento cheese and Wonder Bread sandwiches?"

"Of course. And they still come with a side of barbecue slaw."

"Damn!"

Grinning, J.J. placed his hand at the base of Cheri's spine and waited for her to pass in front of him into the newsroom. He leaned down to whisper in her ear. "And they're still whipping up their world-famous fried pies and their—"

Cheri spun around, threw her arms around his neck, and kissed him deeply. J.J.'s eyes widened in surprise, and though his first impulse was to grab the globes of her ass and throw her down and devour her, he decided he'd be smart to make sure the night copy editors weren't getting a show.

As soundlessly as he could, J.J. pulled Cheri back into her office and shut the door with his foot. He started chuckling beneath her kisses. "If I knew pimento cheese would send you over the edge like this, I'd have mentioned it earlier."

Cheri laughed, too, leaving sweet little kisses all over his cheeks, chin, and forehead. Eventually, she peeled herself off his neck. "Sorry—I've been dying to do that all damn day."

J.J. rested his ass on the edge of Cheri's desk and pulled her between his legs. "Oh, yeah?"

"Yeah."

She tipped her head and smiled shyly, her gaze wandering over his face. Eventually, she raised her hand to bury her fingers in his hair, and J.J. held his breath, as if he were afraid the slightest movement would chase her away. It was nothing less than a miracle, this loving touch of hers. It felt like he'd been waiting for it forever, as long as he'd been waiting for her to tell him she still loved him . . . or loved him at all.

J.J. watched in fascinataion as Cheri's thoughts wandered and her golden eyes darkened.

"Tell me, darlin'," he said.

Her gaze locked with his and he swore he saw fear there. "Please don't say anything to Granddaddy, not yet, but . . ."

J.J. straightened. Whatever Cheri was about to tell him had nothing to do with love or even grilled cheese.

"I think I need to show the *Bugle* books to Turner."

J.J. abruptly stood up, which caused Cheri to stumble backward. He grabbed her hips. "It's that bad?"

She nodded her head and bit her bottom lip. "I'm seeing a pattern. Year after year, the expense vouchers Purnell's been signing off on don't make sense. I swear there's a shitload of money missing, and the pattern stretches back at least five years, probably longer."

J.J. pulled his head back in surprise. "Someone's skimming off the top? Are you sure?"

"No," Cheri said as she pulled away and began to pace, her arms crossing over her chest. "That's the thing—it's been done ingeniously, year after year. Nothing's obvious. It could be possible to miss during an audit."

"I don't follow," J.J. said.

"Okay." Cheri nodded. "Let's say I'm standing in a room and I don't see anyone come in behind me, but I can see their shadow on the wall and I can smell their cologne, so I know they're there. It can be the same way with numbers." She turned to him, her brow creased in concentration. "Does that make any sense?"

"I guess," J.J. said.

"Here's the thing," she continued. "On multiple occasions, expenditures can't be verified. There were huge payouts for a color capacity printer tower that was never delivered. Consultants I can't track down. Increases in our newsprint costs that are way out of line when compared to other newspapers in the region."

"So what do we need before we can go to the authorities? What can I do to help?"

Cheri laughed, letting her arms swing down at her sides. "Nothing. I just have to keep plugging away, and ideally, I should be looking at records going back another twenty years or so, but I don't want Purnell to know what I'm up to."

J.J. pushed up from the edge of the desk and went to her. "How much money are we talking?"

"Depending on how long it goes back, maybe a million or more."

J.J.'s stomach clenched. "Shee-it."

"Yeah."

"But if Purnell's been stealing boatloads of money from the paper, what's he done with it? The guy lives like a pauper, and nobody in his family's doing so hot, either."

Cheri looked up at him, the corners of her mouth

pulled tight. "I know. His house is a pigsty. But let me put it this way—*somebody's* up to something, and maybe it would be best if *nobody* knew I want every record I can get my hands on—not Purnell, not Gladys, not even Granddaddy. So, yes, there is something you can do for me. You can get me the old records."

J.J. felt his eyes go big. "I'll go to the warehouse and see what I can find. But you can't possibly believe—"

"I don't know what to believe," she said, cutting him off. "But those are the only three people involved in accounting and bookkeeping around here since, well, *forever.*"

J.J. tipped his head. "Except your daddy, right? He was publisher for six months back in the mid-eighties, before he . . ."

Stupid. Stupid. Stupid. J.J. knew better than to bring up Loyal and Melanie Newberry, even in passing. Back when they were kids, the subject would turn Cheri to cold, hard rock in a flash—and understandably so. Her parents were young and healthy when they were found asphyxiated in an Outer Banks beach house on their second honeymoon, a faulty gas stove eventually to blame.

And now, as Cheri's spine went rigid and her face lost all expression, J.J. knew nothing had changed for her.

"Yes, my father was publisher from February to September 1987." With that, Cheri retrieved her bag from the floor—where she'd tossed it during the throes of kissing him, an event that now felt like a lifetime ago.

"Cheri—"

"It's okay, J.J.," she said, shaking her head sadly. "It's an important point, actually. When I get the old records I'll focus on that stretch. Maybe I'll see a change in the way business was done or some indication my father knew there was a problem. Thanks for pointing that out."

She turned away and headed for the door.

"So, no grilled cheese?"

Cheri looked over her shoulder. "I'm suddenly too wiped out to eat. See you tomorrow?"

"Tomorrow's Saturday," he said. "Publishers get the weekends off around here."

She offered him a tired smile. "Not this one—not until I sort out this mess."

Chapter 18

"Yoo-hoo!"

Cheri sat up in bed, noting right away how the painfully bright light streamed through the window and how her stomach had clenched in on itself with hunger. And what about that bizarre dream she'd been having? She could swear she heard someone calling out to her clear as could be. The smell of blueberry muffins still wafted through her nostrils.

"Cheri! It's Granddaddy and Aunt Viv! We brought you some breakfast!"

She swung her feet over the edge of the bed and clutched at her aching head. She heard the deep rumble of her grandfather's laughter coming from the living room.

"Plus dinner and supper and snacks and more damn furniture than this place can hold," he said.

"Oh, *hell*, no," Cheri mumbled to herself, wondering what ungodly time of day it was and how Viv could possibly think she was welcome out here after that debacle at the supper table. Forget the books—her priority for the weekend should be buying a big-assed lock for the front door.

She scrambled to find a pair of jeans and a T-shirt, deciding to skip the bra. Who cared?

"Tater Wayne and some helpers are here, too!" Viv announced.

Cheri grabbed a bra. "Coming!"

After a quick pit stop in the bathroom, she stumbled down the hall and into the living room. Cheri shielded her eyes from the light pouring through the front door, and the first thing her vision focused on was a refrigerator sitting in the middle of the living room floor.

"What the—"

"Now come on in here and have a seat," Viv said from the kitchen.

"Mornin,'" Granddaddy said, holding out a Styrofoam cup of what Cheri prayed was real, steaming hot coffee.

She shuffled over to the old oak table and took the cup from Granddaddy. "Thank you so much," she said, pulling back the plastic lip of the lid and taking a sip. Suddenly, a knife and fork, salt and papper, and a paper plate were set down before her. On the plate was a hard-boiled egg, a blueberry muffin, and a banana.

"Nothing fancy, but at least it'll get you going today," Viv said, leaning down and leaving a kiss on the top of Cheri's head.

"Thank you, really, both of you," she said just before she bit into the still-warm baked confection. She moaned in pleasure as the sugary delicacy hit her taste buds. How could she stay mad at Viv when she made these awesome muffins for her? *With* the crumbly tops?

"Oh, I nearly forgot. Here's y'all's pat of butter."
And butter!

"Thank you so much, Aunt Viv," Cheri said. "This is delicious!"

"Well, now, once Tater gets the fridge hooked up, you'll be set for a while." Viv began unpacking covered dishes from a half-dozen brown paper sacks lined up on the drainboard. "I fixed y'all a little bit of everything— a chicken and rice casserole, baked spaghetti, some beef noodles with gravy, and a meat loaf. Oh, and my sweet potato casserole."

Granddaddy rolled his eyes and whispered, "Just in case the Union Army marches through."

Cheri laughed as she crammed another bite of the muffin in her mouth.

"Where y'all want this?" Tater Wayne stood in the doorway holding a chest of drawers.

"Put that one in the back room," Viv ordered. "The bigger one goes in the front bedroom for Cheri. She needs a lot of storage for her delicates."

"You got it," Tater said. "Oh, Cheri, we nearly ran over that damn squirrel just now, standing there hollerin' like it was guarding the driveway or sumthin'."

Cheri spun around in her chair. "Did you hit her?"

"Naw, but I can put a twenty-two-caliber greeting card right between its eyes if you like."

"No!" Cheri was horrified, but realized everyone was looking at her funny. "I don't mind the squirrel much. Thanks, though." She hid her face in her coffee cup.

"Suit yerself," Tater said, carrying the bureau down the hall. Cheri took a moment to assess the growing assortment of household items piling up in the living room. There were several cans of interior semigloss paint, a few secondhand tables, lamps, and a space-age lime green sofa that was so out-of-date it would be considered retro chic in Tampa.

Viv sighed loudly. "I told Garland that couch was enough to make a person queasy but he said you'd like it."

Granddaddy winked at Cheri.

"Everything's lovely," she said. "I truly do appreciate you taking care of me like this."

"Least we could do," Viv said. "We couldn't just let you stay out here without a pot to piss in or a light to aim by."

Granddaddy sighed loudly and began to turn around in his chair but Viv smacked his shoulder. "Oh, hold your peace, Garland. I promised I wouldn't say a thing about Cheri up and moving out like she did, so I won't, and I won't mention the party, either."

Cheri blinked. "What party?"

Granddaddy's face had gone scarlet. "Vivienne, I have half a mind to—"

"Garland's turning eighty in two weeks, and we thought maybe—"

Granddaddy smacked his palm on the old oak table.

Viv waved her hand at him and pressed on. "We thought we'd combine the two monumental occasions into one big *shindig*!"

Cheri felt the half-eaten muffin fall from her grasp to the paper plate. Try as she might, she couldn't prevent the visual from setting up shop in her brain again— Aunt Viv, in her polka-dot bikini, rubbing up against her jazz musician boyfriend, while firing up a Jamaican-sized spliff.

If that wasn't horrifying enough, she was beginning to suspect one of those "monumental occasions" had something to do with her.

"It was just an idea," Granddaddy said, rolling his eyes. "We thought we could jointly celebrate my birthday and you taking over the helm at the *Bugle*."

Cheri swallowed a crumb that had become stuck in her increasingly dry throat.

"And," Viv said, her face lit with excitement, "since the lake house is getting all spruced up, we were thinking we could have the party out here. The water will be warm enough for swimming. Tater Wayne can bring his mobile barbecue pit, the one shaped like a hog. And we can . . ."

Cheri spaced out for a moment, letting the bizarre scene unfold without her. This visit was invasion of privacy jumbled up with too much food, overbearing love, passive-aggressive good intentions, and genuine desire to smooth over old hurts. It was all very Newberry.

Suddenly, Cheri's eyes shot to the blue and white checks over the kitchen sink, and the only thing that made any sense—the only right thing to do—was to hug Aunt Viv.

She rose from her chair, went toward Viv, and pulled her aunt's short, stocky body close to her, which stopped the party planning in mid-sentence. Cheri inhaled the familiar Jean Naté-and-vodka elixir and looked again at the curtains. A worker had tried to take them down and toss them yesterday, but she'd stopped him, and Cheri had washed them out by hand and hung them to dry. Now, as they rippled in the breeze, her eyes began to tear up.

Cheri realized that for whatever reason, she'd woken up without her usual defenses that morning, and it felt like something had softened inside her, like some kind of internal fist had relaxed and opened. She held Viv tighter and let the tears flow and the memories rush through her—raw, alive, and bittersweet . . .

The brush of her mother's lips on her forehead. Her father's voice—a mix of molasses and mischief—as he read to her before bed. The taste of corn on the cob and rhubarb pie at a summer supper. The cries of the loons and the songs of crickets.

And suddenly she knew that her beginnings hadn't just disappeared from the face of the earth, as hard as she'd tried to convince herself otherwise. The truth was a lot of it remained in the people and places she came from. This old cottage, surely. The elderly great-aunt and a grandfather, still right here in her kitchen, loving her the best they knew how. A sweet boy who'd become a man who *fit* her. The *Bigler Bugle*. A best friend who supported her no matter what.

And a sister, so close, and yet lost to her.

"Now, if that don't beat all?" Viv mumbled into Cheri's chest. "Why are you cryin', sugar?"

Cheri couldn't speak.

"Garland? Why's she crying?"

"I was near tears myself listening to you carry on about barbecues and potato salad and whatnot."

Cheri laughed. "No, that's not it. The party is a fine idea. Really." She released her grip on Viv but kept an arm loosely wrapped around her. "I'm crying because y'all brought me muffins this morning. And while I'm at it, I want to say thank you, both of you, for taking such good care of me and Tanyalee when Mama and Daddy died. It couldn't have been easy—I know I wasn't a pleasant child. I hope it's not too late to tell you how much I appreciate what you did."

Cheri smiled down at Aunt Viv's stunned expression.

Garland laughed. "I do believe that's the first time I ever saw Vivienne Newberry at a loss for words."

Viv began to cry, too. She smacked Cheri on the arm. "Now look what you've gone and done." She wiggled free and sniffled as she went back to to her unloading. "I better get these in the freezer before they start to thaw."

Granddaddy chuckled. "The fridge is unplugged in the middle of the livin' room, Vivienne, and its interior is about as frozen over as a bonfire in August."

Cheri began to snicker. Then Aunt Viv's shoulders jiggled, and Granddaddy's booming laughter nearly shook the walls.

In the rich harmony of all that laughter, Cheri couldn't help sense the one missing note—even if it had always been a little off-key.

Tanyalee.

She pressed against the old brass handle and the door to Wimbley Real Esatate opened with a tinkling bell.

The reception area was unusually metropolitan for Bigler, with its dove-gray leather and chrome furnishings, modern art, and animal-print accessories. Even if

Tanyalee herself hadn't been seated at the reception desk—a point of golden light against a muted palette—the space would have had her name all over it.

Tanyalee hid her surprise with a stiff smile. "Come to see one of the lofts?"

"No, actually. I came to see you. Do you have time to talk, maybe go for a walk or something?"

Tanyalee laughed. "Us regular Joes punch a clock. I just got here, and Saturday morning is our busiest time of the week, so I certainly can't just up and leave to take a *stroll*."

"Okay, then." Cheri stepped inside and took a seat on one of the couches. She hardly wanted to hover over Tanyalee's desk—this conversation would be confrontational enough on even footing. "Then we can talk here."

"About what?"

Cheri took a deep breath. "About you and me. About our family—Viv and Garland and Mama and Daddy. About your marriage to J.J."

"Oh, Lord-*ee*, Cheri! You truly are a piece of work, aren't you?" When Tanyalee tipped her head back and laughed, Cheri couldn't help but notice the resemblance between her sister and their late mother. Now that Tanyalee was just a few years younger than Mama at the time of her death, the resemblance was impossible to ignore. Her sister had every bit of Mama's delicate beauty, but not a lick of her gentle nature.

"I just want to talk, Tanyalee."

"No. No you don't." She spun around in her desk chair to face Cheri full-on. "What y'all want is to march into Bigler and get all Dr. Phil on my ass, and I'll tell you right now, I'm not having it." Tanyalee crossed her arms over her chest and lowered her chin, suddenly resembling the petulant five-year-old Cheri had had so much trouble getting along with. All shades of Melanie Newberry had disappeared.

"I had nothing to do with your divorce or miscarriage, Tanyalee."

She blinked her pretty blue eyes. "*Really*, now."

"Really," Cheri said, tossing her purse to the couch. "As you know, I never called J.J. while you were married. There was no secret plot to betray you. Nothing to cause you to miscarry. So tell me what happened to the baby, and why you lied to me about J.J.'s part in the divorce."

Her sister's mouth unhinged, her eyes bugged out, and she slammed her fist on the desktop. "Who the *hell* do you think you are, Cheri? Y'all got a truckload of nerve coming in here and making crazy accusations about something you know nothing about! My God! I don't know if you noticed, but we've all survived just fine here without you and your college degrees and your money and your big house and your high-and-mighty wisdom!"

Cheri kept her voice soft and her anger under wraps. "I'm here to ask you—my only sister—to have an honest conversation with me. Good God in heaven, Tanyalee, we are grown women! We aren't fighting over an Island Fun Barbie here—this is real life, and we need to sort some shit out between us! We should have done it a long, long time ago." Cheri took a deep breath. "Now, why did you tell me I caused you to miscarry? Why did you tell me it was my fault that your marriage didn't work?"

Tanyalee sat frozen for a moment. Cheri watched the tendons in her slender neck tighten.

"You've been talking to J.J." Tanyalee's mouth had gone hard and her eyes blank. "You've already slept with him. I'm sure he's told you things that make me sound like some kind of bitch. Well, it's all lies."

Cheri shook her head. "I did not sleep with him. I was tempted, but I knew it wouldn't be right until I'd cleared the air with you."

One corner of Tanyalee's mouth curled up. "But I *saw* you."

"Yeah, I know you saw us—because you drove out to the lake without an invitation. J.J. was just leaving."

She snorted. "Oh, now I need an invitation? To my own family's land? The lake house is Newberry property, you stuck-up little bitch! And I may not be Queen of the May slash publisher of the *Bigtime Bungle,* but the last time I looked, I was still a fuckin' *Newberry.*"

"After your last felony conviction, Granddaddy put the lake house in my name only."

"Who the fuck cares? Once I'm married to Wim, I'll be richer than even *you.*"

Cheri swallowed hard. Tanyalee had mentioned it twice now. Apparently she was as blissfully ignorant of her financial situation as anyone in Bigler. "I'm happy for you," Cheri told her.

Tanyalee leaned forward on the desk and snarled. "What did J.J. tell you?"

"Not much. He said whatever happened in your marriage was private, and if I had questions, I'd need to ask you."

Tanyalee sniggered. "That sounds like him. He's such a pompous, holier-than-thou dick-face. Oh, but just you wait, dear sister—the day's gonna come when Mr. Perfect's gonna show his stripes to you, and God have mercy on you when he does."

"What happened to the baby?"

"I lost the damn baby."

"How?"

"The usual way—I had a damn miscarriage."

"Why did J.J. leave you?"

"Because he's a phony and a liar, and when there was no baby, he figured there was no reason to be married to my ass."

"No other reason?"

She laughed bitterly. "That's not enough for you?"

Cheri stood up. "Did you get pregnant on purpose to trap J.J.?"

Tanyalee stood up, too. Both her fists were clenched against the front of her nubby knit skirt. Cheri watched the silver necklace tremble against her silk blouse.

"I hate you," Tanyalee whispered. "I've always hated you."

"I know you have. Why is that?"

"Because you've always thought you were so much better than me—smarter, classier, richer, prettier—and because you were so damn *mean* to me when we were kids! You were so nasty that Mama and Daddy had to leave town to get away from you! And they *died* doing it! They died trying to get away from you, Cheri! That's why I hate your skinny little stuck-up princess *ass*."

Those words felt like a knife being forced down her throat and into her chest. But Cheri had asked for the truth, and she'd gotten what she'd asked for, what she'd long suspected. And it all made perfect sense.

"So you trapped J.J. into marrying you to get back at me, is that it? You saw it as the ultimate revenge?" Cheri glared at her. "Answer me one thing—did you know J.J. went to Florida to tell me he'd always loved me?"

One corner of Tanyalee's mouth curled up. "Sure I did."

"And you chose that time to tell him about the baby?"

"Of course."

"Thank you. I get it now." Cheri sucked in a deep breath. "You trapped J.J. You set up that phone call for maximum damage to me. Then you made sure I saw J.J. as an asshole of the first order so that I'd never speak to him again as long as I lived. All that, *plus* you were making sure Viv and Garland thought I was an ungrateful, stuck-up bitch. My, what a busy girl you've been, Tanyalee Marie!"

"I wish you were dead," she whispered. "I wish—" The door to the back office opened and Wim stuck his perfectly coiffed male head into the reception area. "Ah! I thought I heard sisterly voices!"

"Hey, Wim," Cheri said.

"Hey yourself, Cheri. Come to see one of the lofts? I can probably do a month-to-month for you."

"Uh, no, thanks. Not today." Cheri shot a look at her sister—red-faced, shaking, eyes alive with hate.

"She was just leaving," Tanyalee said, turning to Wim with a smile and a flip of her eyelashes.

"Just one more thing, if you don't mind." Cheri reached for her bag and flung it on to her shoulder. "I'm hosting a party for Granddaddy's eightieth birthday in a couple weeks at the lake house. Viv will be sending y'all an invitation."

"How perfectly lovely," Tanyalee said, her words sticky-sweet and her eyes dagger-sharp. "Thanks so much for stopping by. Y'all have a good day."

Chapter 19

"Brought you some flowers."

Purnell watched Wim set the cheap arrangement on the hospital room windowsill. Pathetically enough, it was one of only three he'd received in the days he'd been hooked up to a tangle of tubes and wires and informed that he was not long for this world.

The most extravagant flower arrangement was from Garland and the staff of the *Bugle*.

The scrawniest was some kind of fern sent by his three kids, ten grandchildren, and twenty-two great-grandchildren. Being that he had little else to occupy his thoughts, Purnell had figured out that the arrangement likely cost each descendant a whopping eleven cents. No wonder no one had come to visit him—who could scrounge up gas money after that kind of large-scale family sacrifice?

"What the fuck do you want?" Purnell snapped.

Wimbley broke out in a fake smile. "Can't an old friend pay his respects? Out of the goodness of his heart?"

Purnell groaned. He didn't have the energy to point out that Wim didn't qualify on either count.

"Honestly, I came to do a little brainstorming with you. You're going to help me formulate a plan."

Purnell had no time for this dipshit. "Your threats mean nothing to me, son. I'm going to be dead soon, so go ahead, knock yourself out—tell the world I killed Barbara Jean Smoot. You can even make up some details if you want, seeing as I can't remember half of what happened that night."

Wim shoved his hands in his pockets and rocked back on his shiny shoes. "I didn't come here to threaten you, Lawson, I came to offer you redemption for your sins. Isn't that what the dying want?"

"Get out of my hospital room, you prick."

Wimbley laughed. "Okay, so here's the deal. I sent a threatening letter to the *Bugle* that they'll never trace back to me, because I'm brilliant. And now you're gonna help me come up with something to blackmail Garland Newberry with—something that will stop him from snooping around out at Paw Paw Lake."

Purnell shook his head in disgust—Winston's boy might be handsome, but he was stupid enough to try to alphabetize a bag of M&M's. "Again with blackmail, young Wim? Not looking to branch out? Have you considered counterfeiting? Forgery? Your lovely fiancée could help you with that."

"Funny. You got any better ideas?"

He turned his face away and stared out the window. The first thing that caught his eye was the red brick of the *Bugle* building in relief against the green-blue hills of his little mountain town. He didn't know what to expect in death, but surely hell wouldn't include a view of the Smokies. That would be reserved for the decent folk who made it to heaven, the ones who didn't have so much blood on their hands.

He shuddered. The truth was his most hideous offense was a bloodless crime, perfectly clean, premeditated in the most literal sense. Poor Loyal and Melanie, drawing their dying breaths as Purnell drove through the night, all the way from the seashore to his home in the blue mountains. That car ride seemed to last an eternity, nothing but his self-loathing to keep him company as the hours stretched on.

Just like it had been with Barbara Jean, he'd made it home before dawn to shower out the smell of his crime from his skin and hair. With Barbara Jean, of course, it had been the smell of pussy and blood. With Loyal and Melanie, it had been the smell of gas.

He was squeaky clean when he stood in the middle of the newsroom later that day, his sobbing coworkers gathered near to hear the tragic news—their new publisher and his wife were dead. And Purnell was steady as a rock in Vivienne's parlor later that evening, helping Garland, Viv, and the Newberry girls deal with their shock and grief.

Clean. Steady.

Viciously heartless.

And just like that, it happened again, the way it had been happening since the day Barbara Jean's body had been pulled from the mud. Images flashed through his brain like lightning strikes, bright, shocking, then gone. He didn't know what the hell they were. Memories? Imagination? Fear? His brain going haywire from the liver disease?

But these—the ones he just now experienced—these were new.

Winston Wimbley yanking Purnell's shirt collar and dragging him from Barbara Jean's car.

Wimbley's police baton connecting with Purnell's cheek.

Blood flying past a shiny sheriff's badge before it splattered on the dark road under Purnell's feet.

He thought he might vomit.

"Well?" The young Wimbley sounded impatient. "Tick, tick, old man. Help me figure a way out of this mess."

Purnell turned to face him. "Your father was the biggest son of a bitch I ever knew."

Wim laughed. "Now that's a news flash worthy of the front page of the *Bugle*. I asked you a question, old man. I need you to give me something I can hold over Garland's head."

Purnell closed his eyes for a moment. How had he gotten himself in this mess? How had he allowed his life to be controlled by not one, but *two* Wimbleys?

"Garland ain't even publisher anymore, you ass. Cheri Newberry is, remember? She's the one making decisions over there now, along with J.J., of course, so if I were you, that's who I'd be trying to get to do my bidding."

He watched Wimbley squint and bob his head up and down, as if the act of thinking might be a new experience for him. Eventually, the boy stopped nodding and started smiling. "Now, that sounds like something I might actually enjoy, Lawson, and it's definitely something my lovely fiancée and I could do together for fun and relaxation! You're a fucking genius!"

Right then, Purnell made a decision. He'd keep his gaze focused on the mountains for the remainder of this painful hospital room visit. Nothing else. That way, when he died, the timeless beauty of the Smokies would be the last image to burn itself in his mind, not the moronic look in Wim Wimbley's eyes.

He wondered what was the last thing Loyal and Melanie Newberry saw. Probably each other. The autopsy report said they died in their sleep, tangled up together like teenagers as the gas slowly poisoned them. Without a doubt, their blood was on him. He remembered what he did to those poor kids. He remembered every last second of it.

But what about Barbara Jean? What was the last image she saw? Purnell's angry eyes? His sloppy-drunk smile? Was it the back of his hand? Oh, everybody knew he could be a mean drunk back in those days, but why—*why?*—couldn't he remember the act of killing her?

Unless, of course, he hadn't.

But that would mean he was nothing but a pawn, a spineless man who'd handed over his life without the slightest fight. And the pain of that was too much to bear.

Purnell's body jolted. This time, the flash wasn't a picture. It was words . . . horrible words . . . real . . . and they struck him so clearly he clamped his hands to his ears to block the sound.

"Get out of the damn car, Lawson. Time to share."

When Purnell's hands fell away, Wim was still droning on.

"I think Cheri's full of shit, myself. She came by the office this morning, and I kept looking at her thinking that nobody I know in Florida real estate made it out alive, and she's going around telling everyone she's still living the high life down in Tampa?"

Purnell kept his eyes on the mountains.

"And I thought to myself, *shee-it,* it'd take me about five minutes to get the goods on that bitch."

"Sounds like you got yourself a plan, son," Purnell said, concentrating on the last mountain spring he would ever see. It fascinated him that beauty remained, even in the middle of all the weakness and the killing and the lies. "Time's a-wastin."

Cheri handed Tater Wayne the leftover pizza and a few extra cold beers, then waved to Mimi Grayson as she pulled away from the lake house. "Thanks again for your help, Mimi!" she called out.

Tater Wayne turned to go, but he stopped on the first porch step, giving her a shy smile.

"You're a good friend to me, Tater," Cheri said. "I appreciate every last thing you've done since I came home."

Tater shook his head, his hair sliding over his ricocheting eye. "You know Garland's paying me, right? I mean . . . that's not the *only* reason . . ."

She smiled at him, hoping it would get his eye to settle down.

"I'd do anything for you, Cheri, even if I wasn't getting money, but all's I'm sayin' is—"

She stepped forward and hugged him. "You have a good night, now, Tater."

"Oh. Okay. You, too, Cheri."

Keet, keet, keet!

"Careful not to run over Artemis," Cheri added, nodding toward the squirrel now standing in the middle of the gravel drive.

Tater Wayne shook his head, laughing. "All right now, I'll admit that thing acts like a Doberman, but are you telling me you *named* a damn *squirrel*? Y'all been in the city too long."

Cheri giggled. "Artemis was the ancient Greek goddess of protection. I looked it up."

"Y'all need a dog," Tater said, heading out with a wave. Cheri made sure Artemis darted safely off around the side of the house as Tater drove away. Thanks to J.J.'s reconnaissance earlier in the day, Cheri now knew exactly where her little preggo roommate was headed— the old wood tongue-and-groove soffit under the eaves. J.J. said she'd built an impressive nest of leaves, fur, dried lake grass, feathers, and shredded paper for her brood, and had chewed a hole clear through to serve as her private entrance to the inside of the house. He'd closed it up.

"You sure you don't mind sharing your home with a family of squirrels?" he'd asked her. "I can move the nest—put it in a hollow log or something."

"No!" she'd said. "She was here first, after all."

Suddenly, strong arms slid across her ribs and pulled her close, bringing her back to the present moment. With eyes closed and neck limp with pleasure, she luxuriated in the feel and scent of J.J. She'd spent the whole day in his company for the first time in a dozen years, and it felt comfortably familiar and like an exotic treat all at the same time.

That morning they'd retrieved more than a dozen boxes of financial records from the old warehouse and hauled everything—including what Cheri had accumulated at the *Bugle*—back to the lake house, where they'd set up a makeshift office in the back bedroom.

They had enjoyed lunch at Lenny's in town, and Cheri finally got her grilled pimento cheese sandwich. They stopped off at the house on Willamette to chat with Granddaddy, asking him if her father had left behind any personal record of his time as publisher. Granddaddy had directed them to four boxes in the attic, which J.J. had carried to his truck.

When they'd returned to the cottage to paint, they were thrilled that Tater and Mimi were there ready to lend a hand. Cheri had pulled J.J. aside at one point to ask if the general assignment reporter was trying to suck up to the new boss, and he shook his head. "Nope. Mimi said she admires you and hopes you stay. Personally, I think she's into the 'woman on top' aspect of it all." Cheri had laughed at that.

And now, as she stood on the porch in the unusually warm night air, J.J.'s arms around her, Cheri felt loose and calm. She'd accomplished a great deal in one day. She was physically exhausted. And she'd had two beers with her pizza. But she knew the real reason she felt so peaceful, so outrageously happy, was J.J.

He'd had her laughing all day, reminiscing about their teenage escapades, filling her in on his life between high scool and his return to Bigler, and his adventures as managing editor of the *Bugle*. With frequent contributions from Tater and Mimi, Cheri could now say she had the lowdown on the remaining inhabitants of the newsroom. She found out the graphics editor had five kids and coached in the town's soccer and baseball leagues; the sports reporter ran a statewide foster program for abused hunting dogs; and city editor Jim Taggert was a sought-after banjo picker who'd released three CDs and went on tour every summer. This information did nothing but make Cheri more determined to keep the newspaper in business and her employees' lives afloat.

Despite all the conversation and laughter, the four of them managed to clean and paint the whole inside of the cottage in a day. It would easily be party ready in two weeks.

"You smell so damn good," J.J. said into Cheri's ear.

She laughed, knowing he was exaggerating. "I smell like Sherwin Williams and Murphy's oil soap."

"Eau de manual labor," he said, his chuckle vibrating against the side of her neck. J.J. moved his hands over her belly and cradled her. "With rich undertones of Cheri—pure, sweet *Cheri*."

"Mmm." She snuggled into him closer, enjoying the simple act of breathing the lake air. She leaned into the hard heat of J.J.'s body. She listened to the telltale symphony of a fast-approaching summer—crickets, tree frogs, and even an occasional call of a loon.

"I love it here," she whispered, shocking herself, not because she said those words but because there seemed to be no aftertaste of anxiety. She must be coming to terms with the fact that she loved being at the lake house. She must be getting used to Bigler again. Damn, but Candy was going to *freak* when she told her.

And just like that, Cheri felt her body clench. What the hell was she *doing* letting her guard down like this? Her sister hated her and wished her dead. She was solely responsible for people's livelihoods. And she was living a lie! Tanyalee and J.J. and Granddaddy and Aunt Viv and everyone else in Bigler thought she was rich and successful, and she'd done absolutely nothing to correct them since her return.

And now it was too late! She'd look like a fool if she told everyone the truth now! She was no better than Tanyalee.

"Want to grab a couple beers and sit on the dock?" J.J. asked her.

"You just read my mind," she said, pushing the uneasiness away again, if only for the time being.

Chapter 20

J.J. looked down at their naked toes drawing cirlces in the dark water and sighed. "This whole day has felt like a dream, Cheri."

"A real good one."

He felt her nudge closer to his side and rest her head on his shoulder. They were now hip to hip, their arms forming an X behind each other's backs, just like they used to do back in school. The moon was up, a sliver above the trees, but it was enough to light up each other's faces.

"I heard you paid a visit to the Wimbley Real Estate offices this morning," J.J. said.

"How'd you hear that?"

He laughed. "You can't be serious. This is Bigler, sweetheart."

"Hmmph."

"Not going to tell me what transpired?"

"Just more of the same ugly stuff, I'm afraid." When Cheri looked up into his face, J.J. was startled by the intense sadness he saw in her expression.

"Baby, what—"

She shook her head and looked away. "I confronted her," Cheri said, her voice barely a whisper, her eyes focused out across the dark lake. "I don't know what I expected, but all I got was more bullshit about how you failed to live up to your sacred vows."

J.J. put his beer down on the freshly sawed boards of the dock. "That's a fair statement."

"What?" Cheri turned toward him again, her eyes flashing.

"I did fail. Miserably. I stood there like an idiot and said I promised to love and cherish her till death do us part when I knew it was impossible, since I couldn't even manage it for the ten minutes it took us to get hitched. I never loved Tanyalee. Marrying her was the biggest mistake I ever made—well, second only to sleeping with her without protection."

Cheri stayed quiet a long moment, looking down at her feet. "Did she tell you she was on the pill?"

J.J. shook his head. "I'm not going there, Cheri. Please don't ask me to."

She let go with a suddenly icy laugh. "Well, *she's* sure as hell not going there, so if you want me to know what happened, if you want me to know the truth, you are the only way I'm going to get it."

"I won't ruin your relationshp with your sister. It's between the two of you."

He watched Cheri shake her head. "It's already ruined, J.J. She flat-out told me today that she hated me and wished I was dead and that I was to blame for Mama's and Daddy's deaths."

J.J. jerked his head back in horror. That was pure

evil, even for Tanyalee. "You know that's ridiculous, baby."

Cheri shrugged. "It's something I've always carried around with me. She was just rubbing it in."

"That's the craziest shit I've ever heard." J.J. brought his face down close to hers, trying to get her to look him in the eye. "You were seven years old, Cheri. Your parents went to the beach and there was a gas leak in their rental—how in God's name was that your fault?"

She flashed her eyes at him briefly, then looked away. "I've heard it from Viv, too."

"Heard what? That you were to blame for them dying? Why the *hell* would Viv lay that guilt on a little girl? You've got to be wrong about that."

Cheri shook her head, looking off across the lake. "The night after the funeral, I snuck down to eavesdrop on the grown-ups. Viv, Granddaddy, and Purnell were sitting in the parlor. Viv said it. I heard her. She said that Mama and Daddy needed to get away from me and Tanyalee because we fought so much, because I was such a belligerent and stubborn little girl who'd always resented sweet little Taffy, and the constant yelling and fussing was enough to drive my parents crazy."

J.J. held his breath. All he could think was, *Oh, God, no.*

"Viv said that all my parents wanted was a moment's peace." Cheri paused, swallowing hard. "And Purnell . . . Purnell said, 'They got it, the poor souls.' "

J.J. brought his arm up around her shoulder, but Cheri remained stiff against him. "That was an incredibly insensitive and stupid thing to say," he whispered. "Sometimes people lash out in their grief, and don't realize what they're doing. I'm so damn sorry you heard that."

They sat quietly for a moment, their toes still circling in the water. Eventually, he felt Cheri's breathing slow.

"That's not the only thing Tanyalee told me today, J.J. She warned me that you would turn on me one day and she hoped that God had mercy on me when it happened."

J.J. shook his head. "Of course she did."

"Tanyalee told me she had a miscarriage and that was all she'd say."

Cheri looked up at him again, her face a mask of resigned sadness. "I want to know what's possible for you and me in the future, but I have to know the truth about the past first. You're the only place I can go to get it."

J.J. sat perfectly still for many long seconds, until he knew he had no choice. Cheri deserved the truth. "Yes, Tanyalee told me she was on the pill. She miscarried a few weeks after the wedding but it slipped her mind to mention it to me. I only found out because her doctor's office left a message on the answering machine."

"Oh, Lord."

"So I went looking for her. With a heads-up from Turner, I tracked her down at the Tip-Top Motel."

"Where?" Cheri's eyes squinted in disbelief.

"Room 34 to be exact. With some guy."

"Huh?"

J.J. tilted his head back and laughed. "That's what I said." His laughter mellowed into a sigh. "Yeah. Ugly, ugly, ugly. She never admitted it, but I'm pretty sure she was trying to get pregnant again real quick, thinking I wouldn't notice it was the world's first twelve-month human gestation."

Cheri tilted her head and stared at him, her nose and mouth scrunched up. It made him chuckle. He kissed her wrinkled nose. "The answer to your unspoken question is no—we never had sex after that first time, so she had to go elsewhere for what she wanted. I couldn't do it, Cheri. I didn't love her—I didn't even like her. But, I gotta admit, there was a part of me that . . ."

J.J. managed to stop himself, but knew he'd gone too far, and now Cheri was staring at him. She expected him to finish his thought. "Part of me wanted to get you out of my system, I guess. After what happened in Florida, I knew I'd be dead to you, that this town would be dead to you. I wanted to burn it all away."

She raised a single eyebrow at him.

"I think I saw those months with Tanyalee as a way to punish myself."

"For what exactly?"

"For ruining my chance with you—forever."

J.J. gasped when Cheri slipped her small hand over his. Her skin was so smooth and warm. The delicate bones of her hands wrapped around him like a velvety ribbon, and her thumb rubbed the top of his wrist. "But she trapped you, Jay. She wanted revenge against me. You were just caught in the middle."

"I wasn't exactly a victim," he said softly. "It was my decision to sleep with her in the first place. My penis. My mistake. My responsibility."

With his free hand he reached over and touched the side of her face. He smiled at the smear of eggshell white that went across her cheek like war paint. Then he ran his hand over her paint-speckled hair.

"What?" she asked, slowly returning his smile.

"You're covered in paint."

"Really? Well, so are you. Here, let me help you clean up a little."

Cheri was suddenly on his lap, her arms around his neck and her lips opening to his. J.J. grabbed her, the need in him immediate and fierce—until he felt himself falling straight over the edge of the dock and into the water.

"Hey—" The cold slapped him and he surfaced with the sound of Cheri's laughter ringing in his ears. She was already swimming away, though she was laughing too hard to make headway with her sloppy strokes.

"Y'all in a load of trouble now, girl," he said, heading after her.

"No!" she shrieked. "Stay away!"

A few loons decided to join in her protest.

"You want to play, do you?" As J.J. closed in on her, Cheri began kicking her feet hard and fast, shooting water into his face.

"No! Stop!" She was laughing so hard she could barely get the words out.

J.J. was suddenly aware that all this noise was the most beautiful music he'd ever heard, a crazy cacophony of loons, laughter, and lake water. He began laughing, too, gasping for breath as he reached one of her flipping feet.

"Gotcha!" He yanked her toward him and her sweet ass slammed into his belly. J.J. flipped her over and got an arm under her back, reached his feet down into the muddy lake bottom for leverage and began hauling her out through the reeds.

"Where are you taking me?" she asked, her fingers already tearing at his shirt buttons.

"Somewhere warmer and drier."

"What y'all fixin' to do with me?" When J.J. saw the mischievousness in her eyes, his heart nearly broke apart. Here she was—tight in his arms, joy in her heart, her fingers doing their best to get his clothes off—and he wasn't sure he could handle this much luck. He hadn't felt this hopeful since the day he stood on her front porch in Tampa, and she'd answered the door, smiled, and threw her arms around him. "Ain't made up my mind yet, sugar," he said. "You got any ideas?"

"Yeah, I got a few," she said, just before she put her hot lips on his cold, wet chest, and began kissing down his sternum, her tongue flicking at his ball bearing of a nipple until bolts of pleasure shot through his boxers.

J.J.'s feet hit hard ground and they cleared the water without a moment to spare. His knees were on the edge of giving out, not because the woman in his arms was a burden—Cheri barely weighed anything—but because his dick was getting so hard he had forgotten how to put one foot in front of the other.

"I thought maybe we could take a shower together," she said, biting down on his other nipple. "The grout's dry."

"Oh, fuck, that's the best grout-related news I've ever heard."

She giggled, and the second her lips left his flesh he pulled her higher and clamped his mouth on hers as they tackled the front steps.

"Keet!"

The squirrel had returned to lodge her most recent complaint with the landlord. J.J. paused the kiss long enough to address her. "Now you just hush for once, you bossy thing. This is none of y'all's business."

He placed Cheri down on the porch and they both began ripping their sopping wet clothes off their bodies. As he peeled everything off, J.J. was suddenly relieved that he'd left his wallet, phone, and keys inside the cottage before they'd gone to the dock.

Moments later, he was still struggling with his boots and socks as he watched Cheri scurry through the living room, bare-ass naked, past the ugly green couch under a clear plastic drop cloth, and down the hall to the bathroom. The vision of her pink and perfect little body made his hands shake, which only added to the frustration with his wet bootlaces. He grabbed the wet condoms from his jeans pocket, and ran through the living room, water flinging with every step.

The feel of J.J.'s solid flesh under her soapy fingers was glorious. The sensation of hot water pounding onto their cold skin made her shiver with pleasure. The erection pressing up against her belly had her dizzy with lust. It had been many months since she'd been with a man, but it had been many long years since she'd been with J.J., and she had no intention of waiting a second longer.

"Have you figured out what you're going to do with me?" she teased him.

"Hell, yes," J.J. said. "I'm gonna make up for lost time, Cheri. I'm gonna make up for every month that went by that I didn't have you to laugh with and love and make hot and wild love to."

"That sounds like a big job."

"Fortunately, I have everything I need."

"Yes, you do," she said.

J.J.'s hands slid up and down the sides of her body. His palms cupped her ass, pressed into her hips, brushed down her thighs and up again. She was well aware how hungry he was for her—he was eating her up with his hands, devouring her with his eyes, consuming her with his lips.

"I want you bad, Cheri."

"I want you, J.J." Her pussy throbbed. She felt like she was going to come just by being in close proximity to the heat and desire shooting off his body.

"Tell me," he growled into her ear.

"I always have. I always will."

"What? You *what*?"

"I love you, J.J."

He moaned into her mouth as he kissed her. She threw a thigh up around his hip. After many long moments of that kiss—building up, mouths on fire with the taste of each other, tongues pushing and teeth nipping—the mood switched. The kiss slowed. The touch was loving and gentle.

J.J. pushed her away slightly, then spun her around so that her back faced him, and pressed her shoulders down. Cheri gasped as she felt him spread her thighs apart with his knees. She slapped her hands against the tile wall, and shuddered with pleasure at the feel of his hands sliding down the back of her legs. He was kneeling behind her . . .

The instant his hot tongue slid between her pussy lips, she came, bucking and moaning and pressing back against his mouth. It was too much! Too fast! She laughed at herself at the crazy pace of this! It usually took her a long time and lots of concentrated attention to get her to orgasm.

With J.J., it was nearly automatic.

He chuckled softly, his mouth still pressed to her sex, the vibration tickling her as she came down from the orgasm. Slowly, he removed his lips from her, slid his hands up her legs and stood, reaching over her to turn off the water. He threw the shower curtain open and grabbed a towel, helping Cheri to stand upright as he dried her off, alternating swipes of the soft towel with soft kisses. She did the same for him, and then he picked her up and carried her across the hall into the bedroom.

Dark. Silent. Peaceful. No curtains on the windows. No neighbors. Not a stitch of clothing between them. J.J. laid Cheri down on her back and got up on top of her. He was there, so solid, so warm, so loving and gentle, as he scooped her into his arms.

"Don't take yourself away from me again, Cheri. Please don't do it."

She shook her head, tears welling in her eyes, overwhelmed by the feel of this moment. Somehow she'd come full circle in the span of a week—home, love, a place in the world, the right man to belong to. She opened her legs to J.J., as if she were opening herself up to the possibility of being completely alive, completely present. Her heart felt so full she thought it might burst at the seams.

J.J. braced himself on his knees, grabbed a condom and slipped it on, and in seconds he had his hands under her bottom and was lifting her up. There was just enough moonlight for her to see the outline of their joining. She felt speared into—all heat and stretching and pushing deep into her being. J.J. started slowly, careful with her, careful that his hardness and his thickness wasn't a shock to her system. Once she'd accepted him, he dug his fingers into her flesh and pulled her away and against him, in and out, the music of their bodies meeting the only sound in the world.

Pulling her legs further onto his thighs, J.J. leaned forward and grabbed her behind her back. He pulled her up, balancing her weight on his thighs, pushing deeper, his mouth going to her breasts, her nipples, the orgasm building so slow and hard inside her she had to gasp for air.

Cheri heard a long and high-pitched wail and it took a moment for her to realize the sound was hers, coming from her body, her soul.

She flung her arms around J.J.'s neck and let her head fall back as he continued to ram into her, call out that he loved her, and the force of his explosion was enough to send her over the edge yet again, harder this time, wilder, higher . . . she was lost in it.

Lost, and found.

The next morning it rained. They slept in as the water beat down on the tin roof of the cottage, waking only to make love and fall asleep again. They made love two more times—just to be sure neither of them were imagining anything, J.J. pointed out. Eventually, they went rummaging for warm clothes. It was quite a sight watching J.J. build a fire in the skintight outfit that was his only option for the moment—a pair of Cheri's baggiest sweatpants, her largest sweatshirt, and her roomiest socks. Once the fire was going, he grabbed their wet clothes and shoes from the porch and draped them on the hearth and mantel.

Meanwhile, Cheri put Aunt Viv's sweet potato casserole in the oven along with some leftover ham and set about tidying up the cottage. She dragged the drop cloths out to the back porch lean-to, set the table with mismatched dishes, and placed the canning jar of the still-perky flowers in the center. She opened the kitchen window for fresh air, and smiled at the blue and white checks in the breeze.

Cheri wandered back into the living room and stood behind J.J. as he placed another log on the fire. "I never did thank you for the bouquet," she whispered in his ear, wrapping her arms around him.

"I never did tell you they're from me."

"Of course they are."

"Damn. I wanted to be a man of mystery." J.J. spun her around in his embrace. He pulled her tight, and Cheri could feel his heartbeat, slow and sure.

"I don't want any more mystery," she heard herself say. "I just want to know things, to be sure of a few things in life for a change."

He kissed the top of her head. "You've come to the right place, then," he said.

"You sure?"

He laughed. "I'm sure you can be sure about me. I love you, Cheri." He brushed the hair from the side of her face and planted a kiss on her lips. "I'll always be straight with you. I promise. These are my real stripes you're looking at. There's nothing about me you can't see or don't know. As usual, Tanyalee was wrong about that."

She nodded, resting her head on his chest once more.

By the time they finished eating, J.J.'s clothes were dry and he emerged from the bedroom looking relieved. "Never was big on cross-dressing," he said with a grin.

Cheri had already arranged piles of financial documents on the living room floor, the couch, the coffee table, and on top of several turned-over bankers' boxes. She'd sorted them into general categories: year-end income and expense statements, ad revenue summaries, contracts for ad sales, monthly bookkeeping reports, and the newspaper's state and federal tax returns.

For about two hours, Cheri went over the oldest of the financial records, and found the first indication of missing money was in July 1964. From there it looked like hundreds of dollars were skimmed off ad revenues, month after month, year after year, until 1971, when questionable expenses began to show up. There were breaks in the pattern in 1987 and again in the early 1990s.

She took notes. She entered numbers into the spreadsheet in her laptop. When her brain began to hurt, she decided she'd start in on her father's things. It would be hard, but it had to be done.

Cheri sat curled up on the end of the couch with the floor lamp nearby, four boxes of her father's personal belongings arranged at her feet. Granddaddy had said that inside the boxes she'd find everything that was in his office at the time of his death.

Cheri upacked all the things a businessman in the 1980s might cling to even as the world went digital—a Rolodex, a desk blotter and calendar, a datebook, a wall clock, a business card collection, a small leather notebook with phone numbers and birthdays, and a stack of paper expense reports. She also found several framed family photos—one of her daddy and mama on their wedding day, Mama's lacy confection of a princess dress spread out around her in the grass, Daddy standing tall and handsome and proud; one of Granddaddy and Gramma a few years before she passed; one of Aunt Viv in her twenties, a knockout in a tight pink Jackie Kennedyesque Easter suit and matching pillbox hat; and a photo of Cheri and Tanyalee.

She placed that photo in her lap, angled it toward the floor lamp, and studied it. She remembered the day the photo had been taken.

They'd gone to the Cataloochee County Fair. She was six and Tanyalee was four. They'd begged long and hard to be allowed to have a Sno-Kone and so sported the telltale blueberry-blue and raspberry-red rings around their lips. They had their arms linked over each other's shoulders—which must have been a rarity—and they were smiling and laughing like little girls who hadn't a care in the world.

That would all come the following year.

But for the moment, there was Cheri with her missing front teeth and Tanyalee with her hacked-off front bangs (Cheri had needed a client for her pretend beauty shop), and they were the picture of summertime sisterly bliss.

Cheri remembered seeing this framed photo propped on a corner of Daddy's desk, one day in particular. She'd been playing hide-and-seek in the publisher's office as Daddy and Granddaddy talked business. She'd just turned seven, but even she could detect an odd nervousness to her father's voice and a rare undercurrent of irritation in her grandfather's.

She'd sat as still as could be in the corner next to the copy machine, hardly breathing. She stared at that photo of her and Tanyalee while she listened. Granddaddy had said, "That can't be right," and her daddy kept saying, "*Follow the money. Follow the money.*"

As a child, she had no idea what the phrase meant. Now she knew it was the infamous tip from Deep Throat to Washington reporters looking into the Watergate cover-up. It had long ago become a cliché in investigating any kind of political corruption or corporate crime. But what had her daddy meant by it that day in 1987, in the publisher's office of the *Bugle*?

Cheri placed all the framed photos back in the box and closed the lid. She checked on J.J., stretched out on his back on the floor, a leg crossed over a knee, a stack of papers held up over his face, lost in concentration.

She'd forgotten. It was really that simple. All the time she'd been in Florida chasing and pushing and fighting for money and success—both before and after J.J.'s disastrous surprise visit—she'd forgotten what it felt like to be comfortable and at ease and in love with a man.

She didn't have anything to prove with J.J. There was never a balance sheet with them, one that tracked the giving and the taking and checked for inequities. Maybe it was because they'd known each other so long. Maybe it was because they were just right for each other. Maybe she'd never understand it, and didn't need to.

His eyes flashed her way and he smiled. "See anything that's knocked your socks off yet?" he asked.

Cheri smiled back. "Yep."

"Yeah? What?"

"You."

He shook his head. "Besides that."

"Nothing really. But I've been thinking about something and I'd like to run it by you."

"Sure." J.J. effortlessly sat up, spun around on his butt, and crossed his legs. She loved watching him move. It had to be all the mountain biking, hiking, and weight lifting he'd been doing since he was a kid, but he moved like a wildcat.

"If the possible theft was a story you were reporting for the *Bugle* or for your New York news service, what would be your basic approach?"

J.J. shrugged. "Follow the money."

"I knew it!"

He laughed. "You getting all Woodward-and-Bernstein on me?"

She laughed, too. "No, but listen, seriously. Where did all this money go?" She got up from the couch and walked into the kitchen. "You want coffee?"

"Sure," J.J. said. "But keep talking."

Cheri put the water on to boil. "From what I can tell,

somebody was skimming off the top of advertising revenues from the mid-sixties to the early seventies, but then suddenly switched it up and starting padding expenses." She grabbed the coffee from the cabinet. "With a few exceptions, this has continued month after month, year after year, until very recently."

"Then what happened?" J.J. asked.

"Well, the books got so fucked up it was like Purnell just gave up trying."

"But how could that have happened?"

She shrugged. "Granddaddy never had the books audited. And basically, until the newspaper business as a whole started going into the toilet, nobody paid much attention. If the *Bugle* had eight million in revenue and seven million in expenses, there was still one million in profit, and nobody asked any questions."

"So you're sure it was Purnell. And all these years—"

"He was stealing. I'm fairly sure of it. Which brings us right back to my original question—where did it all go?"

Cheri set out two mugs and the sugar and cream. "If the guy had been squirreling away money all these years, wouldn't now be the time to tap into it? To fix up his house, maybe? To retire with? To run off to Bora Bora? Why is he still working when he's obviously so ill and way past retirement age?"

"I'll go to town hall tomorrow and look up Purnell's property tax records, see if he still carries a mortgage."

"You should probably do the same with Gladys and Granddaddy—just so we can rule them out."

"Will do, but I think it's time you take this to Turner. If you give him enough for probable cause, he can get his hands on all kinds of information—Purnell's personal tax returns, investments, bank balances."

"Absolutely, but I'm going to visit Purnell in the hospital first. I have to at least give him an opportunity to explain."

"Better do it soon," J.J. said, frowning. "He's not long for this world, I'm afraid."

With a sigh, Cheri plopped down into the kitchen chair across from J.J. As the water heated, she let her thoughts wander. "So, hypothetically . . ."

He raised a brow and nodded.

"Who in this town *does* have money?"

J.J. shrugged. "Same as always. The owners of Amos Paper and Fiber. The Wimbleys. The Gladsen Tannery family. The doctors and the lawyers. Cataloochee County's pretty much like the rest of the country—the top one half of one percent's got more than the rest of us combined."

Cheri nodded.

"I'm sorry, sweetheart, but I'll need to take that coffee to go." J.J. reached across the table and stroked the top of Cheri's hand with his thumb. "I got to go into the newsroom. We're running a wrap-up feature on Barbara Jean tomorrow—you know, trying to get our sexy back when all we're doing is rehashing the same, worn-out information."

Cheri looked up at him and smiled. "I was entertaining my first day on the job, wasn't I?"

His eyes sparkled. "Not nearly as much as now."

She giggled as she rose from the table to pour the water through the drip filter. "Can you come back tonight?"

"If you'll have me again."

"That was my plan."

Cheri was grinning as she returned to the table and poured out two mugs of coffee. The little drip pot and a pound of Folger's gourmet blend from the Piggly Wiggly had been her first official household purchases with Friday's paycheck.

"So why isn't there anything new with the Barbara Jean story?" she asked.

J.J.'s sigh was tinged in frustration. "Turner says there's going to be a break in the case this week." He took a careful sip of his coffee. "Whoa! This is delicious, Cheri!"

"Really?" It was the first cup of coffee she'd made in close to eight years, and it was a relief to know she remembered how.

"I have a hunch they've already ID'd her body but there's something they don't want made public quite yet. That's what I gather from talking to Turner, anyway."

"So he doesn't give you scoops, even though he's your best friend?"

J.J. thought that was funny. "Sure, but not when it comes to a story this big. I can't say I blame him. He says that as the county's first black sheriff he's got to do everything better, faster, and with a big smile. Plus, he's got a lot of eyes on him right now—regional media, the Feds, the state." J.J. grinned. "He's playing this one by the rules."

Cheri watched J.J.'s smile fade. He lowered his gaze and stared at the scarred old wood of the tabletop. "What's wrong, Jay?" she asked.

He raised his dark blue eyes to her and tried to smile, but she noticed the tension in his mouth. "I've scoured every public record I can get my hands on that's related to this case, but nothing is jumping out at me. Until they declare it a homicide, Barbara Jean is just another cold disappearance case, and the information's been gathering dust for more than forty years. Anyone who had firsthand knowledge of the investigation is dead. Sheriff Wimbley died back in 2001. The witness is gone, obviously, and so are the state troopers who had the case, the workers who dragged the lake, the people who owned homes out at Paw Paw Lake— everybody's dead. But . . ." He shook his head.

"What?"

"I know I'm missing something. I'm not seeing something that's right under my nose, and it's making me crazy, Cheri. I don't miss shit as a rule, but I'm missing it now, when I can least afford to."

"It's the sister," Cheri said. "The old lady who was crying at the crime scene. She's still alive."

J.J. chuckled. "And she's as jumpy as spit on a hot skillet. She won't have anything to do with us. She sicced her dogs on me last time I showed up, and she's no nicer to Mimi. But we'll keep trying."

"Maybe I should talk to her."

J.J.'s coffee mug stopped in midair.

"Or I could call her."

"No phone," J.J. said.

"I could just stop by and say I was in the neighborhood."

"No neighborhood. She lives so far out in Maggie Valley that the postman delivers once a week."

"I'll write her, then."

J.J. nodded. "No harm in that. I'll take the note next time I venture out there, but I wouldn't get my hopes up." He stood to go, grabbed his jacket from a hook near the fireplace and turned to Cheri, his face suddenly soft and innocent because of his smile.

"Cheri, I'm so glad you're here."

She rose from her chair and went to him, finding her place in his open arms. "I'm glad, too."

"But you look exhausted, sugar."

"I'm fine."

J.J. placed a finger under her chin and lifted her lips to meet his. He gave her a generous, slow kiss that sent a rush of warmth through her whole body.

"Maybe you should take a nap," he said, his voice a husky whisper.

"Because it's a rainy day?"

He chuckled. "No—because I doubt you'll get much shut-eye tonight."

Chapter 21

Cheri woke with her heart about to rip through her ribs. She knew if she didn't concentrate on breathing she might faint. The dream had been so real.

The girl with the ponytail had walked alone in the mist, back and forth on the pier of Paw Paw Lake, wringing her hands as she looked into the black water.

Cheri felt such sadness for her, because she knew poor Barbara Jean would never find what she was looking for, no matter how long she searched. It was futile. Heartbreaking.

Then Cheri *was* Barbara Jean. *Her* eyes stared into the depths. *Her* nervous hands pulled and tugged at each other. *Her* thoughts were frantic. And she knew with certainty that she must keep searching . . .

And suddenly, there had been a sound like an explosion of glass as Tanyalee's face soared up through the depths of the lake, glowing with an eerie light, breaking the surface and coming right at her . . .

Now fully awake, Cheri shook her head to drive away the image. With a quick check on the soundly sleeping

J.J., she slipped from the bed, put on her sweats, and headed for the front porch. She needed air.

Cheri walked out onto the front lawn in her bare feet. The cool night grass tickled the tender skin between her toes. The breeze cleared her head. She looked up and took in the sight of the sky above her—a big black bowl filled to the brim with cosmic glitter.

That's when it occurred to her—it wasn't Tanyalee's face that had burst from the dark water of her dream.

It had been her mother's.

She wiped her eyes and went back to bed.

J.J. bolted up from a dead sleep, unsure of his surroundings until he heard the sound again.

"Chit! Chit! Keek! Keet!"

Cheri sat up, too. She clutched at his arm. "Ohmigod, what's that?"

"Stay here." J.J. had barely thrown the covers off his legs when the sound of shattering glass made him jump.

Cheri screamed.

"Call Turner on your BlackBerry."

"Okay. Okay. But be careful!"

J.J. pulled on his jeans and ran into the hallway. He pressed himself against the wall in the shadows, feeling pretty damn useless without anything to protect himself or Cheri. He fell to his hands and knees and crawled toward the fireplace, grabbing the poker and crouching behind the far end of the couch. It had sounded like the breaking glass had come from the kitchen, but he didn't see anyone.

"Keet! Chit!"

The squirrel squatted not three feet away, her little paws rubbing together in nervousness, staring right at him in the darkness. Even if he'd managed to hide himself from the intruder, his cover had just been blown.

Or maybe there was no intruder. Maybe this damn squirrel . . .

That's when J.J. saw that the room had been trashed. Papers were everywhere. A side table was smashed. A loud *bang!* echoed from the back of the house, followed by the slam of the lean-to's screen door. He raced toward the kitchen but skidded to a stop when he saw broken glass all around his bare feet. He looked up to see that the kitchen window had been smashed.

J.J. turned and exited the front door, went down the porch steps, and ran around the side of the house. Loose gravel cut into the soles of his feet. The poker was clutched in his hand.

"Keet! Keet!"

The squirrel was at his heels.

"Dammit!" J.J. hissed, spinning around trying to get his eyes to adjust to the dark. He heard no car leaving. He saw no one on foot. Whoever had broken in—for whatever reason—had gotten away.

"What the hell is all this?" Turner stood in the open front door of the lake house and gestured to the papers tossed all over the living room. "Everybody okay?"

Cheri nodded from her place on the floor, where she sat cross-legged and slumped over.

"Come on in and join the party," J.J. said.

Cheri watched Turner take careful steps into the room and assess the situation in seconds—broken kitchen window, vandalized personal belongings, family photographs tossed in the smoldering ash of the fire.

Turner whistled long and low when he noticed that last bit.

Cheri fessed up. "I probably shouldn't have touched anything, but I pulled the picture frames out of the heat. I wanted to save them."

"Understandable," he said. Cheri didn't miss the silent exchange between J.J and Turner.

"Anything missing?" Turner asked.

"Not that I noticed," she said.

"Time this occurred?"

"I'd say about two-fifteen, " J.J. said.

"Did you see anyone?"

"The breaking glass woke us up," J.J. said. "I heard the door slam out on the lean-to, but by the time I got outside no one was there. No car, that was for sure."

"We would have heard a car," Cheri added.

Turner wandered into the kitchen, stepping over glass. He examined the drainboard and the windowsill, then tapped his boot against the large creek rock sitting in the middle of the kitchen floor.

He turned toward them, an eyebrow raised. "Looks like whoever stopped by wanted to make some noise and a mess. Looks like they were leaving you a message."

"No kidding," Cheri muttered.

Turner walked back into the living room and smiled down at Cheri, still sitting cross-legged by the fireplace.

"You know you got a rabid squirrel on your property?"

"She's not rabid. She's pregnant."

"I stand corrected." Turner tugged on his gun holster and obviously tried to suppress a smile. "But if you're gonna be living all the way out here on your own you might want to get yourself some protection other than a pregnant squirrel. The sheriff's department sponsors gun safety classes for citizens."

She groaned. "I hate guns."

Turner squinted, trying to get a better look at what Cheri cradled in her hand.

"Oh," she said, sighing. "Yeah. I found this on the floor. Whoever broke in must have dropped it."

Turner came closer and peered at the lustrous mother-of-pearl hair comb in Cheri's hand. "Very pretty. Looks antique. You recognize it?"

"Sure," Cheri said, figuring that was a rhetorical question she didn't need to answer. "Any suggestions on what I do now, Turner?"

He pulled off his ball cap and sat down on the couch, leaning his elbows on his knees. "Well, I can call in the evidence techs to dust for prints on the rock and on the picture frames and such, and I can head over to get a statement from—the suspect—and see if they can account for their whereabouts, but the real question is, do you want to press charges or do you want to handle it more, uh, privately?"

Cheri glanced at J.J.

"I don't want to press charges," she said.

Turner shrugged, hopped up from the couch, and put his cap back on. "Then, as long as no one is hurt, I'd say y'all get the window fixed and set about having a little heart-to-heart with your . . . uh . . . the suspect."

"Thanks for coming over," J.J. said, giving Turner a quick man-hug.

"I do love my job," Turner said with a dramatic sigh. "But I gotta be honest, with the threatening letters and the break-ins, y'all at the *Bugle* are making my life a living hell." He winked. " 'Night."

Chapter 22

The next morning, Cheri sat in the brightly lit waiting room of the intensive care unit of Western Carolina Medical Center, patting Granddaddy on the shoulder.

Purnell had drifted into a coma overnight, and the doctors said he had only a twenty percent chance of coming out of it.

"I'm sorry, Granddaddy," she said again.

"Well, shee-it," he sighed. "Hardly worth getting up every day once everyone you came up with has kicked the bucket." His vacant stare fell on the elevators out in the hall. "My brother was first, you know, dying in the war, and then your gramma, and your daddy and mama, then old Chester, now Purnell."

She slipped her arm up and around his bony shoulder.

"At least I still got my girls," he said, a hint of a smile at his lips.

"Yep. All three of us—Tanyalee, Viv, and me."

He laughed.

"Granddaddy? What exactly did Tanyalee do that you had to file charges against her?"

"What's past is past," he said, tapping her knee with his big, spotted hand. "She's human and she made a mistake. She paid for it. It's over. She's family, and family forgives."

"All right." Cheri sat for a moment, thinking about last night's break-in and preparing for her next question. "What has Tanyalee been telling you and Viv about me over the years?"

He turned his head and searched her face. "Nothing I paid any attention to, Cheri. Now, Vivienne is another matter. She's a flibbertigibbet, you know, into the girlie things like weddings and babies and such, things she got to experience with Tanyalee, at least for a bit. So that brought them closer."

Cheri blinked.

"But she loves you something awful," he said, one corner of his mouth twitching. "She ran around like a headless chicken when I told her you were coming home. Should've seen the old gal . . ."

Cheri chuckled. "Like she is right now getting ready for this party we're having."

"Lord-a-mighty! Half the town is coming! I told her we might as well host my wake while we're at it since I won't have two dimes to rub together after this blow-out."

"I thought you called them shindigs back in the day."

One of Granddaddy's bushy white eyebrows floated high on his brow.

"Gladys told me all about your legendary get-togethers at the lake."

He laughed and shook his head, embarrassed. "There was no call for that."

"It certainly sets the bar mighty high for any future parties I might host."

Granddaddy pulled her tight to his side, and Cheri leaned her head on his chest.

"Your daddy would be so damn proud of you, Cheri," he whispered. "I've heard nothing but good things about your instincts, and your energy, and your willingness to try new things. I told you this publisher thing was in your blood."

She didn't move. She didn't breathe. She wanted to blurt it all out right there. *I'm broke. I lost everything. I'm not the successful businesswoman you imagine me to be. I'm a phony. Don't trust me. I'm a failure.*

"And I have to admit, I'm damn glad you and J.J. are getting along so well."

Cheri rolled her eyes. It was like Bigler had its own Homeland Security division, focused exclusively on her home, her land, and her private comings and goings.

"Now all we have to do is get Tanyalee to settle herself with you being back. Because we would sure like it if you stayed, sugar. We'd like you to come on home for good. *I* would like you to stay."

Cheri steeled herself. She sat up straight and looked into her grandfather's tired eyes. She owed him the truth.

"Mr. Newberry?"

Cheri and Granddaddy whipped their heads around to face the nurse who'd just spoken.

"Yes?"

Cheri helped Granddaddy to a stand.

"The doctors wanted me to tell you to go on home now. Mr. Lawson's unable to see visitors and it's not expected his status will change in the near future."

"But I just—" Cheri felt Granddaddy's body tremble. "I wanted to say good-bye to my friend."

"I understand," the nurse said kindly. "But that's not possible."

"Just let me say something to him before I go. No one has to know."

The nurse looked around her and sighed. "All right, but y'all will have to be quick about it."

Cheri walked with him to a room down the hall and waited while the nurse opened the door and gestured for them to go in. Granddaddy came to a stop by the bed and Cheri remained behind him. She couldn't look at Purnell. Her grandfather was whispering good-bye to a loving friend, a friend he didn't know had been stealing him blind for forty-plus years. She couldn't watch.

She drove him home in the pimpmobile. He remained silent for most of the twenty-minute trip. Cheri knew that everything about this was wrong—the timing, the message, the way she was going about it. But she had no choice. It would be far worse if he found out indirectly that his granddaughter had handed his lifelong friend over for prosecution—while the man lay in a coma.

"I know you think of Purnell as family and you believe in forgiving family, but what he's done to the paper is really bad."

He turned his face toward her. She could see he'd been crying. "Your daddy tried to tell me the same thing, just before he died. I thought he was being too hard on Purnell. I thought he was overreacting."

Cheri's spine stiffened. *Follow the money.* "What did he tell you, exactly?" Her mind immediately went to all her father's personal documents in a box at the lake house. Had she missed something?

Granddaddy shook his head as he tried to recall. "Only that there was money missing. He didn't know how much or where it went to, but he implied Purnell was up to no good."

Cheri's hands gripped the wheel. "I don't understand," she whispered. "Why didn't you get the paper audited right then? Why didn't you confront Purnell? He was stealing from the *Bugle*!"

Granddaddy shrugged. "Things happened so fast, Cheri. Your daddy and mama died. There was the funeral. Raising you girls. And Purnell was right next to me the whole time. Then his wife died of cancer. His health started to fail. I know you don't understand, but I just figured if he was skimming a few thousand off the top here and there it wouldn't kill us. So I just let it go."

Un-fuckin'-believable. The time had come for a little rendezvous with reality.

"It was closer to three quarters of a million dollars over the course of forty-seven years."

Granddaddy said nothing. She glanced over at him and his face had blanched. Even his lips had drained of color. For a second, Granddaddy looked as sickly as Aunt Viv's Caucasian lawn jockey. Cheri checked the road and looked to Graddaddy again. "Breathe," she told him.

He sucked in a lungful of air.

"You okay?"

He nodded. The color slowly returned to his face.

"There's something else you need to know."

He nodded.

"I'm obligated to take my findings to the police."

"Sweet baby Jesus," he said.

Cheri's BlackBerry rang. She reached in her purse and answered the call.

"Hi, J.J.—I'm driving back from the hospital with Granddaddy and I have you on speaker."

There was an instant of silence. Obviously, J.J. was revising his greeting for general audiences.

"They've ID'd Barbara Jean's body," J.J. said. "We now have an official homicide investigation."

"Bad news always comes in clumps of three," Granddaddy said to no one in particular. "I wonder what's next?"

"Wim!"

"Find something else?"

"Oh, hell's bells, yes," Tanyalee said. She waited for Wim to poke his head out from the back office door. "I couldn't make this shit up if I tried," she said, pointing to the computer screen, so excited her hand shook.

"Cheri and Candy are b-r-o-k-e, baby," she said, her voice a reverent whisper. "They're being sued by six different companies for nonpayment. Cheri's house is in foreclosure and Candy unloaded hers in a short sale. Both their cars were repossessed. They're in arrears out their asses."

"Damn," Wim said. Tanyalee felt him move closer to the back of her chair. "You sure know your way around cyberspace, baby."

"I also found their joint eBay account. In the last year they've sold everything from jewelry to gym memberships under their real names. They're living in some six-hundred-dollar-a-month furnished studio in a big-box building in a not-so-great section of Tampa. I'm telling you, Wim . . ." Tanyalee spun around in her chair to find him right up against her, breathing heavily. "She's not rich. She's got nothing—less than nothing."

It was then that Tanyalee realized she'd started to unbutton her own blouse.

"She's not smart," she added.

Tanyalee pulled at Wim's belt and unzipped him.

"She's not classy."

She spread her legs wide and hiked up her skirt.

"She's just a total failure, baby. A damn loser."

Wim scooped her up with one hand while he un-hooked her bra and mauled her breast with the other. Somewhere in the back of her mind, Tanyalee realized it was the smoothest move she'd ever seen him execute.

"I'm gonna fuck your brains out," Wim growled into her ear.

Tanyalee nearly swooned, then remembered it was not even ten A.M. on a Monday and the front door to the real estate office was unlocked. "We should—" Wim slammed his mouth down on hers, cutting her off.

"Get back there in my office, you fuckin' brilliant little tart," he said. "Bend over the desk. Pull your pant-ies to the side. Do it." Wim glared at her. "Now."

"Oh, God, yes." Tanyalee ran into the back office and assumed the position. When she heard the click of the lock, she nearly came all over herself.

Chapter 23

In between editorial meetings, special project planning sessions, gun shopping, meet-and-greets with potential advertising clients, a speaking engagement at the Lion's Club, and three more visits to Purnell's intensive care room with Granddaddy, Cheri completed the financial analysis by Thursday afternoon.

She left a copy on J.J.'s desk. She kept a copy for Granddaddy. And she drove over to the municipal complex to deliver a copy to Turner, but he was out on a call.

"Frankly, I wouldn't count on him getting back to you on this right away," his secretary told Cheri. "The homicide case has him going twenty-four hours a day. He'll have to review it and determine if it should go to the district attorney over in Waynesville."

"I understand," she said.

As planned, she swung by the house on Willamette to meet Aunt Viv for another party-planning session. She nearly turned around in the driveway when she saw that Tanyalee was there.

But what did it matter? Cheri would see her next

week at the party anyway. It wasn't like she could avoid her for the rest of her time in Bigler, whether another week or the rest of her life.

On her way to the front door she patted the lawn jockey on the head and thought of Candy. Their conversation last night had been a little rocky. In fact, Cheri would have to classify it as an argument, a rarity for the two of them.

She told Candy that she'd gone ahead and had her lawyer file her personal Chapter 7.

"I had to. Every day I feel like more of a hypocrite," she'd told her best friend.

Candy sighed. "So are you going to tell everyone?"

"I don't know. But here I am, running a newspaper dedicated to finding out the ugly truth behind a murder and I'm pretending to be something I'm not. I'm digging to expose decades of employee theft and I'm a walking, talking lie myself!"

"Then just tell everybody."

"But it's too late."

"Then don't tell them."

"But I can't live with myself!"

Candy sighed louder at that point. "Listen, if it's killing you, then you have no choice but to tell everyone. Besides, the world is going to catch up with you soon anyway. You're the publisher of a small newspaper in North Carolina, not living in a cave in Botswana. You're still on the grid. And now that you've filed, it's public record."

"But what about your mom?"

"Oh, the hell with it," Candy said. "If she finds out I lost her nest egg, then she finds out. She was going to have to know sooner or later. I can't protect myself if it hurts you."

"Maybe I should just tell J.J. Honestly, that's what bothers me the most. I've been sleeping with him almost every night. I'm falling in love with him—no, I *am* in love with him, Candy. No doubt about it. He deserves to know. I love that man."

That was when Cheri thought the call had been dropped from Candy's new pay-as-you-go cell phone. "Hello? Candy? Can you hear me?"

"Uh, yeah."

"What?"

"You just said you're in love with J.J. You've been there a grand total of two weeks!"

"I know."

"Be careful," Candy said, her voice suddenly stern. "J.J. and Bigler have a lot in common."

"Meaning?"

"Well, they both look really charming from a distance, but once you get settled in, something always happens to make you wish you'd just kept on driving."

No, Cheri hadn't exactly hung up on her, but it had been a curt good-bye.

"Hello?" Cheri popped her head in the door and found Viv and Tanyalee all cozy on the sofa together, looking over a large sheet of paper. From where she stood, Cheri swore they were poring over some kind of seating chart.

A seating chart at a barbecue?

"Cheri!" Viv said, jumping up. "Come on in here! I'll get you some sweet tea!"

"No, no, that's okay, Aunt Viv." For once Cheri

managed to stop the pink tornado from spinning out of the parlor and into the kitchen. Cheri put her hands on Viv's shoulders. "I can just stay a minute. Really. Just sit down."

Viv frowned a little but took her seat.

"Hey, Tanyalee."

"It's my brilliant sister!" She jumped from the couch and came at her with such enthusiasm that Cheri felt compelled to check for sharp objects. "So good to see you!" Tanyalee planted a kiss on her cheek and looked her in the eye.

Her sister looked positively manic. Her chignon was lovely as usual, but she was one hair comb shy of a matched set. Lucky for her, Cheri had the other tucked safely in her purse.

"Oh, this is gonna be such a fabulous party!" Tanyalee said. "We're gonna have a live band and Wim's gonna trailer his party boat out to the lake so we'll have that, too. Have you ever seen Wim's pontoon boat? It is just fabulous!"

Cheri froze where she stood. Why the sudden change in Tanyalee's demeanor? Was she medicated? No longer medicated? Thrilled to have gotten away with breaking and entering? Or was this an act for Viv? Regardless, it was godawful embarrassing to witness.

Suddenly, Cheri had a stab of sympathy for Tanyalee. Maybe there was something wrong with her and, as her sister, it was her responsibility to get her help.

The sympathy was fleeting.

"We have tables of eight, which is turning out to be a little tricky with seating for the head table," Tanyalee said.

"Why is there a head table?" Cheri asked. "Why is there seating at all? I thought this was a casual barbecue."

"Oh, it is," Viv said. "But Taffy and I were thinking that with the mayor coming and so many older people invited, we had to have tables and chairs, so it just kind of grew from there."

"Please don't call me that," Tanyalee snapped.

Aunt Viv's mouth fell open, then closed tightly. She nodded. "Well, now."

"You know I don't like that name, Aunt Viv." Tanyalee caught herself and continued on in a much sweeter tone of voice. "Now, I've asked you about a million times to stop calling me that, right?"

Aunt Viv shrugged, obviously hurt.

Cheri dared look over at Tanyalee. Her smile was way too cheerful and her eyes far too bright for the topic at hand. She then clapped her hands with an unnatural amount of enthusiasm.

"So," Tanyalee said. "Y'all will be over here at the table *next* to the head table." She pointed to the chart with a long, frosty fingernail.

"Hmm," Cheri said, trying not to laugh at the idea that the new publisher—one of the intended honorees of this *shindig*—would be seated at the kiddie table. "You can put me wherever you'd like, Tanyalee. I'll probably be mingling and running back and forth from the kitchen most of the time anyway."

"We have caterers," she said.

"Huh?" That was news to Cheri. She looked at Aunt Viv and frowned. "I thought Tater Wayne was cookin' up a mess of pork ribs."

"Oh, he is," Viv said. "But we're having all the extras catered."

Cheri's head began to spin. When had Aunt Viv ever allowed anyone else to cook for her? Granddaddy wasn't kidding when he said he'd be broke after this affair.

"Well, this all sounds great. Glad to know you two have everything under control."

"Of course we do!" Tanyalee said, an abnormal amount of giddiness in her voice. "We know how busy you are juggling your publisher duties with all your business dealings down in Florida. Y'all have plenty on your plate without having to bother with this little ole party."

Cheri nodded. She kissed Aunt Viv on the cheek. Then she stuck her hand inside her bag and pulled out the comb.

"You left this at my place when you popped in the other night," she said, tossing it onto the seating chart. "Y'all have a good day."

"I'm kidnapping you."

Cheri looked up from the figures she'd just received from Gladys and tried to shift her focus to J.J.

"What did you say?"

"Kid. Nap. Ing. *You.*"

She laughed.

"We're playing hooky." J.J. held out his hand and scanned the newsroom behind him as if to be sure no one had heard of his secret plans. "But this is a limited-time offer, so you'd best be getting a move on."

Cheri looked at the jumble of papers spread all over her desk and knew that she needed a break. In fact, if she didn't take one, she might just scream.

Besides, this latest news was so bad she'd best approach it with a clear head. She grabbed her purse. "Where you taking me?"

"No questions. Hurry."

J.J. grabbed her hand and pulled her through the newsroom. They got out to the employee parking lot and J.J. opened the passenger door of his truck for her, but Cheri couldn't help but notice what he'd stashed in the truck bed. It made her heart soar.

"Are you serious?"

"Serious as a heart attack—which is what we're both going to have if we don't slow down for a few hours. Boss's orders." He closed her door and ran around to the driver's side.

"But I'm the boss," Cheri said

"I'm talking a higher authority here." J.J. started the engine and swung the pickup onto Main Street. Cheri figured they were headed up Randall Road and their usual put-in place.

"I've never heard you talk about God," she said.

J.J. tipped his head back and roared. She enjoyed the view—his thick black hair blowing back from his face in the open window, his Adam's apple dancing. Truly, when Jefferson Jackson DeCourcy smiled and laughed it was as if everything else in the world fell away, leaving just happiness and joy. She loved him something awful.

"God? Hell, no. I'm talking about *Gladys*. She said you'd been grumpy the last few days and that today was bound to be the worst yet."

"Hmph," Cheri said. Of course Gladys would want her out of the office today—those reports she'd just handed her were dire. Cheri had promised that no one at the *Bugle* would lose their jobs this month, and now, somehow, she'd have to keep her word.

The only way she saw to do it was to stop paying somebody.

That somebody was going to be herself.

"Want to talk about it?"

"No, I do not," she said, closing her eyes against the wind as they climbed the hill. "I'm sick of talking about serious shit. I'm in the mood for something else entirely."

"Oh, yeah?"

"Yeah." She turned to look at J.J., and found him all smiles and sweet, sexy eyes. Of course he knew what she was about to say, so she paused for effect, then shouted out, "I'm in the mood for . . ."

"The tube!" they hollered in unison.

"Perfect!" Gladys stepped back and examined the handiwork of the maintenance staff. Every frame was perfectly level and perfectly spaced, just the way J.J. had wanted it, and seeing the Newberry history displayed like this was almost like seeing the history of her own life.

She'd been there for Garland, for Loyal, for Garland again, and now Cheri. the *Bugle* had been her life, her love.

Looking at all those photos on the wall like this—set off so pretty in the bright white frames J.J. had chosen—it was enough to make an old broad tear up, it truly was.

Gladys straightened the brass nameplate one last

time before she turned off the lights and closed the door to the publisher's office.

Cheri looked like an angel over there in her inner tube, all loose and relaxed in the bikini top and cutoff shorts he'd grabbed from her dresser, limbs askew, a Miller Lite dangling from her fingertips as it cooled in the gentle current of Little Pigeon Creek.

Sure, there may have been men in her life down in Miami and Tampa who knew how to show her a good time—fancy meals and champagne and sparkly gifts— but J.J. had no doubt that this date beat them all to hell.

Cheri opened her eyes and smiled at him. She parted her lips to speak but seemed to decide it was too much effort, so she just closed her eyes again and let her head fall back against the old patched-up Michelin forty-six-incher.

The sun itself was his sparkly gift to her today.

And what a perfect day it was. In the mid-eighties already, not a cloud in the sky, the light dappled by miles of overhanging trees. J.J. reached behind him into his specially designed beverage cooler and cracked open a fresh one.

"That right there is beautiful music," he said.

Cheri laughed dreamily. "Damn, this is awesome, Jay."

"Yep," he said, taking a swig.

"You did arrange for someone to pick us up down-river, right?"

"Of course I did! You think I'm some kind of ama-teur?" J.J. retrieved his BlackBerry from its waterproof holder and called Turner. "Can you swing down to the

Little Pigeon basin off the state highway and pick us up in about two hours?"

When he completed the call he found Cheri staring at him in amusement.

He shrugged. "I got so excited about kidnapping you that I forgot a few details."

She shook her head. "Can I tell you something?"

"Anything." He paddled closer to her so he could reach out with his non-beer hand and mesh his fingers with hers.

"I've never known a man who could play like you."

J.J. wasn't sure what she meant by that, but he was counting on it being a good thing.

"What I mean is that you're just damn goofy, Jefferson Jackson. You're playful. You can just be fun—and I've never found that kind of playfulness in any other man I've ever dated."

J.J. hated to ask, but now was the time.

"How many was that?"

Cheri shrugged and took a sip, spilling a little down into her cleavage. Not that he minded. "Not so many. At first, they were older, a lot older. I thought it made me look more mature if I was dating a man in his forties when I was twenty-five. It didn't hurt with the promotions, either."

"Right."

"But my last boyfriend—Evan—he was younger than me, and the most uptight, materialistic, shallow man I've ever come within arm's distance of."

"Sounds like a real winner."

Cheri shook her head and suddenly looked solemn. "I think I chose him like I'd choose a nice watch—I wanted people to see that I accessorized myself with only the most beautiful and expensive things."

"Did Evan know that?"

Cheri laughed. "Of course he did—he chose me for the same reason. But—" She looked down at their intertwined hands. "I was lost back then. I'd forgotten what it was like to be myself. To be a kind and real person."

"Something must have happened to change that. You're not like that now."

Cheri's eyes locked with his. This was it, he knew. She was going to tell him the truth, and God, how relieved he was. All this love he felt for her needed a side dish of honesty to feel like a complete meal to him, and besides, he knew she'd have to shed her façade before she'd ever consider staying in Bigler.

Cheri smiled softly. "I came back home—to you."

J.J. raised her hand to his lips to hide his disappointment. Clearly, she'd tell him the whole story when she was damn good and ready, and not a moment sooner.

Chapter 24

It took about forty minutes for Cheri to reach the small dirt road in Maggie Valley where Carlotta Smoot McCoy lived. Since she'd already passed plenty of shacks and trailer homes on the way, she should have been prepared for the spectacle of Carlotta's living conditions.

She wasn't.

Cheri slowed the pimpmobile to a crawl, swallowing hard, looking around at the scene. Mimi Grayson had prepped her for the interview. In addition to outfitting Cheri with a crisp new reporter's notebook and a new pen, she'd explained that Carlotta had been a widow for twenty-plus years and that her kids were nowhere to be found.

It certainly showed.

The property was strewn with gutted cars and pickups of every description, discarded appliances, tire rims, bed frames, and mounds of garbage obviously picked through by wild critters. At the center of it all was an orange-and-yellow striped trailer home that might have been at the height of double-wide fashion a few decades ago, but was now a pile of sagging vinyl and rusted metal, and, she suspected, unfit for human habitation.

In comparison to this dump, the cottage on Newberry Lake was gracious Southern luxury, and Cheri's former Harbour Island home had been the freakin' Biltmore Estate.

The screen door opened, and the small lady Cheri had seen at Wim's construction site two weeks ago appeared, hand on hip. Several dogs began barking and growling behind Carlotta, trying to jockey for a spot at the door and a shot at the trespasser.

Cheri exited the car and cautiously approached the trailer. "Good afternoon, Ms. McCoy. I'm—"

"Garland's oldest granddaughter. I know who you are."

Cheri tried to smile, but knew she probably looked as uncomfortable as she felt. Despite the invitation, Mimi had warned her not to expect a warm welcome. She hadn't been joking.

Shouting over the dogs, Cheri said, "Is this a good time? I would have called ahead but you don't have a phone!"

Carlotta kicked at the dogs and stepped outside on the tiny metal stoop, closing the door behind her, which muffled the racket. She took a moment to look Cheri up and down.

She must look ridiculous to this woman, Cheri realized. Her hair was perfectly styled and she'd worn a pair of sleek black trousers, boots, and a tailored silk blouse—an outfit Cheri had considered an embarrass-

ingly off-the-rack budget ensemble back in Tampa.
Carlotta wore a dirty and torn housedress. Her collar-
bones jutted out from her wrinkled skin. Her legs were
thin as twigs, her wrists large knots of bone under
wasted flesh. The lady looked like she was quite ill, or
just plain starving.

"I got damn little to say to you newspaper people
after all this time, but if you're suddenly gonna decide
to do your job, I won't stand in your way."

Cheri nodded, trying to appear polite and professional when she wanted to scream—how was it that
human beings were left to rot like this in Cataloochee
County? Of course she knew there was hunger in Ap-
palachia, like everywhere on earth, but she'd never
thought much about it. She'd never let herself.

She looked around nervously, seeing nothing but
poverty and decay, and Cheri had to wonder, how had
she let herself get swallowed up in crap that didn't
really matter? For so long? The shoes, the cars, the collection of man-accessories she'd called lovers? And after
it all disappeared, why had it been so easy to wallow in
a puddle of self-pity and shame? At the time, Cheri had
seen the Tampa studio apartment and the temp jobs as
deprivation, when she'd still had a clean and safe place
to live, a best friend, nice clothes, and food. Clearly, the
lady scowling down at her from her trailer doorway
would have been grateful for a scrap of that life.

How had she ever allowed herself to get so fucked up?

"Yes, well, forgive me if it seems like an invasion of
your privacy, but I have a question about Barbara Jean's
personal life before she disappeared."

Carlotta looked disgusted. "I said I'd give y'all a quote about my sister being a decent and lovely young woman—I ain't airing out her dirty laundry. If that's all y'all want, you can turn that pink car right around and head back to town."

Cheri looked around for somewhere to sit, and motioned to a still mostly intact picnic table. "Do you mind if we sit for a spell? It's important."

Carlotta scowled at her, but gingerly stepped down from the stoop and headed to the table. Coming closer, Cheri could see her shins were covered in scabs and her nails were yellow and broken.

"So yer the one who got all rich and fancy down in Florida, right?" Carlotta sat down across from Cheri and produced a grin. That's when she saw that the woman had about four teeth left in her head.

"Uh, yes," Cheri answered her. "I was an accountant and then went into real estate."

"But you're stayin' in Bigler now?"

Cheri pulled the new reporter's notebook from her bag and flipped it open. "I'm not sure about my plans yet, Ms. McCoy." She clicked on her pen. "Now, I understand you were willing to talk to me and I appreciate that very much. I have a couple specific things I'd like to ask you."

She shook her head and looked around the land. Granted, it was a lovely natural setting, in a fertile dip in the foothills, surrounded by trees, the mountains hovering just to the west, but Cheri wondered if the current state of things made Carlotta sad. She hoped the old lady at least had the comfort of good memories.

"This place was always a hole. Once he got ahold of

this land, my husband became a lazy good-for-nuthin'
who never lifted a finger to feed his family. He only
lifted his hand to—" Carlotta paused. "Anyway, my
three sons grew up to be just like their daddy, sad to
say. One's in prison down in Charlotte now. Twenty-
five to life. "

"Oh," Cheri said. *So much for that fantasy.* "So, Ms.
McCoy, about Barbara Jean. Do you know if she was
seeing a man at the time of her death?"

Carlotta turned her head slowly and examined Cheri
again. "I can't say."

"All right, well, the reason I ask is that now that the
police are sure they've found her, they are exploring
who might be responsible for her murder."

Carlotta frowned. "Honey, I'm old and poor—I ain't
soft in the head. I know what the police are lookin' to
do. All of 'em been out here enough times—the FBI,
the CIA, whatever they are."

Cheri felt frustrated. Her first foray into reporting
wasn't going so great. And she was about to ask a question that was none of her business, but the issue was so
glaringly obvious she couldn't stop herself.

"Why in the world don't you sell this property?"
Cheri spat out. "It must be worth a fortune, Ms. McCoy.
You could get yourself a little place in town, have a very
comfortable life, instead of living out here like this."

Carlotta's mouth tightened and her eyes went wide.
"Don't ask me any more about that. It's none of your
goddamn business. It's nobody's business. If you bring
it up again, I'll throw you off this land."

Cheri leaned back, surprised by the vitriol of her
response. She knew how people around here felt about

land that had belonged to their families for generations, but Carlotta had just said her husband bought this property. So why was she so attached?

"Of course. Forgive me," Cheri said. "J.J. DeCourcy said you'd read my note and agreed to be interviewed, but maybe there was a misunderstanding. I'll go ahead and leave."

That's when Carlotta chuckled. "Lord-a-mighty, Miss Newberry. You sure are a stuffy one, ain't ya? I did say I'd talk to you, but that's because I knowed you have a sister. Everybody around here's heard about the two baby girls that got left alone in the world back when your mama and daddy died. I thought about you girls when I saw your sister's engagement announcement in the *Bugle* the other day."

Cheri straightened. "I see."

"That's why I said I'd talk to you. I figured you'd understand how bad it hurt to lose my Barbara Jean."

Cheri sat frozen on the rickety picnic table bench, unsure how to respond. But Carlotta was waiting. "Yes, Tanyalee is two years younger than I am."

"I know she's had trouble with the law, but did you'uns get along when you was little? Me and Barbara Jean was like Frick and Frack, I'll tell ya. She was my big sister, like you are to Tanyalee, and I loved her with every bit of my heart. We lived outside of town, so she was also my playmate, my friend. I looked up to her. I wanted to be just like her."

Cheri tried to smile when what she really wanted to do was cry. Obviously, the Newberry girls had little in common with the Smoot sisters. Tanyalee never loved

Cheri, or looked up to her, or wanted to be like her. Cheri never considered Tanyalee a playmate or friend. "How lovely for you," was Cheri's response.

Carlotta shrugged. "I was sixteen when she up and went missing. I never finished school, and got myself married a few weeks after she disappeared. Never had a friend like her since."

"She was very beautiful," Cheri offered, sensing that Carlotta might be thawing a little. "I remember as a kid thinking about her and what she had planned for herself, how she wanted to move to the big city. I sort of identified with her."

The old lady nodded. "She had big plans, that was for sure. Wanted to be in the pictures. But she shoulda got out while she had the chance."

"What do you mean?"

"I mean she shoulda finished school and left instead of . . ." Carlotta stopped herself, looked at Cheri briefly, and dragged her eyes away. She almost looked ashamed.

"Instead of what?"

Carlotta shook her head. "Oh, you know how girls can fall for fancy-talkin' fellas. I suppose you could say she was a bit of a wild child."

Cheri smiled. "My aunt Viv was one of those, I hear."

Carlotta's head snapped around. She nodded, lips curled. It was only then that Cheri saw a hint of Barbara Jean's beauty in her little sister. "She was older than us, but yes, we all knew about Vivienne Newberry's *rep-yoo-tay-shun,* as they called it back then."

Cheri laughed, and before she knew it, she'd laid her

hand on Carlotta's, and the old lady was laughing, too. But not three seconds passed before Carlotta removed her hand and went silent.

"That's all I can say today." She got up from the picnic table.

"But—"

"Good-bye, Miss Newberry. I enjoyed the visit."

Cheri scrambled to her feet and followed her toward the trailer, the dogs renewing their racket. She had to scream over the noise again. "But I thought you were willing to tell me something, Carlotta! I thought you were willing to help us!"

"Help you?" She wheeled around, her eyes suddenly angry. "Help you make money off my dead sister's bones? I don't see that happening, no, I do not. Y'all should've did yer job the first time around." She reached for the trailer's door handle.

"Please—"

Carlotta Smoot McCoy looked over her shoulder. Her face was not kind. Her voice trembled. "This county is rotten to the core, girl. Look around you." She waved a skinny arm over her property. "All these fancy new houses they're puttin' up look nice, but it's all rotten underneath. Same for all this beautiful land everywhere the eye can see!"

Cheri took a step back.

Carlotta pointed a spindly finger down at her. "Believe me, Miss Newberry, anything good and true in this town is buried under a mess of thick, black mud, just like my pretty, pretty sister."

She slipped inside the door, leaving Cheri standing

with her mouth open, confusion the only thing she'd be taking back to the newsroom.

The new reporter's notebook and pen? She needn't have bothered.

"Are you absolutely certain?" Cheri scribbled on her legal pad and circled the information about ten times while the Cataloochee County clerk double-checked the information.

"I'm sure," she said. "On July 1, 1964, Wesley McCoy purchased the thirty-two-point-six acres in Maggie Valley from Winston Wimbley for a sum of ten dollars, thereby owning it outright. Everything is in order."

"But . . ." At the risk of sounding like a dolt, Cheri just had to ask again. "Ten dollars? For that much land? Wimbley basically gave it away."

The clerk sighed, clearly at the end of her patience. She'd already given Cheri about ten minutes of her time and the office sounded terribly busy. "Ms. Newberry, I can only tell you what the land records show—Mr. Wesley McCoy paid Sheriff Wimbley ten dollars. The sale was duly recorded and the property hasn't changed hands since."

"Who owned it before Wimbley?"

"Well, let's see . . . it looks like the land had been in the Wimbley family for at least a hundred years prior. I have a property tax notation here from right after the War of Northern Aggression."

"So, Winston Wimbley is referred to as 'sheriff' on the deed transfer? And the sheriff gave away his family's land to McCoy for almost nothing?"

"Look, Miss Newberry, hill people haven't always done business like the rich and famous down in Florida. Transactions haven't always been straight dollars and cents. Sometimes a deal includes barter or services rendered."

Cheri didn't miss the swipe. "I understand, but I had Mimi Grayson, one of my reporters, check into Wesley McCoy, and he had no relationship with Sheriff Wimbley that we could find. He worked on the line at the tannery and got fired for chronic lateness. What kind of services could he possibly have offered to—"

"I have no idea," she snapped. "And just so you know, Mimi Grayson used to date my son back in school and broke his heart, so if y'all be needing any additional information, our property records are available for public inspection from nine A.M. to five P.M., Monday through Friday. Take care, now."

Click.

Cheri hung up the phone and shook her head. Why would Sheriff Wimbley give such a valuable gift to McCoy? And just weeks after McCoy's sister-in-law up and disappeared? Was it a wedding gift? A bribe? That Maggie Valley acreage wasn't just another piece of property Wimbley had bought and sold. In fact—Cheri flipped through her notes to be sure she was right—Wimbley hadn't even started buying and selling land until late 1965.

What the *hell* was going on here?

Cheri fell against the back of her chair. The fine hairs on the back of her neck suddenly stood erect, electrified with a very ugly thought.

What had Carlotta said? *"Y'all should've did yer job*

the first time around . . . this county is rotten to the core . . . look around you."

Cheri stood. She walked to the window. *The money. Follow the money.* Her eyes wandered to the Smokies, a melancholy shade of gray today, and she thought . . . that Maggie Valley land was a payoff. McCoy knew something about the sheriff that Wimbley didn't want spread around, something terrible enough that he'd give away his family legacy in exchange for McCoy's silence. The connecting thread was Barbara Jean. It had to be.

" . . . anything good and true in this town is buried under a mess of thick, black mud . . . like my pretty, pretty sister."

Cheri began to pace the publisher's office, her head spinning. Was it possible that everything was somehow connected, part of the same giant, dirty lie that started with Barbara Jean getting thrown into the lake?

Here's what she knew for sure.

Purnell started stealing money from Granddaddy right after Barbara Jean went missing.

Wimbley paid off McCoy to keep him quiet.

Wimbley directed the search for Barbara Jean's car, but the police managed to miss it after four drags of the lake.

A year after the disappearance, Wimbley suddenly had enough money to start buying and selling land from Asheville to the Tennessee line.

When Daddy became publisher, he found something wrong with the *Bugle*'s accounting. He died before he could expose Purnell.

Or somebody killed him. Wimbley? *Purnell?*

Cheri suddenly had trouble breathing. "Oh, shit," she whispered aloud. "Oh, shit. Oh, shit."

She spun around and stared at her family photos. A wedding. Children. A family. Normal—before it was torn apart from the outside. It did not happen the other way around. *It was not my fault.*

Just then, Gladys poked her head in the door to the publisher's office. "I'm sorry, Cheri, but there's a gentleman on the phone who insists on speaking to you."

Cheri looked at her but didn't say anything.

"You all right, child? You look like you just saw a ghost!"

Cheri blinked. "I did. More than one, actually." She snatched her bag and notepad. "I'll be out for the rest of the day."

"What should I tell the man on the phone?"

Cheri shook her head to clear her thoughts. "I'm sorry, who did you say it was? Where was he calling from?"

"He wouldn't give a name but he sounded like a foreigner. His number came up as *Incomplete Data.*"

Cheri rubbed her forehead. Something about that turn of phrase made her stomach flip, but she didn't have time to dwell on it. There was something really important she needed to ask Gladys.

"You said you remembered being here in the newsroom the day Barbara Jean disappeared."

Gladys frowned so hard her penciled-in brows formed a black vee over her face. "Yeah. I was here."

"Okay, good." Cheri knew she couldn't make Gladys feel like she was ratting out her boss of nearly fifty years. She was loyal to Purnell, that much had always been obvious.

"Tell me, as quickly as you can, what you saw."

She cocked her head. "When?"

"That day! That day Barbara Jean went missing!"

Gladys shrugged. "No need to shout. Well, it was crazier than a run-over dog in here, is all, with people hollerin' at each other and the phones ringing and the typewriters bangin'. Garland was shouting out assignments to everybody left and right."

"I see. And everyone was at work as usual?"

"What do you mean?"

"Oh, I'm just curious about how the paper operated back then, you know, whether people outside of news operations would come to work in a time of crisis." Cheri nearly rolled her eyes at how stupid she must sound.

Gladys shook her head. "I can't see what that has to do with the price of eggs, but as far as I remember, the business end ran same as always that day. Purnell was at his desk. Chester Wollard was at the circulation desk. Everybody was here as far as I could tell."

"Were there any visitors to the newsroom?"

Gladys nodded. "Well, I remember Sheriff Wimbley came in right early. We exchanged pleasantries."

"He went to see Granddaddy?"

"Yeah, but he stopped off at Purnell's office first—they were all close since school you know, the three of them, Garland, Purnell, and Winston."

Cheri smiled, trying to hide the panic now rising to high tide inside her. "Um, Gladys? Was there anything unusual about Purnell that morning? Anything you might remember?"

"Huh," she said, shaking her head. "Nothing out of the ordinary. He was a little hungover and he'd cut himself shaving again. I remember because he asked me if I had a Band-Aid and I was rooting through the first-aid kit when someone came by and told him about Barbara Jean."

"What did he do?"

"Nothing. He was horrified like all of us and walked away without taking the bandage, went into his office and shut the door."

"Thank you."

"That's it?" Gladys stood with her hands open at her sides.

"Yes. I appreciate your help."

"But what about the caller?"

"Take a message, please," Cheri said, walking around Gladys and into the newsroom.

"But what do I tell him?"

"Anything you want."

"Well, all right," she said with a shrug. "You're the boss."

Chapter 25

When Cheri arrived at the lake house, Tater Wayne was busy setting up the barbecue, a huge barrel-shaped contraption with a decorative sheet-metal pig snout and ears at one end and a curly metal tail at the other. The rental people were unloading tables and chairs on the lawn. The liquor store deliverymen were rolling the kegs up onto the porch.

It suddenly occurred to her that two hundred people would be here by noon tomorrow. How was she supposed to throw a party and deal with all this crap at the same time?

Cheri saw Turner's SUV and J.J.'s pickup parked in the grass near the dock. She could see the two men standing in conversation by the water, and she ran toward them.

"Whoa!" J.J. said, laughing as she raced their way. The smiles they'd had on their faces faded fast—she must have looked as shell-shocked as she felt.

"Are you all right?" J.J. caught her as she came to a stop at the dock edge.

Cheri shook her head. "No. Yes. I'm fine." She planted a quick kiss on his lips, then looked to Turner. "Did you ever wonder how Sheriff Wimbley got the money to start his real estate business?"

Turner's hazel eyes immediately lost their friendly sparkle. It was as if a shade had just been pulled down. "Why do you ask, Cheri?"

"I mean, where did Wimbley suddenly get a bunch of cash to go out buying up land and making real estate deals in 1965? He couldn't have made a lot of money as sheriff, right?"

"Nope," Turner said. "The pay sucked just as bad back then as it does now."

"So where did he get the money?"

Cheri heard J.J. chuckle. She turned to him.

"You see where I'm going with this?" she asked him.

J.J. nodded.

"No," Turner said. "Fill me in."

"She's following the money," J.J. said. "All the cash missing from the *Bugle*—"

"Have you examined the report I gave you?"

"Yes," Turner said, his voice clipped. "I sent it on to the district attorney. You've definitely got something."

Cheri laughed. "No—*you've* got something, Sheriff! Don't you see? All the money Purnell stole went to Wimbley! Wimbley must have been blackmailing Purnell. Do you think it's possible Purnell has gone all this time thinking he killed Barbara Jean, and that's why he was paying Wimbley?"

"Still paying," J.J. added.

Turner didn't say anything, only stared at her, and

Cheri worried he didn't believe her hypothesis. But then he said, "Go on."

"All right." She took a breath. She was going for it. "Here's the real question. Have you found any evidence—anything at all—that would indicate Sheriff Wimbley made sure the car was never found? Have you found anything tying Wimbley to Barbara Jean's actual murder? If you have, then all the pieces fit."

Turner's usually handsome and friendly face pulled into a blank mask. It was a transformation both startling and fascinating to watch.

"Wh-whaaat?" J.J. managed to get out.

Turner stayed silent.

"Yeah. See, after Barbara Jean disappeared, Wimbley gave his family's Maggie Valley land to the boyfriend of Barbara's little sister, a slacker named Wesley McCoy, who promptly married the girl. Why would Wimbley do that, unless he was paying McCoy off for something? Maybe to make sure Barbara Jean's sister never pushed for answers in the case or went above his head to get justice?"

"Hold up, sugar," J.J. said. "You're swinging mighty wide here."

"Or not." Turner's eyes flashed at J.J. "Listen, De-Courcy, you can't use—"

"No." J.J. shook his head with conviction. "There is no way in hell that whatever you're about to say is off the record."

Turner scrunched up his lips. "Fair enough. Then I have no comment due to the fact that this is an ongoing federal homicide investigation."

"Shee-it!"

"But thank you, Cheri." Turner reached out and gave her a good squeeze and kiss on the cheek. "If things don't work out over at the *Bugle* you can come to work for me."

"Halliday!"

Turner waved over his shoulder and started down the dock, but didn't look back.

"Fine!" J.J. called out. "We'll run what we got and we'll get our own comment from the FBI!"

Turner looked over his shoulder and winked at him. "It's a free country, DeCourcy."

J.J. began chuckling.

"What?"

"Oh, that was Turner's way of telling you that you got the story right."

"*We* got it right."

J.J. smiled down at her, the water shining in his dark eyes. "I think *we* need to make a run out to Maggie Valley."

Cheri agreed, but told him to wait a moment. There was something she wanted to bring along.

Carlotta Smoot McCoy greeted them halfway down her drive, legs spread wide, arms crossed over her chest. She was already shaking her head.

"I just shooed the sheriff and those snooty federal people away," she told them, scowling. "You think I got anything better to say to you? You might as well just stay in your pickup and turn right on around."

"Let me handle this," Cheri said to J.J.

She exited the truck, bringing the box with her. "You got a freezer, Carlotta?"

The lady nearly growled at her.

Cheri looked up at the power lines running along the lane. "You got the electric turned on out here?"

"Of course I do!" she said. "I ain't country trash!"

"Fine. Let's walk to your trailer. I've got some things to put in your freezer."

Carlotta's eyes darted to the box in Cheri's hands and then to her face. "I don't take charity."

Cheri laughed. "Have you ever sat down to supper with Vivienne Newberry?"

Carlotta nodded. "Yes, but it was a long, long time ago. She's one hell of a cook."

"And she cooks a hell of a lot of food—too much." Cheri kept walking and Carlotta kept pace. "Look, I won't beat around the bush with you, Ms. McCoy. I'm stinkin' rich. I've got everything a person could want. I've frittered away so much it would make your head spin. You, however, are living as poorly as anyone I've ever seen. So, in this box there's lots of food and some nice clothes—you're probably about my size when you're not malnourished—so this stuff is for you."

Cheri kept her eyes looking straight ahead and didn't slow her walk.

"What in the name of—"

"Don't argue with me, Ms. McCoy. Don't tell me you don't need help, at least for the time being, because that would be a bunch of bullshit."

They'd reached the trailer. Cheri put the box on the metal stoop. The woman's face was stoic as stone. "Oh, and I brought this for you."

Cheri reached in the box and pulled out the black-and-white photograph of Barbara Jean the newspaper had kept filed away for more than forty years. Cheri had put a nice frame around it.

Carlotta frowned but reached out for it.

"We scan all pictures digitally now, so we don't need the original. I thought it was only right to return it."

"I'm so grateful, Miss Newberry." The words came out in a barely audible whisper.

"I don't deserve your gratitude. You've been through a lot, probably more than anyone will ever know. And you were right—the *Bugle* failed you. We didn't do our job. We didn't dig deep enough to find out what happened to your sister, even when the answers were right in front of us."

Carlotta's jaw dropped.

Cheri smiled. "But we're getting there."

Her eyes bugged out. "You are?"

Cheri nodded. "Listen, Ms. McCoy, we know Sheriff Wimbley sold this land to your husband for a pittance, probably to keep him quiet. We think the sheriff had something to do with Barbara Jean's death or at least had a hand in covering it up."

Carlotta swallowed hard.

"It's all about to come out, Ms. McCoy. It's okay if there's something you want people to know about Barbara Jean, or the circumstances surrounding her disappearance. Your husband is dead. Sheriff Wimbley is dead. Nobody can hurt you or take this land from you. I checked, and you own it outright, so it's yours to sell or live on as you choose. You're a wealthy woman."

She blinked. "I am?"

"Absolutely."

"I gotta sit." Carlotta's knees buckled as her little

rump hit one of the metal stairs. Her body began to twitch. Then she began to cry. She grabbed Cheri's hand and looked up at her. "Wimbley told us we'd lose our land and he'd make the rest of us disappear too if we ever raised a fuss about Barbara Jean."

Cheri sighed. Wimbley had been such a bastard.

"He always reminded us that he owned us and his son would own us after he was gone. You see, Barbara Jean . . ." Carlotta shook her head, the tears streaming down her face. "She told me once that she was running with Wimbley and his friend Purnell Lawson at the *Bugle*. I knowed they did something to her. But I always figured if the law *and* the newspaper don't want something to come out in this town, it ain't never coming out. *Never.*"

Cheri put a hand on her shoulder. "I'm sorry it's taken so long."

Carlotta clutched the framed photo of her sister to her belly and softly cried. "Can y'all give me a ride into town?" she asked. "I want a copy of my deed and then I'm going to talk to the police."

Chapter 26

"There isn't enough coffee in all of Cataloochee County to get me through this party." J.J. stumbled in the front door of the lake house, crumpled and red around the eyes.

Cheri handed him a mug anyway. "Then you'll have to rely on—what did you call it?—the adrenaline of a great news story. Just be careful who you go around kissing today."

J.J. pulled Cheri to him and kissed her hard. "We doubled our print run this morning, just like you told us to do, you sexy thang."

She giggled. "Good."

"The story is awesome. Mimi did a hell of a job helping me put everything together after you left late last night, plus she got the FBI to give us a statement—a real one. Cheri, I've got a huge surprise for you. Ready?"

She nodded.

J.J. reached behind him and pulled a rolled-up copy

of that morning's *Bugle* from his belt. Cheri opened it but could barely believe what she was seeing.

"He *did* do it." She glanced up at J.J. with her mouth ajar. "They found Wimbley's nightstick rammed between the dash and the gas pedal of Barbara Jean's car? Are you *kidding*?"

"Turner came through at the last minute—he got the FBI to give us what we needed in exchange for bringing Carlotta in to make a statement—and for all your research. Look at this—" J.J. tapped his finger on the third paragraph and read aloud. " 'An FBI spokesman said that Wimbley, a Bigler real estate developer who died in 2001, is now considered the only suspect in the murder. According to investigators, Ms. Smoot had a sexual relationship with Wimbley during his tenure as Cataloochee County sheriff, and forensic examination revealed that prior to her death, Ms. Smoot sustained a blunt force injury consistent with the shape and weight of the police baton found in the vehicle. However, officials said the forensic evidence indicated the injury was not fatal and that Ms. Smoot likely lost consciousness and drowned.' "

Cheri stared at him. "Poor Barbara Jean!" she whispered.

"At least we have answers now."

"What's Turner going to do about Wim?"

"Right," J.J. said, scrunching his nose as if the mere sound of the man's name left a bad smell. "We agreed to leave out any mention of the blackmail payments. The FBI is still investigating and the district attorney is putting together a case on Wim as we speak—they didn't want to spook him."

"He's supposed to show up here with Tanyalee today."

"This is sure gonna be interesting."

J.J. had no idea just how interesting. Cheri had been anxious all morning, knowing that she'd only cleaned up one part of the mess. She still had her suspicions about her parents' deaths to sort through, which would be no easy task with Purnell still in a coma. Plus, there was her own confession to make. She'd decided the ruse had gone on long enough—she would tell J.J. now and everyone else would find about her financial troubles back in Florida at the picnic. She'd just give them the facts, then ask to be forgiven for taking so long to come clean.

"What's up, sugar?" J.J. peered down into her face with concern. "Are you worried about Garland? How hard he's going to take the news about his old friends?"

"Oh, absolutely," Cheri said. "I plan to sit down and hash it out with him before the party, but it's more than that, really."

"You gonna tell me?"

She nodded. "I am. But first, there's something I want you to see."

Cheri relieved J.J. of his coffee cup, spun him around, and directed him out the front door. When they hit the porch they were greeted by a wall of dark clouds coming in over the lake.

"Uh-oh," Cheri said. "It wasn't supposed to rain today."

When J.J. didn't concur she found him checking out the kegs of beer sitting in ice on the porch.

"Nothing to fear. Where there's beer, there's a way."

Cheri tugged on J.J.'s hand and dragged him down

to the gravel drive and around to the ladder against the side of the house.

"Oh, boy," he said as he began to climb. "When did you make this discovery?"

"About an hour ago. I hadn't seen Artemis for a couple days, so I figured I better make sure she was all right."

J.J. peered up into the soffit and was greeted by a loud *"Chit! Chit!"* He immediately climbed back down, a huge smile on his face. "I counted five. You know, she's not going to like our party very much."

Cheri checked out the gathering clouds again, knowing that the squirrel was the least of her concerns.

Suddenly they heard the crunch of gravel beneath car tires and turned to see who was arriving so exasperatingly early. Cheri's money was on Aunt Viv when a strange rusted-out Chevrolet Caprice topped the hill and coasted toward the house. It almost looked like a junked police cruiser. Cheri squinted to get a better look.

"Anyone you know?" J.J. asked. "The Blues Brothers, perhaps?"

That was when Cheri got her first peek of blond curls and big, dark sunglasses. The horn began to blast. *"Candy?"* she yelled out. "No way! It's Candy!"

"Cherise! I made it! Am I too late for the party?"

For the first hour or so, the picnic was smooth sailing. There were several reasons for this, and Cheri was thankful for each and every one of them. Most importantly, the rain had held off. Also, the side dishes were plentiful, the keg taps worked, and Tater Wayne's pork ribs and barbecued chicken were so good everyone agreed they should be illegal. It didn't hurt that Jim Taggert's bluegrass group—the Sardonic Beaver Band— had the place rockin'.

Oh. And Tanyalee and Wim hadn't shown up.

"Where do you think they are?" Viv asked Cheri for the tenth time in as many minutes. "She's not answering her phone. I'm worried sick."

Cheri put an arm around Viv's pink blouse and squeezed her tight. "Please don't worry." She nodded toward Turner, standing with a few FBI agents and J.J. over by the hog-shaped barbecue. "If there'd been an accident or something, Turner would have already found out."

"All right," Viv said, wandering off.

Granddaddy was her main concern. He hadn't recovered from hearing everything Cheri had to tell him about Winston Wimbley and Purnell. It broke Cheri's heart to hear him blame himself. Before the guests arrived, he'd sat at the old oak table and cried his eyes out, saying that if he'd let his friends dupe him like that he had no right to call himself a newsman.

Thank God Candy had shown up when she did. Granddaddy had always adored her, and she had him laughing and reminiscing by the time the party was in full swing.

At one point, Candy took Cheri aside and whispered, "I just *knew* you needed me here for this. Was I right or what?"

And now, since everything seemed to be going

smoothly, Cheri decided she'd get herself a beer and mentally review everything she needed to say to J.J. before anything or anyone else could distract her.

I'm broke. I lost everything in the Florida real estate crash. Please forgive me for not telling you sooner, but I wasn't ready until now. I don't want there to be any more secrets between us. I'll tell you all the details after the party.

A quick peek confirmed that he was now standing on the dock with Turner and the FBI agents. J.J. must have felt her gaze on him because he turned at that moment, unleashing a wickedly sweet smile in her direction.

Cheri took a step toward him. It was going to feel so good to get this off her chest.

Then her BlackBerry rang.

"Incomplete Data" was on the line.

"No. No. No. This cannot be."

Tanyalee slapped a hand to her chest. She was having heart palpitations. She was going to die. She should call an ambulance.

It was all gone. Everything Wim had ever given her was gone.

Her two-carat marquise-cut diamond in its platinum setting. Her pearls. Her gold and silver. The emergency cash envelope she kept in her underwear drawer.

He even took his great-grandmother's hair combs! She loved those things! She hated that bastard!

He'd run all her credit cards through the shredder, which was her first clue that today would not be going as planned.

She'd woken up at eleven. She went into the bathroom and there it was, a little shredded bird's nest of plastic on the bathroom rug, tiny slivers of what had once been her lovely, smooth, gleaming American Express Gold Card, her Visa card and MasterCard, and her Home Depot card. He'd even shredded her Sears card! Really—like she'd suddenly have the urge to go out and purchase appliances?

Two hours had passed since that initial shock, but she was still sobbing. What had happened? Everything had been going so well—he was so happy with everything they'd discovered about Cheri! Where had this all *come* from?

And, oh no, she didn't even want to look in the attached garage, because if he'd taken her Mercedes, she might as well just hang herself.

Tanyalee looked in the bedroom mirror and swore that if she ever saw Wim Wimbley again, she'd put her hands around his spindly neck and cut off his air supply.

"Hello?"

A man's thickly accented voice said, "Is this Cherise Nancy Newberry?"

"Who's calling, please?"

"Am I speaking to Cherise Nancy Newberry, formerly of 4761 Belinda Lane in Harbour Island, Florida?"

"Who is this? How did you get this number?" Cheri abruptly turned away from the dock and swiveled her head around to look for Candy. She found her over by the barbecue hog chatting up Tater Wayne.

"Cheri!" Aunt Viv had just jumped up and down

waving a pink arm in the air. "Cheri, come on over here now. We're gonna have a little presentation!"

"I need to speak with Miss Newberry regarding a matter of—"

"Cheri! Come on now!"

"Listen, I can't talk at the moment, but I'm doing the best I can to deal with my debt situation. You have my word."

Viv began swinging a little metal noisemaker over her head.

"I've really got to go."

She shoved the BlackBerry in her pocket.

The douche bag had taken the singles from her wallet. He'd even taken the change from the kitchen junk drawer, her house key, her cell phone, her laptop, her iPod.

Feeling a lot like Bigler's version of Cindy Lou Who, Tanyalee walked down to the end of their lane and stuck out her thumb.

A couple of Bubbas in a beat-down pickup offered to take her anywhere she might be wanting to go. She politely declined. More than five minutes went by and no one else stopped for her. That just couldn't be. Then the Bubbas came back.

"Sure I can't change your mind, honey?"

Tanyalee sighed. "I am armed. Touch me and I'll shoot you."

The two men looked at each other and busted out with a rebel yell. "Well, we'll get along real well, then! Come on up here!"

Tanyalee felt herself being swung into the cab of the pickup. She immediately clamped her nose shut against the odor of what could only be a combination of chew and dead fish.

"Where's a pretty little bit like you goin' on a Saturday afternoon?"

Tanyalee was roughly deposited on the seat between the two men, whom she could now see were no older than twenty. "Take me up to Newberry Lake."

The driver hit the gas and let out another rebel yell, then handed her a Budweiser. The passenger stuck a pinch between his cheek and gum.

In an unexpected twist, Tanylaee briefly prayed she'd live to see her family again.

"Now, y'all know how much it means to me that you came out to spend your Saturday with us Newberrys." Granddaddy had decided that he and Cheri should hold court up on the top porch step, and since he'd already taken an inordinate number of trips to the keg tap, Cheri stood right next to him, basically propping him up. She tried to maintain her smile while her BlackBerry continued to vibrate in her pocket. She didn't bother to check who was on the line.

"As y'all know, we're celebrating the end of my fifty-three years as publisher of the *Bugle* on a significant day. On our front page this morning is—easily—the biggest piece of breaking news we've ever published."

Murmurs and whispers went through the crowd. Granddaddy held up an unsteady hand.

"Yes, we're all still in shock. It's going to take a while to come to terms with all this. To think that a man we counted as a friend and considered a linchpin in this community would do such—" He stopped, shook his head, and took a moment to regain his composure. Cheri squeezed his arm. Granddaddy winked at her before he continued.

"Now, here's what I want to tell ya'll—the *Bugle* will continue to cover this story. We will be there to give you every twist and turn in the news of the day. You can count on us to keep you informed."

Tater Wayne and Candy cheered from their posts over by the barbecue hog. The mayor clapped.

"And now I'd like to thank everyone involved, especially my managing editor, J.J. DeCourcy, and reporter Mimi Grayson, and everyone in graphics and page design and, of course, our law enforcement professionals, for all their hard work."

Granddaddy paused and looked down at Cheri with a smile. He started to lose his balance but she caught him. Her pocket buzzed again. She felt a bead of sweat roll down the center of her spine. She shot a look of alarm to J.J. who began to edge closer.

"I got this," she mouthed.

"But the real news today is my granddaughter, Cheri Newberry, who's come all the way up here—" he gestured so grandly that his plastic beer cup sloshed all over the porch steps—"from Florida and grabbed the bull by the horns, showing all of us that she's made of tough Newberry stuff! I can't tell you how proud she makes me."

Granddaddy kissed her.

"Maybe you should sit down," she whispered to him.

But he looked out at the crowd and chuckled. "Now, here's the ironic part! I never would've even thought of asking her to come back here if J.J. hadn't twisted my arm."

Cheri felt the first raindrop land right between her eyes. The crowd laughed uncomfortably. *What had he just said?*

She braced her leg to hold him up, and Granddaddy fell against the side of her body, which must have hit the speaker button on her BlackBerry, because suddenly, a man's voice rose from Cheri's pants pocket.

"*. . . and because your account is more than eight months overdue, we will now begin legal proceedings to—*"

Cheri fumbled around inside her pocket and hit the off button.

The partygoers had gone silent. They stared up at the porch.

"Who in heaven's name was that talking?" Aunt Viv asked.

"Oh, shit," was Candy's pronouncement.

Cheri looked nervously toward J.J., who had started to frown.

None of it slowed down Granddaddy, however.

"Yep," he continued waving wildly again, beer flying everywhere. "J.J. came to me one day and told me Cheri was flat busted—lost damn near everything down there in that housing . . . the housing . . . what the hell was it? A crash? And then he told me she was sellin' her underwear over the computer and staying in some flophouse and . . ."

"Oh-fuckin'-hell, no!" Candy called this out at exactly the right instant during the pause in Granddaddy's incoherent rant.

Cheri's face went up in flames. Slowly, ever so slowly, her swimming vision began to find its focus again, and it zeroed right in on J.J.

"So you like guns, do you?"

Tanyalee lifted her chin and stared straight ahead, estimating she had only another five minutes until they'd get to the lake. She didn't have the energy to deal with these idiots. And she was way too pissed off to be scared.

"Rifles? Pistols?" The driver wouldn't drop the subject. "You know, a lot of people assume women should carry around a little twenty-two, or a twenty-eight, or even a thirty-two. But I know better, see, 'cause that small shit ain't gonna stop two hundred fifty pounds of criminal element, if you get my drift."

"Right on!" his buddy said.

Tanyalee took a deep breath. She counted to three.

"Nope," the driver said, putting his hand on her knee. "I think the ladies would do best to keep a nice little thirty-eight snubnose in their panties. Heh, heh, heh."

"All right, that's it!" Tanyalee straightened up in the seat and looked from one Bubba to the other. "You have no idea who you're dealing with here, do you? I'm Tanyalee Marie Newberry, of the *Bugle* Newberrys, and my dipshit of a fiancé just took away my diamond engagement ring, my cell phone, and my credit cards, and I am about to spit nails I'm so angry, so if either of you fuck with me, you're going to live to regret it. Now, hand me another Budweiser and step on it. I'm late for a party."

There was no response. The only sound in the truck was the metallic *crack!* of a beer can opening.

"Why, thank you very much," Tanyalee said.

"Damn," the driver said, stepping on the gas.

"Yee-haw!" Bubba Number 2 yelled out the open window.

Wim stood up to his shins in the mud, Purnell's old revolver cradled in the palm of his hand. It was loaded. He'd checked. But he wasn't sure the thing would still fire.

Only one way to know for sure. He raised the gun to his head, removed the safety, and reviewed all the reasons why doing away with himself seemed like a good idea.

The Wimbley name was shit. That story on the front page this morning had ruined any hope he had of making this retirement project fly—or anything fly, ever again. Purnell had been right. Once the whole story came out they were going to take everything from him because of the blackmail. He might even be sent to jail, which hardly seemed fair. Wim had worked his ass off to keep Wimbley Real Estate going in this economy. He hadn't even started this mess! His father had, that black-hearted bastard.

Wim cocked the trigger, knowing that what bothered him the most was his father. The old prick had died without giving him a heads-up on the little problem he'd be leaving him. How hard would it have been to speak the words? *By the way, son, you might want to avoid digging in Paw Paw Lake. There's a dead girl in a car down there. My department-issued nightstick happens to be holding down the gas pedal and there's a nice baton-shaped hole in her skull, too, details that*

may cause you a bit of undue embarrassment in the
future, should anyone ever discover that car.

Prick.

Not to mention that Wim had been too embarrassed to
go to the bank, so he had only six-thousand and change
to his name at the moment, all of it from Tanyalee's secret stash. Once a thief, always a thief, he supposed.

Fucking Newberrys.

Wim took what would be his last breath. He pulled
the trigger and waited for the great black empty nothing to swallow him whole.

Click.

But he still stood there in the mud, seething at his father, Tanyalee—all the fucking Newberrys!—and still
breathing.

A big, fat raindrop hit him on the forehead. Well,
shee-it. If he was still breathing, he might as well kill
someone else instead of himself. Someone who really
deserved to die. He ran to the car, pulling his suit jacket
over his head to keep his hair dry. He wanted it to look
nice for his entrance at the barbecue.

Chapter 27

"Now, hold up," J.J. said, throwing his beer cup to the grass and jogging toward the steps. "Dammit, Garland, why did you have to go and do that?"

Granddaddy's face had fallen. "Oh, hell, son, I'm sorry. It just slipped. I've had a rough morning."

Tater Wayne and Turner, bless their hearts, got to the porch in time to scoop Granddaddy from the stairs and get him to his banquet chair.

Cheri blinked in the rain, trying her best to let the impossible sink in.

J.J. twisted Granddaddy's arm?

J.J. was the one who wanted me here?

J.J. already knew about what had happened in Florida?

Cheri looked around until her gaze locked with Candy's.

"Oh, shee-it," her best friend said.

Suddenly, Cheri felt like she was choking, like invisible fingers had grabbed her by the throat. It was the stranglehold of this small town, these people and their good intentions gone bad. Without a doubt, she'd made a horrible mistake coming back to Bigler. She'd made a horrible mistake trusting any of them. Coming back had just made things a million times worse.

She looked out at the silent crowd. She heard her own small voice say, "I'm in hell."

"Listen, sweetheart, it wasn't really like that," J.J. said, arriving at her side. Cheri knew she should grab J.J. and drag him inside, down the hall, and into the bedroom so they could deal with this in private. But she was too stunned to move, and besides, she didn't want him in her bedroom. Ever again.

"Really?" she asked him. "Then by all means, set the record straight."

"He . . . I . . . I only told Garland that it would be good to give you an opportunity to come home and take your rightful place at the *Bugle.*"

"You told him I was selling my underwear on eBay?"

"Hell, no! I told him you were selling your purses and garden gnomes and shit and that you and Candy had gone under in the real esate collapse."

Aunt Viv gasped. Turner mumbled something unintelligible. Tater Wayne's mouth hung ajar and his eyeball had gone on the fritz.

"So, you set a trap for me, then. You admit it. This whole little episode has been some kind of game for you."

"No! Cheri, I wanted to give you an out that would save your dignity, give you a way to get back on your feet. Listen to me, I—"

"You used me like I was some kind of plaything. You manipulated me! Oh my God! And to think, I was really starting to love my job at the *Bugle.* I mean, for the first time in my life, I felt like I was doing something real, something that made a difference, something other than just shuffling cash around from one account to the next!"

"Cheri—"

She cut J.J. off as tears burned in her eyes. "I got suckered in, didn't I? Y'all wanted me to feel like I was an important part of this family, but it was all a setup, a joke. And to think, I was stupid enough to believe you instead of my sister, stupid enough to fall completely in—"

Just then, Cheri realized the crowd had gone silent. All eyes were on her. Candy was jumping up and down and waving her arms over her head, mouthing the words "stop" and "now."

"I did it because I love you," J.J. said, his voice barely above a whisper. "And really, if you think about it, what I did only makes us even, because you weren't exactly forthcoming with me, either."

Cheri flinched. "Excuse me?"

"You never fessed up about your troubles. I waited for you to tell me, sweetheart. I kept hoping you'd feel comfortable enough to—"

"I have an announcement to make." Cheri turned to face everyone. "I am bankrupt. My business failed in Florida."

"This ought to be fun," Candy mumbled.

"Here's the real story—I am being hounded by bill collectors as we speak. My phone's been going off all damn morning. Candy and I lost about fourteen million dollars when the market tanked. We've got nothing."

A collective gasp went up through the group. The

rain started to come down. People began gathering their things. The musicians hauled tarps over their equipment and started loading up the van.

Suddenly, a trashed old pickup came barreling down the drive, Lynyrd Skynyrd blasting, smoke coming from the tailpipe. Guests scattered when the truck careened dangerously close to a group of tables and chairs.

The passenger door flew open and out fell Tanyalee.

"She's a damn liar!" she shouted. There wasn't a closed set of lips for miles. Tanyalee was a mess. She was missing a shoe. Two very rough-looking men tumbled out behind her.

"Let's party!" the driver yelled.

"Somebody shoot me."

That comment happened to come from J.J., but it was Cheri's thought exactly.

Tanyalee ran on her one shoe toward Cheri and began pulling on her sister's shirtsleeve. "You lying, cheating, selfish . . ."

Thank God a full contingent of law enforcement professionals was present, because Tanyalee was dragged away almost immediately, and Cheri straightened her shirt, trying with all her might not to break down into deep sobs.

It had all gone to shit. Just like that.

The rain poured. Lightning cracked. The crowd scattered. The ones who could run to their vehicles did so, while the older people scuttled up the steps, shoving Cheri aside to get under the tin roof overhang.

Her eyes locked with J.J.'s. The two of them just stood there, rain beating down on them, staring at each other in shock.

Turner reached J.J. and yanked him away without any warning. J.J.'s head twisted around and he stared at Cheri in alarm, then listened to whatever else Turner was telling him.

"Hey, everybody!" Tanyalee was doing her best to wiggle free from the FBI agents. "Cheri's not rich! She's broke! She's nothing! She's a loser!"

Cheri hung her head. Just then, she smelled something expensive and felt something warm against her arm. She looked up to see Candy's clear blue eyes. "Tanyalee," Candy said protectively, "as usual you are a day late and a dollar short. Now, come on, Cheri, let's get you inside."

"Wait." Turner and J.J. approached them. A quick glance was exchanged between Turner and Candy before the sheriff cleared his throat. "Ah, look, Cheri. I just got a call from the hospital. Purnell's out of his coma and insisting that he has to talk to us—me, J.J., and Garland, but especially you. He said he has something horrible to confess to you in particular."

She couldn't. She couldn't do it. Her heart was in a shambles already. "It's about my parents," Cheri whispered. "He killed my parents. I'm pretty sure that's what he wants to confess. He killed them so Daddy wouldn't expose him. Just take good notes."

"Oh, no. Oh, sweetheart—" J.J. grabbed for her but Cheri shook him off.

"No!" she snapped. "All y'all—I think it's best that you just leave."

Purnell Lawson used his last seconds of life to set the record straight, and for that, J.J. respected him. He just as easily could have died and taken his secrets with him, like Wimbley had done—or at least thought he'd done.

When Purnell said Wimbley killed Carleton Johnston, Turner nodded sadly. Next, Purnell claimed he wanted Garland and the girls to know the truth about Loyal and Melanie. He didn't ask for forgiveness and he couldn't look Garland in the eye. Garland couldn't look at him, either—the old man stood several feet from the bed as tears slipped down his face.

Then Purnell told J.J. that in his house, under his bed, he would find a second set of books that accurately recorded every dime he'd ever stolen from the *Bugle* and handed over to the Wimbleys.

The whole encounter lasted but a minute, but it was a minute of pure pain for everyone.

"I didn't kill that girl. I didn't kill Barbara Jean," was the last thing Purnell said before he slipped away.

By now, the FBI was already crawling all over Purnell's place. Turner and J.J. had just dropped Garland off at the house on Willamette, and J.J. spent a few moments with Vivienne, telling her the essence of Purnell's confession while she fed them red velvet cake.

"You got to help Cheri through this," she pleaded with him. "She's the one with the strength and the heart to keep this family going. Please, J.J., love her and stand beside her through this."

He'd kissed Viv on the cheek and promised he'd do his best.

Of course, Cheri wasn't answering her phone. He didn't blame her, but it still bothered him enough that he'd convinced Turner to swing by the lake house.

Instantly, Turner and J.J. glanced at each other. "Damn," Turner said. "Wim. Where the fuck is Wim?"

"You don't think he'd . . . ?"

Turner floored it.

Alcohol was a magic thing, Cheri figured. It could destroy lives and take down businesses yet it could subdue even the most batshit crazy, demon-possessed of sisters.

Tanyalee was sprawled out on the floor of the living room, one hundred twenty pounds of deadweight. Cheri had no idea what she'd do with her when she came to, but she'd worry about that later.

She'd managed to calm Tanyalee enough to explain to her what Purnell had done to their parents. She'd cried like Cheri had never seen a person cry. At one point Cheri had held Tanyalee's head in her lap as she sobbed. Strangely enough, it was the only time Cheri could remember ever feeling like a real big sister.

It had taken forever to shoo the Bubbas—as Tanyalee had called them—off her property, however. Candy sent them off by telling them they could take the remaining keg of beer and enough leftover barbecued chicken to choke a horse.

Everyone else had gone when the lightning started coming too fast to count to one one hundred.

And now, she and Candy sat at opposite ends of the couch, their feet propped up, a half-empty bottle of José Cuervo between them, a fire going in the fireplace.

"I prefer to see it as half full," Candy said aloud. "I'm an optimist at heart."

Cheri snorted.

"You should answer your phone. You know J.J. wants to talk to you."

"Who cares? I don't want to talk to him."

"You don't love him anymore?" Candy tried to refill her plastic beer cup with tequila but was having trouble navigating the individual actions required. Cheri helped her.

"I still love him," she admitted. "I just can't trust him."

"He did it because he wanted to help."

"But don't you see?" Cheri was starting to feel a little nauseous. Maybe beer and tequila weren't supposed to be consumed together under duress. "He had to have been collecting information on me for a long time to know all that shit about eBay and our garden gnomes!"

Candy nodded. "You're right. But it could have been a good-hearted kind of stalking, Cheri."

Cheri hiccupped.

"So I can call you Cheri now? For real? You're not gonna knock me upside my head?"

"Sure. Go ahead. Whatever."

"Oh, thank God. I hate callin' you Cherise. I've hated it for over five damn years."

Both of them cocked their heads at the sound of a car coming down the lane. "What now?" Cheri moaned.

"What if it's the Bubbas?"

"Oh! I've got a gun!" Cheri hopped up and headed down the hall.

"Oh, shit—wait!" Candy called out. "I think combining guns with tequila is frowned upon!"

When Cheri returned to the living room not thirty seconds later, she was greeted by the oddest sight: Wim

Wimbley stood over the couch, a hand slapped over Candy's mouth and a gun pointed at her head.

"Look, it's the Rags to Bitches!" Wim said, laughing. "Back together again for a limited time—and I do mean limited—and they've brought along Tanyalee, Bigler's most infamous gold-digging ho! She's flat on her back even as we speak!"

He was a little surprised to see Cheri's arm swing up, a gun pointing at him. *"Rrriiight,"* he drawled. "I'm stone-cold sober, Cheri, and you're not. My reaction time is quicker than yours, so Candy here will be dead before your finger touches the trigger."

"Git out!"

"You know, it's funny, but I'm noticing that your accent has come back."

"I'm warning y'all."

"Oh, God, just shut the fuck up, would you?" Wim straightened, leaned in, and acted like he was going to pull the trigger. Cheri dropped the handgun on the floor and shrieked. This was just too damned easy.

"Move." He grabbed her by her wrist and threw her down on the couch next to Candy. "Now here's how it's gonna be . . ." Wim untucked his shirttail and used it to pick up the tequila bottle. He splashed a little on Candy's blouse. "It's a good look for you," he said, laughing as he turned the bottle on its side on the coffee table.

"This is going to be a murder-suicide thing." He put Purnell's useless, piece-of-shit gun in his pocket, retrieved Cheri's gun from the floor, and wiped his prints from it as he explained. "Cheri, I'm going to put this in your hand and make you shoot Candy, then you're going to turn the gun on yourself. Just another failed business partnership that ends in tragedy."

"And who gets to shoot the hairspray off your pinhead?" Candy asked.

"Hilarious. You haven't changed at all, Candy Carmichael—still more boobs than brains. And from what I can tell, you've had about as much luck holding on to businesses as men lately."

Wim took great pleasure in watching Candy's pretty bow-shaped lips lose their smirk. "What? No snappy comeback? Come on now. It'll be your last, so make it a good one!"

Suddenly, Cheri gasped and lowered her gaze to the floor near the open front door. Wim knew it was some kind of trick, so he didn't bother to look behind him.

"Oh, please, Cheri. You think I'm that stupid? You think you're going to distract me so you can try something? You Newberrys have always underestimated us Wimbleys." He grinned. "But not today, right?"

Cheri then quickly glanced toward Tanyalee's lifeless form.

"Oh, God. This is pathetic." Wim began to laugh, but stopped when he heard some kind of strange, high-pitched *chit! chit!* sound coming from behind his head. Suddenly, he felt a painful pinprick in his shoulder. He twisted around to see that he'd been attacked by a fucking *squirrel*!

"What the—?" He tried to brush it off, but its teeth were buried in his flesh. He grabbed it by the tail and pulled. "Help! Somebody help get this thing off me!"

"Now!" He heard Cheri scream. "Do it *now*!"

* * *

Those few seconds raced by in a horrible blur. Cheri watched Artemis leap into the air and sink her teeth into Wim's dress shirt, causing him to spin around wildly and wave the gun in the air. Candy jumped up from the couch and tackled him around his knees just as Tanyalee rose from the floor and bashed him over the head with the tequila bottle.

That's when Wim crumpled, hit his forehead on the corner of the coffee table, and the gun went off.

At exactly that moment, Turner and J.J. busted into the room. Turner threw himself over Wim and J.J. collapsed on his knees next to Cheri.

"Are you okay?"

She nodded.

J.J. grabbed her. "Oh, my God, sweetheart. Oh, my God."

"Anybody hit?" Turner asked, looking from Tanyalee to Candy to Cheri.

"I'm fine," Cheri said. Tanyalee wobbled a bit and then fell to the floor in a cross-legged position, but gave a thumbs-up. Candy remained propped against the couch, breathing hard.

"Candy?" Turner's eyes burned with intensity. "Are you wounded?"

She shook her head. "Just my pride."

Turner's body loosened with relief. Cheri thought he even laughed a little as he cuffed Wim, holstered his weapon, and called for backup.

Epilogue

"You better let me fill 'er up, because we've got a lot to toast to tonight."

Cheri giggled and held out her champagne glass, pleased that the full moon had provided the finest romantic lighting available anywhere. And all she'd had to do was get in her own little rowboat and head out to the center of her own family's lake.

She sighed, absolutely content.

"First, to us," J.J. said, raising his glass to clink with Cheri's. "To forgiveness and patience and love—and sex hot enough to melt house paint."

"I'll drink to that. And to living together," Cheri added. "To the happiness found in waking up with and falling asleep with the one you love."

"Amen to the *Bugle*," J.J. said. "To its remarkable publisher and to continuing growth in its sales, revenue, and excellence in news reporting."

"And to Tanyalee," Cheri said.

J.J. lowered his chin and sighed. "Here we go."

Cheri laughed as she watched J.J. steel himself for

the jab he knew was on its way. "Well I'm sorry, but you guys took your sweet damn time rescuing us, so here's to Tanyalee and her tequila bottle!"

"And for checking herself in to rehab!"

Clink. They each took a sip.

Everyone knew it had taken a lot of courage for Tanyalee to make the decision to seek inpatient treatment for compulsive stealing, codependence, and a few other "issues" she didn't want to share. Granddaddy said he didn't need to know the details, then whipped out his checkbook.

"To the memory of brave Artemis."

"Of course." Cheri sniffled. It still hurt that her friend had died protecting her home, her friends, and her babies. They found the squirrel shot through near the fireplace, the night's only victim, killed when the gun in Wim's hand discharged. Cheri and J.J. had been hand-raising her babies in the week since, but knew they'd need to send them out into the world eventually.

"To my debt repayment plan."

J.J. smiled. "To your courage."

Cheri shrugged. "Oh! And to Wim."

J.J.'s laugh echoed across the lake and was answered by at least three loons. "May he enjoy his three-hots-and-a-cot while awaiting trial."

"Which one?" Cheri asked.

"All of 'em," J.J. said.

"I'll drink to that."

Wim was being detained in Charlotte on federal kidnapping charges for holding the women at gunpoint at the lake house, but according to Turner, he also would face a federal grand jury on multiple blackmail and extortion charges.

"Oh, and we can't forget to toast Candy." Cheri raised her glass high. "To my best friend and her willingness to stay in Bigler and keep me company—at least temporarily."

J.J. giggled. "For as long as she can stand rooming with Gladys, you mean."

"Yes, there's that," Cheri acknowledged.

Candy had chosen Gladys's offer of housing over Aunt Viv's, but was beginning to regret it. "She keeps borrowing my clothes without asking," Candy reported just the other day. "It's disturbing."

"And to the memory of Barbara Jean," J.J. said.

"And to Carlotta and her brighter future," Cheri added.

They clinked their glasses, but Cheri hesitated before taking another sip.

"J.J.," she said. "I think what we're toasting tonight is the truth, making things right. You know what I mean?"

He smiled at her then, the moon bright in his dark eyes, and he leaned closer and tugged on her free hand. The boat began to rock. A bit of champagne splashed from Cheri's glass.

"I know exactly what you mean," he said, planting a kiss on her lips. "Now, I got a little surprise for you. Here, give me your glass."

J.J. poured what remained in both glasses into the lake, put them aside, then began to roll up the sleeve of his denim shirt.

"What in the world are you doing?" Cheri asked, giggling.

"I think the moon's bright enough for you to read this."

Cheri burst out laughing. Written in big bold letters along the inside of J.J.'s forearm were the words, *"I'll love you forever, CNN."*

"I can't believe you did that," she said, shaking her head and smiling.

"It's in permanent marker, and that means it's forever." J.J. flashed a devilish smile as he began to roll the sleeve up even further. "Just like I hope this will be."

Cheri leaned forward in the moonlight, not sure she could trust her eyes. It almost looked as if J.J. had taped a ring inside of the crook of his arm.

It dawned on her that she'd seen correctly as he pulled off the tape and slipped the ring on her finger.

"Say yes," J.J. whispered, cradling her hands in his. "Say yes to putting things right with the world and with us. Once and for all."

She gazed at the sparkle on her left hand and then at the sparkle in J.J.'s eyes.

"Yes," she whispered. "I thought you'd never ask."

Read on for an excerpt from Susan Donovan's next book

I WANT CANDY

Coming soon from St. Martin's Paperbacks

It took a few attempts, but the gearshift eventually slipped into reverse, and the car began to lurch down the driveway. Candy bit her lip in concentration and craned her neck out the window. This was going to be a challenge, she knew. The driveway wasn't straight, and it was lined with boxwoods. Plus, it was the dead of night, and she'd opted to forgo the headlights so her escape wouldn't be detected.

No, this wasn't the most mature way to deal with a roommate conflict. There was just no way Candy could handle another scene with eighty-year-old Gladys. The old gal had been kind to take her in rent-free when she came back to town, but when she'd started to "borrow" Candy's lingerie, it was time to hit the road.

Almost there.

She squinted into the dark, delicately adjusting the car's course as it scraped against the bushes. Not that anyone would notice additional scratch marks on this beast, a 1997 discarded police cruiser she'd bought at auction with her last three hundred bucks. Candy sighed. Sometimes she couldn't even *believe* how fast—and how spectacularly—her perfect life had imploded.

Just a few more feet.

Slowly, the Chevy's rear end slid onto the dark country road. Candy wrestled with the gearshift until it slipped into drive. She carefully pressed down on the gas. If she could just make it to the state highway before the thing backfired . . .

Bam!

"Shee-it." Candy floored it. The old car's worn tires screamed against the asphalt as they fought for traction, just as the engine released a series of cannon-fire belches, each one more obnoxiously earth-shattering than the last.

She fought for control of the wheel as the car careened forward, an automotive version of the *1812 Overture* providing the soundtrack for her escape. A peek over her shoulder revealed that Gladys's bedroom light had just come on.

Candy hunkered down, put the pedal to the metal, and headed toward Highway 25. She took a right at the stop sign, careening away from the Town of Bigler, proper. Her heart pounded in her chest. Her hands shook. And suddenly, it occurred to her that she was having difficulty seeing. *Well, duh!* She'd forgotten about the headlights! With a groan of frustration, she turned them on. That's when red and blue flashing lights appeared in her rearview mirror.

"Shee-it," she said, louder this time. "You've got to be kidding me!" Candy's gaze darted from the alarming swirl of color in her mirror to the contours of the winding country road. Where was she supposed to pull off? It was guardrail and woods as far as the eye could see. The quick blast of the siren made her jump in her seat.

"OK! OK!" she yelled out. "I'm fixin' to pull over, you idiot! God! Give me a freakin' *break*!"

Suddenly, in her peripheral vision, she noticed an open patch by the side of the road. It happened to be on the *other* side of the side of the road, but she decided it was still her best bet, and whipped the car around to a skidding stop. Unfortunately, all the whipping and skidding hadn't set well with the engine, which began to spew smoke into the air along with another volley of backfires.

"Uh-oh," she whispered. It seemed the officer wasn't happy with all the commotion either, and the large, black SUV did a U-turn, the siren now *whoop-whooping*, and slammed to a stop in front of her, blocking any attempt she might make to get back on the road. Then a spotlight flashed on, so blindingly bright she had to shield her eyes.

Briefly, Candy thanked God for small favors. At least this wouldn't be Turner Halliday pulling her over. He was the actual sheriff in Cataloochee County, and the sheriff didn't work nights. He had deputies to take those less desirable shifts. So at least Candy would be spared the additional misery of being pulled over in the middle of nowhere at four in the morning by her childhood friend, especially since they were supposed to get together that night with Cheri and J.J. out at the lake house, and, boy, wouldn't *that* make for some interesting dinner conversation.

The siren went silent. Candy heard the door of the SUV slam shut, and she blinked against the intense light. She could barely make out the figure of a man advancing toward her, but she heard him cough and saw him wave his hand in front of his face, chasing away the smoke. She cut the engine, thinking . . . wondering . . .

Since this wasn't going to be Turner strolling up to her window, she might be able to buy herself some mercy. She decided to get out the big guns. Shameless? Absolutely. But what choice did she have? Candy began undoing two additional buttons of her blouse and arranged her weapons to their best advantage. Then she fluffed her hair and licked her lips. She hated to do this, but she didn't have the money to pay for a simple parking ticket, let alone a moving violation. She took a deep breath and prepared herself for the dumb-blonde-from-out-of-town defense.

That's when the officer reached the driver's-side window, leaned in, and grinned at her.

"License and registration, ma'am," Turner said, his eyes and smile gleaming in the spotlight. "And you can put your ta-tas away. They're not gonna do you much good in this particular situation, and besides—I'm more of an ass man, myself."

Candy groaned and fell back against the driver's seat. "Ah, come on, Turner. Have mercy on me."

He shook his head and chuckled. "Candy Carmichael, this car you're driving is a public safety hazard of the first degree—and that's *with* the lights on! Lord have mercy, girl! What are you doing driving around in the dark in this piece of shit with no headlights? You could've killed someone, or gotten *yourself* killed!"

She sighed as she reached up to button her shirt. "Yeah. I know. Sorry. I was trying to escape Gladys and forgot to turn on my lights once I hit the main road."

Turner laughed again and leaned an elbow on the open window. "She finally scare you off?"

Candy rolled her eyes. "I had to get out of there. She's a nice old lady, but she has absolutely no respect for my personal space. Thirteen days was all I could take."

Turner made a soft humming sound in his throat and looked away, nodding all the while. It seemed to Candy that he was contemplating her dilemma, and her heart leapt at the thought that he'd decided to take pity on her. Then she noticed that Turner had been scribbling on an official-looking pad of paper all the while.

"Please, no," she whispered. "Come on, Turner. Would you just cut me some slack, just this once? I swear to God I will always remember to put my headlights on in the future."

He carefully pulled the top layer of paper from the pad, and handed it to her through the open window. "It's just a warning, but it's not just for the headlights. You've got a serious exhaust problem, and I'm ordering you to have your North Carolina emissions inspection completed within seven days. Plus, you're not wearing a seatbelt." He shook his head, slowly scanning her. "You're a hot mess, girl."

"Yeah," she said meekly, accepting the paper. *Truer words had never been said,* she thought to herself as she looked away.

Candy refused to cry. There was no way she'd let her old friend see her fall apart. That had never been her style. She was a survivor. A fighter. Hell, she was a woman who knew how to take care of business! She would simply laugh this whole thing off. That's right. That's what she'd do.

Candy looked up again—and stared. While she'd been busy with the self-coaching, Turner's entire demeanor had changed. The corner of his mouth had curled up mischievously. His hazel eyes smoldered. His masculine face had softened and he'd tilted his head slightly.

She'd known this guy since elementary school. Sure, she'd noticed that Turner Halliday had taken the route from cute boy to handsome teenager to helluva-hunky man, but something about the sight of him right at that moment was a shock to her system. Exactly what was going on here? Was it the light? Was it the fact that Turner was an authority figure actually being decent to her, offering her the first break she'd had in what seemed like *forever*? Was it the way he was trying his best not to smile? Trying not to look down her shirt?

Maybe it was just the alluring shape of his mouth, that little dip in his top lip, the strong, full line of his bottom lip, those little dimples that bracketed both.

Who knew? But the fact remained that Turner Halliday was leaning into her car window all big and brown and sexy and powerful—and wearing that cute little badge—and Candy actually heard herself suck in air at the shock of it all.

She tossed the traffic warning to the car seat, and before she could give any decent amount of thought to what she was about to do, she pushed herself up, grabbed him by his fine-looking face, and planted a big, juicy kiss on her lifelong friend's lips.

Hello.

Shee-it.

This was interesting.

The kiss kept going. That hadn't been her intention. This was supposed to be a simple, friendly, spontaneous expression of gratitude, a genuine burst of affection for a fellow human being who had been kind enough to cut her some slack.

Right?

Which was perfectly understandable given the context. Candy was practically penniless. She'd lost millions in the Florida real-estate crash and was about to declare bankruptcy. She'd lost her luxury home in Tampa. Her Infiniti had been repossessed. She had no job. She'd mishandled her mother's retirement nest egg, a pesky detail her mother remained blissfully unaware of. And Candy had recently crawled back to her hometown in the western hills of North Carolina, where she'd been taken in by her best friend's receptionist, an octogenarian floozy who couldn't seem to stay out of her guest's underwear drawer.

Was it any wonder she felt compelled to kiss an old friend who'd just shown her a modicum of kindness?

Fine.

Then why were her arms now around Turner's neck? Why was she hanging out of the car window with her boobs arched out and pressed up against his hard, muscled chest? Why was one of Turner's hands buried up under her hair while the other was on its way down her spine, headed directly to her—?

"Holy hell, girl."

"Hmm?"

Candy felt herself being pushed away from the heat, pressure, and exquisite juiciness of Turner's mouth. She blinked. The spotlight nearly blinded her. She'd forgotten where, exactly, she was, and why, exactly, she was there.

Turner stared at her, his eyes wide and filled with surprise. He pulled one hand from her hair and the other from the small of her back and stepped away from the car. Candy slid back down into the driver's seat.

"Oh, God. Sorry," she mumbled.

"Right. No. *I'm* sorry. My bad."

Candy looked up in time to see Turner execute a series of moves more suited to a baseball coach on the sidelines than a cop. First there was a quick removal of his ball cap. That was followed by a sweep of his hand across his close-cropped hair, the return of the ball cap, a fast rub of his chin and mouth, and a few taps of his feet in the dirt. The routine was topped off by an adjustment of his gun holster.

"Drive safely," he said as he turned away.

Candy peered out the driver's-side window and watched him practically jog to his SUV. "Uh, thank you!" she called out, feeling ridiculous. What exactly was she thanking him for, anyway? Not arresting her?

Or was she thanking that man for giving her the finest, hottest, most bad-assed-open-mouthed kiss she'd ever had in her freakin' *life*?